New Worlds

C000063151

Brian W. Aldiss
Graham Charnock
John Clute
Jack Deighton
Paul Di Filippo
Peter F. Hamilton
Simon Ings
Gwyneth Jones
Graham Joyce
Paul J. McAuley
Michael Moorcock
Charles Stross

Edited by David Garnett

Also edited by David Garnett

NEW WORLDS
NEW WORLDS 2
THE ORBIT SCIENCE FICTION YEARBOOK
THE ORBIT SCIENCE FICTION YEARBOOK 2
THE ORBIT SCIENCE FICTION YEARBOOK 3
ZENITH
ZENITH 2

New Worlds 3

Edited by David Garnett

Consultant Editor: Michael Moorcock

VGSF

First published in Great Britain 1993
By Victor Gollancz
An imprint of Cassell
Villiers House, 41/47 Strand, London WC2N 5JE

With thanks to Michael Moorcock, Richard Evans and Faith Brooker

New Worlds is Registered Trade Mark of Michael Moorcock
New Worlds Vol. 62 No. 219

A catalogue record for this book is available from the British Library

ISBN 0 575 05146 9

Printed in Finland by Werner Söderström Oy

Contents

And the third is in thanks
for the tambourine

Introduction

David Garnett

I get letters. People write covering letters with their manuscripts, most of which are quite straightforward, although some are more interesting or amusing – while some are totally crazy (and therefore even more amusing). I receive letters about *New Worlds*, which are always welcome, and there are also letters from friends. One of these arrived this week, from someone who published a number of stories in *New Worlds* in the 1960s and 1970s: 'Needless to say, I have not yet seen the second *NW* in a bookshop.' And I know exactly what he means because I've seen copies in very few bookshops, and for this I had to travel to London and really *search*...

The chances of finding a copy of *New Worlds* on sale in your local bookshop are remote – unless you happen to live in Antwerp or Vancouver or Melbourne. Almost as many copies of *NW* have been sold overseas as in Britain. So why isn't it available in Norwich or Tewkesbury or Haverfordwest?

Authors complain; it's a fact of life. They complain about the covers they are given, about the low advances they are paid, about the lack of publicity for their books – why aren't they advertised in the commercial break during *Coronation Street*...? But probably the one thing that writers complain about most is distribution, of not seeing stacks of their books piled high in every bookshop in the country.

The majority of book sales are impulse buys. The potential reader does not intend to buy a specific book, perhaps not even any book. People in bookshops browse. They scan the shelves and might recognize the name of an author, someone they have read before or someone they have heard of, or else they are attracted by the cover. (And the price and number of pages. Every regular browser has seen people calculating which book is the 'best value': never mind the quality, just buy by weight!) It's an obvious thing to say, but readers can only buy what is available. As I said in the introduction to *New Worlds 2*: 'Books cannot sell unless they are in the shops. If the country's largest book chain decides not to stock a title, a huge slice of the market is immediately denied and potential sales are reduced.'

New Worlds is a short story collection, and it is a rule of publishing that short stories don't sell as well as novels. Except that the best-selling

British paperback of 1989 happened to be a book of short stories: Jeffrey Archer's *A Twist in the Tale*. But of course Archer is a 'bestseller' and therefore whatever he writes is inevitably derided by the critics. The same is true of every type of popular fiction, almost all of which is either ignored or disparaged in the belief that if a book is appreciated by the general public it is inevitably inferior. (Those who sneer at books that people buy and read and enjoy usually have a few unpublished, unreadable and definitely unenjoyable novels of their own gathering dust after being rejected everywhere.)

Go into any bookshop, and which is the largest category on display? It's the science fiction/fantasy/horror section (why they should be lumped together is another matter). And when do any of these get reviewed on the book pages of newspapers and magazines?

Not only is *New Worlds* a short story collection, it's an *anthology*: it has stories by *different* authors. But there's no *category* for this. Where does a shop put it on the shelves? And then it's the wrong *shape!* It doesn't fit in with everything else. Much easier not to put it on the shelf, not to try and sell it at all.

In fact, it would be much easier for bookshops if they sold only newspapers and magazines, video cassettes and CDs, toys and games, stationery and greetings cards. You know where you are with products like those. That's how books should be: the same size, the same number of pages – an identical product, in other words. Unfortunately, however, books cannot be the same because they are written by different people.

But there are ways of getting around this...

The decline of Britain's manufacturing industry is generally attributed to lack of long-term investment. If a new venture isn't guaranteed to make a profit within a year or two, then the company involved will not give financial backing to such a project. The most important person to any company is 'the shareholder'. Staff (apart from the directors, of course) who operate the business and customers who buy what the company makes are very low on the list of priorities.

The capitalist justification for profit, of high dividends for shareholders, is that this is a reward for risk taken. But shareholders now expect regular and growing dividends as a matter of course, and also that the value of their 'investment' will continue to increase. Companies have the same perspective: no matter what, shareholders must receive a substantial dividend every year. This is because shareholders have no loyalty. They don't work for the company, they don't buy the product. Their only interest is financial, and without sufficient reward they will sell their shares and the price will fall – which is perceived as the worst thing that can happen to any business.

It isn't only businesses that surrender long-term development for the sake of short-term interests, of course. This is exactly the way that the British government has behaved ever since 1979. Companies abandon spending on research and development, preferring to distribute 'profits' at twice the rate of other industrialized nations; and the government refuses to invest in the future, sacrificing the health and welfare and education and employment and environment of its people on the altar of 'market forces'. The government's dividend is referred to as 'tax cuts' – which are more than made up for by increases elsewhere.

The 'privatization' of public assets inevitably leads to higher prices, a reduced workforce and poorer service, because these companies need profit to provide dividends for the 'risk' taken by new shareholders. In fact, the only ones who gain from such asset-stripping are those who have a monetary interest: the City firms of brokers and merchant bankers who buy and sell what once belonged to everyone, and the financial institutions in whose hands most shares are finally concentrated.

Despite the myth of a share-owning democracy, only twenty per cent of shares in British firms are owned by individuals. The rest are controlled by other businesses, mainly pension funds and insurance companies, which also own huge slices of overseas corporations. Such British interests are the largest foreign investor in America, for example. These, in effect, are the multinational mega-corporations which are so often the faceless villains in derivative, third-generation cyberpunk. Pension-punk, cyber-insurance? All controlled by megalomaniac accountants and psychotic actuaries...

One of the few parts of British industry that is willing to invest in the future, in the hope of long-term profits, is the publishing business. An author will be commissioned to write a novel, given an advance on a book which he or she may not deliver for two years, which may not be published until a year or two later, and which may not show a profit for another two, three, four years – if at all.

Publishing is usually regarded as an old-fashioned business, where nothing is rushed, where decisions take months, even years to be made. Perhaps it is only because publishers behave as if they are living in the past that they are still prepared to invest in the future: they don't know things aren't supposed to be like that any more.

Every book a publisher brings out is different, has a different chance of being a commercial success. A book by a new author is more likely to make a loss than a profit. It takes time to develop a new writer, and a good publisher is prepared to take that time, to issue an author's first novel, the second, the third, however many are necessary until the writer is properly established as a 'name' who is recognized and appreciated – and bought! – by readers.

This 'publisher' is not (usually) a corporate entity but the editor who works for the company. There are numerous science fiction publishers, both in Britain and the USA, but perhaps only half a dozen editors of any real significance in each country. Most of these have been sf editors for over a decade, although they may have moved from one company to another. Others appear on the scene for a few years, have their brief moment of fame, then vanish without trace.

The same thing happens with authors, the majority of whom have a relatively brief career. Many first novels are published, but very few tenth novels. Only a fraction of writers keep on turning out book after book, either because their unique vision fades away – or because they cannot afford to continue writing.

Considering the time it takes to write a book, the amount of money paid to most authors is very low. It has to be, because the sales of most books are equally minimal. A few writers become best-sellers, but the majority earn very little and need another income. If an author is trying to make a living from writing, he or she has to be very lucky or very fast: to be a quick success under their own name, or else to write a lot of commercial material.

Publishers finally begin to make a profit from established authors, those who have been writing for years. Bookshops know their 'brand names' and will stock anything by them, and readers will also recognize these authors.

There are always new writers around, anxious to have their work published, but there are relatively few profitable names. Most of these have grown old and they turn out books more slowly. It would be ideal for publishers if these brand-name writers could produce books as quickly as new writers.

And, with a little bit of licence, why not...?

The biggest-selling novel of the last few years has been *Scarlett*, the 'sequel' to *Gone with the Wind*. The next such book to look out for – or avoid – will be the sequel to *Rebecca*.

The originals are famous titles, important properties. They were both written over half a century ago, and by now both authors, Margaret Mitchell and Daphne du Maurier, have died. In the world of publishing, however, death is no obstacle and so the sequels have been written by other authors.

Similarly, Virginia Andrews died in 1986, but this does not prevent regular publication of 'the new Virginia Andrews', a series written by a 'carefully selected writer to expand on her genius'. And despite his death in 1987, new books with the name Alistair MacLean on the cover have continued to appear. The name of the real author was printed in smaller letters, which led to a court case in 1991. Under the Trades Descriptions Act, the publisher was found guilty of misleading readers, with fines and costs totalling over £10,000.

The new Alistair MacLean books have been written by Alastair MacNeill; in court, the publisher described the similarity of their names as 'a happy coincidence'. MacNeill, according to his biography in these books, 'showed a great interest in writing . . . and won several school competitions'.

Gone with the Wind, *Rebecca*, Virginia Andrews (known in America as V. C. Andrews), Alistair MacLean — all these have become brand names, recognized by bookshops and readers. There is very little risk involved in publishing such books. A publisher offered a million pounds for the sequel to *Rebecca* before a word was written, even the title — and it was probably a bargain.

In a similar way, publishers have tried to establish various sf authors as brand names — even while they are still alive. John Clute refers to this as 'sharecropping' in his article at the end of this volume, and name-leasing is also known as 'franchising'. This is when a more famous author is persuaded to put his name above the title of books by other writers, usually younger, usually poorer. Such books are likely to be based on a novel or short story that the original author wrote twenty, thirty, forty, even fifty years ago.

The only people who have anything good to say about franchising are those with a financial interest; they are the only ones who profit. Readers are cheated because they are sold retreads for the price of new work, and even the authors make relatively little money compared with writing a novel of their own. This is because the publisher's advance has to be split three ways. Most of these deals are set up by middlemen, known as packagers. They come up with the idea — if it can be called that — of cashing in on a famous author's work. They pay for the use of that name, they hire another author to write the book, and they divide up the payment from the publisher.

The only reason for any author to do such work is for the money, which is a perfectly valid reason. That's why publishers publish such books; that's why packagers package such books. The people who write the sequels to *Gone with the Wind* and *Rebecca* make a *lot* of money, but those who write books based on some ancient, creaky sf story don't usually make very much. If a publisher does offer a large advance in one of these deals, then it won't be a new author who is hired to write the books. When three of Isaac Asimov's most famous stories were expanded into novels, it was Robert Silverberg, the ultimate sf professional, who was contracted to do the job.

While Silverberg writes Asimov books, Jeremy Kingston writes 'Robert Silverberg's *Time Tours*' books. But will anyone ever write Jeremy Kingston novels – even Kingston himself?

This is perhaps the most important factor to be considered in any debate about franchising, not the derivative work that is being written and published, but the work that *isn't* being written and published. If a new author is writing a book based on what someone else produced half a century ago, then he or she is doing this instead of creating their own unique vision. In science fiction, writers often produce their best material when they are young, but franchising means they are being denied this opportunity. They cannot sell their own books because publishers know it is much less risky to bring out a franchised product. The only way an author can earn any money is by becoming a writer for hire, producing the very books that are stopping his or her own individual novels from being published.

If this system had operated in the 1940s and 1950s, writers like Isaac Asimov and Arthur C. Clarke would have had far less opportunity to publish their own fiction. More than likely, they would have been hired to write franchised books based on what was produced by the authors of the previous generation. Their own 'classics' would never have existed because they were too busy regurgitating second-hand material.

Reading is a minority interest, and those who read science fiction are in an even smaller minority. To the majority of people, sf means 'space fiction'. The most familiar names are not those of authors but of 'sci-fi' titles associated with film and television: *Star Trek* and *Star Wars*.

Without written science fiction, without the hundreds, the thousands of authors who have created stories and novels, each developing and expanding from what has gone before, there would have been no vast treasury of ideas and imagery for the television and film industries to plunder and exploit. The sf magazines are the ancestors of media science fiction. In turn, media sf has spawned countless novelizations.

There has been an endless line of *Star Trek* novels, based on both the old and the new series. The three *Star Wars* films inevitably meant books-of-the-film, but now there is a new sequence of books written to take advantage of the familiar trade-marked name. The latest series of such spin-offs is *Aliens*, although these books are based not on the film – but on a comic developed from the film...

All of these are even more derivative than franchised books, but they sell better than the majority of original sf novels. It is probably the commercial success of such brand name series that has encouraged publishers to issue so many franchised novels, hoping that this is what the reader wants: a famous name, and more of the same. Or at least the bookshops will recognize that name and put such books on their shelves. Then it's up to the readers. They can take what's on offer – or buy nothing.

Publishers might argue that because of the money they make from recycling the past, they can afford to subsidize the authors of the future; if a franchised series makes a profit, however, it is far more likely that they will publish another set of reworkings of antique material.

Even if only one such book is published a year, that's one too many. Every product currently being spewed out means that there is one less original novel available, one more author who is denied a chance to find an audience and build a reputation through his or her own individual contribution to science fiction.

Franchising is where science fiction asset-strips its past and denies itself any future. Everything that has been written before is repeated, with a sequel or as a series. The gene pool is starved of fresh talent by a lack of investment in the new writers upon which every literature depends. A few of those involved will make a short-term profit – the publishers, packagers and copyright holders – but the cost is paid by those who are exploited: the authors and the readers.

Just as franchised novels prevent new writers getting their books into the shops, the same is true of brand name anthologies. *New Worlds* may not have been available in your local bookshop, but you might have been able to find something entitled, perhaps, *The Super Big Book of New World Science Fiction Stories*, 'edited by' a famous author. The only contribution this author would have made to the book, however, was to allow his name on the cover. He wouldn't have written an introduction, wouldn't even have selected the stories. But because his name was familiar, the bookshop could easily have decided to stock this anthology instead of, say, *New Worlds*.

Such a commercial decision would be entirely understandable, particularly as the other book would be 'better value' – more pages for the same price. To produce this imaginary book for the same price, the costs would need to be reduced. The typesetting has to be paid for, so does the artwork for the cover, the publisher's overheads, the paper – and there's more of that in a bigger book. The best way to cut costs is to pay the authors less, and that can be done by using reprinted material. In order to be profitable, this hypothetical book would consist entirely of fiction twenty to thirty years old. Why bother to publish new stories when it costs far less to buy old ones?

Just as every franchised book means that there is one less original novel, so every reprint anthology, every cheap exploitation of the past, means that there is less shelf space in the shops for new material, for new ideas, for new authors.

Now for the good news:

British sf has never produced so many new writers as in recent years. In the first *New Worlds*, I wrote: 'At least seven new British authors will be having first novels published during 1991 and 1992 – an unprecedented number.' This turned out to be an underestimate. If those dates are stretched over a further two years, the number of first novelists is around twenty, which is a phenomenal figure.

At least half of these writers developed their early potential through publishing short fiction in the original anthologies and sf magazines. Without the chance to practise their skills through writing short stories, and the confidence gained by publication, many of them would never even have attempted a novel.

In Britain at the moment, 'original anthologies' means only *New Worlds*; and 'sf magazines' is also in the singular and means *Interzone*. One of the most important elements in British sf over the last decade has been the regular publication of *Interzone*. Britain being Britain, however, the achievements of the magazine and its editor/publisher David Pringle are all too often ignored and even disparaged.

Starting as a quarterly in 1982 and moving to a bi-monthly schedule for a number of years, *Interzone* has appeared monthly since May 1990. During this time it has published scores of new authors, and many of the companies which publish sf novels (in America as well as in Britain) owe *Interzone* a great debt for finding and encouraging writers whose books they have subsequently brought out. Some of these debts are repaid when the publishers advertise in the magazine, helping to finance its continuing publication.

Some of these debts, however, are never paid. One publisher that is bringing out a number sf novels by authors who began their careers in *Interzone* has never advertised in the magazine. This is yet another example of a refusal to invest in the future, of a company that exploits the past – the recent past, in this case – and the work of others for its own short-term profit.

Just as some publishers refuse to support *Interzone*, so others have never published original anthologies. Although these companies make a great deal of money out of their sf lists, they will not invest any of this profit in books such as *New Worlds*. And because bookshops and distributors prefer to play safe, not to handle something they regard as 'uncommercial', there was never any doubt that this new series of *NW* would be a risky proposition. But any publishing editor who has faith in the future, who wants to develop new authors who write their own books instead of repeating those of the past, who plans to build up a successful list of truly imaginative writers, should be more than willing to take the risk.

The editor who took that chance was Richard Evans of Gollancz. As for the others, where do they think new authors come from? Maybe they'll find people who have won school competitions, or with names that happen to fit.

Here's *New Worlds 3*.

Another investment in the future.

Available only from a few select outlets.

Spare Capacity
Peter F. Hamilton

Eason careered out of the pub in Peterborough's Millfield district, the noises of the fight rolling after him – roaring voices, the crash of breaking glass. The five musclemen he'd hired would lose eventually, they were just ordinary street bruisers; the enforcers chasing him had God knows how many lethal implants and adaptations. But the delay was going to be crucial.

That final image of Tenvis's horrified face stalked his mind, his hands closing on the chubby merchant's cheeks as though bestowing some pagan invocation. Tenvis had been the final fall-back to offload his stash. And if Layia, his kestrel, hadn't been hovering overhead he would have had no warning of the three enforcers closing on the pub. He had reacted instinctively, the long strands of electroplaque cells implanted in his forearms firing a two-thousand volt charge through organic conductors which protruded from his fingertips like eight small warts. A sparkling purple-white corona had flared around Tenvis's head. The merchant was dead before he hit the ground.

Eason positioned himself underneath a shrieking Layia as she tumbled chaotically out of the bright azure sky, catching her with lazy grace before she hit the pavement. Her dead adversary, a Cooper's hawk belonging to one of the enforcers, smacked on to the slabs, a flurry of rusty-brown chest feathers fluttering up like mangled butterflies.

Then he was off, streaking down the side street, boosted reflexes reducing his peripheral surroundings to blurred streaks of primary colours. People solidified in mid-step as he pirouetted round them, the craziest expressions locked on to frozen faces.

There was a boulevard ahead, cutting through the heart of the city's eastern quarter. It was lined with newgene sequoias, only seventy years old but already towering above the old brick houses and new post-Warming whitewashed Spanish-style apartment blocks.

He slammed into the crush of pedestrians and bicycles that thronged its length, his immediate universe dissolving into jabbed elbows, snarls and furious cycle bells. He coaxed Layia on to his shoulder with one hand; she had fallen silent, her broken wing a dull star of pain burning at the back of his mind. His other hand gripped the canvas shoulder bag which contained three hundred ampoules of Wine.

A silent instruction to his infuser implant cancelled the nerve-booster extravasation. His senses immediately started to curve down off their paranoia high.

He tried to see if he was being followed, slowing his walk to match the grudging pace everyone else was using. Limbs trembled in reaction to cold-turkeying the nerve booster. The enforcers were nowhere to be seen, but they weren't the major problem. Avian senses insinuated their way into his brain, sliding out of the neurone symbionts in his medulla, the impulses received from their clone analogues in Layia. The bird was scanning the sky with her enhanced retinas, alert for predators, watchers like herself. But there was only the eternal whirls of gulls gliding above the tapering treetops, their usual cries drowned out by the racket around him. He hurried forwards.

The boulevard delivered him direct to the harbour: a circular, mile-wide deep-water basin, with glistening white polyp walls. Half of it extended out into the quagmire which laid siege to the city's eastern boundary, with a single gap for the channel which led away to the Wash, while the other half had eaten into the urban districts, where it had been surrounded by a dense conurbation of warehouses, taverns, marine supply shops, brothels and a giant fish market. Quays stabbed out into the murky brown waters like spokes from a wheel rim. Right in the centre, forming its own sad island, was the roofless hulk of the city's old cathedral.

A ship out should be easy to find. Destination wasn't important, as long as it left soon.

But after making some quick enquiries he found that none of the merchantmen was leaving until late that evening. The tide was ebbing, and the captains wouldn't risk sailing the channel fully laden.

He started down the southern wall, towards the smaller boats; fishing ketches, coastal sampans, and traders which cruised between the city and the archipelago. They could handle the channel at low tide, although they rarely took on deck hands; they were nearly all family concerns. He didn't have much cash left, certainly not enough to buy passage anywhere. It was going to have to be force again, he realized grimly, which would be chancy in broad daylight.

He saw the girl before he had walked a hundred yards along the wall. She was in her mid-teens, tall bordering on gawky, wearing a loose topaz-coloured cotton shirt and turquoise shorts. Thick auburn hair fell to her hips, styled with an Egyptian wave; but the humidity had drawn out its lustre, leaving it hanging limply. Dermal tailoring had stained her skin a rich walnut to ward of the UV infall.

She was staggering under the weight of a near-paralytic old man. He looked as though he weighed twice as much as she did, wearing baggy olive-green shorts and a sweat-stained vest. A few licks of oily silver hair were plastered back over a dark-brown pate.

'Please, Ross,' she implored. 'Mother'll sail without us.'

His only answer was an inebriated burble.

Eason trotted over. 'Can I give you a hand?'

She shot him a look which was half guilt, half gratitude. He had guessed her face would be narrow, and he was right: a small flat nose, full lips and worried green eyes were cocooned by her disorderly hair.

'Are you sure?' she asked.

'No trouble.' He put his bag down and relieved her of the old man. Layia squawked a brief protest as he slung the old man's arm around his shoulder, then fluffed her feathers out and settled back. With his muscle grafts and reinforced skeleton, Eason could haul the bulky old man along without any trouble. But the girl must have been stronger than she looked.

'This way,' she said, squirming with agitation.

'Take my bag, would you, and the name's Eason,' he told her as they started off along the wall.

'Althaea.' She blushed as she picked up the bag. 'I'm really grateful. I should have been back on the *Orphée* quarter of an hour ago.'

'Is it a tight schedule?'

'Oh no, but Mother likes to get home before dark.'

'Should he be sailing in this condition?'

'He'll just have to,' she said with a sudden flash of pique. 'He does it every time we bring him. And it's always me that has to go looking in the taverns for him.'

'Is this your father?'

She let out a guffaw, then clamped her hand over her mouth. 'I'm sorry. No, he's not my father. This is Rousseau. Ross. He lives with us, helps around the house and garden, things like that. When he's sober,' she added tartly.

'Where do you live?'

'Mother and I live on Charmaine; that's out in the archipelago.

Is your bird all right?'

'Yes, thank you.' He thought quickly. An island would be an ideal place to drop out of sight for a while. And his options were shrinking with each step. The enforcers wouldn't be that far behind; he would never make it back to the city now.

'Her wing looks damaged,' Althaea said.

'She got in a bit of a scrap. I'll fix her up later. Hey, how did you know Layia was a lady?'

'I know about birds.' Her angular shoulders jerked in what he thought was supposed to be an apologetic shrug; it was more like a convulsion. Eason couldn't recall meeting someone this shy for a long while. It made her appealing, after an odd sort of fashion.

The *Orphée* was tied up to a quay near the gap in the harbour wall. Eason whistled in appreciation when he saw her. She was a trim little craft, six yards long, with a flat-bottomed wooden hull and a compact cabin at the prow. The two outriggers were smaller versions of the main hull with room for cargo; all archipelago craft had them, the Fens sea wasn't deep enough for keel fins. Standard bioware fittings were dovetailed neatly into the wooden super-structure: a nutrient supply with ancillary organs in the bilges; a powerful-looking, three-yard-long, eel-consanguineous tail; an eight-yard-high sail membrane mast, whorled into a lean cone.

Althaea's mother was sitting cross-legged on the cabin roof, wearing a faded denim shirt and white shorts. He had no doubt she was Althaea's mother, the resemblance was remarkable: her hair was shorter, and she didn't have her daughter's half-starved appearance, but the delicate features were identical.

She was holding up an odd-looking pendulum, a slim gold chain that was fastened to the centre of a polished wooden disk, three inches in diameter and quarter of an inch thick. The disk must have been perfectly balanced, because it remained horizontal.

When Eason reached the quayside directly above the *Orphée* he saw the rim of the disk was carved with spidery hieroglyphics. It was turning slowly. Or he thought it was. When he steadied Ross and looked down properly, it was stationary.

The woman seemed absorbed by it.

'Mother?' Althaea said uncertainly.

Her gaze lifted from the disk and met Eason's eyes. She smiled.

He found it hard to break her stare, it seemed almost triumphant.

Rousseau vomited on the quay.

Althaea let out a despairing groan. 'Oh, Ross!' She was close to tears.

'Bring him on board,' her mother said wearily. She slipped the disk and chain into her shirt pocket.

With Althaea's help, Eason manhandled Ross on to a bunk in the cabin. The old man groaned as he was laid on the grey blankets, then closed his eyes, asleep at once.

Althaea put a tin bucket on the floor beside the bunk, and shook her head sadly.

'What's the pendulum for?' Eason asked quietly. He could hear her mother moving round outside.

'Mother uses it for divining.'

'On a boat?'

She pressed her lips together. 'You can use divining to find whatever you wish, not just water – stones, wood, buried treasure. It can even guide you home in fog, just like a compass.'

'I'll stick with an inertial guido.'

Althaea's humour evaporated. She hung her head.

'My name's Carnea,' the woman said after Eason stepped out of the cabin. She stuck her hand out. 'Thank you for helping Althaea.'

'No trouble,' Eason said affably. Carnea had a firm grip, her hand calloused from deckwork.

'I was wondering,' he said, 'do you have any work available on Charmaine?'

Carnea's eyes narrowed. 'Why would you be interested?'

'I'm a drifter, I'm always interested in work.'

'A drifter? Is that kestrel affinity bonded?'

Of course she would spot that, a set of neurone symbionts was expensive. 'Layia and I go back a long way. Before I hit the road.'

Layia showed him Althaea emerging from the cabin behind him. He could put his arm around her, and threaten to snap her neck unless Carnea got underway. Nobody nearby would see anything amiss in that pose, not a man embracing a pretty girl.

'It would only be food and board,' Carnea said. 'In case you haven't noticed, we're not rich.' There was the intimation of amusement in her voice.

He stopped his glance from flicking around *Orphée*; she must have cost ten thousand pounds at least.

'And *Orphée* has been in the family for thirty years,' Carnea said briskly. 'She's a working boat, the only link we have with outside.'

'Right. Food and board would be fine.'

Carnea ruffled Althaea's hair. 'No need to ask your opinion, is there, darling? A new face at Charmaine, Christmas in April.'

Althaea blushed crimson, hunching in on herself.

'Okay, *drifter*, we'll give it a try.'

Orphée's tail kicked up a spume of foam as she manoeuvred away from the quay. Carnea's eyes were tight shut, steering the boat via her affinity bond with the bioware's governing processors. Once they were clear, the sail membrane began to unfurl, a brilliant emerald sheet woven through with a hexagonal mesh of rubbery cords.

Outside the harbour walls they picked up a respectable speed. Carnea kept to the deep-water channel for five miles, then changed course to the south, giving the mudbanks and ruins of the Whittlesey shoals a wide berth.

Eason went into the cabin to stow his bag. Rousseau was snoring fitfully, turning the air toxic with whisky and bad breath.

He unzipped the bag to check on the Wine ampoules in their foam-lined boxes. The neurochemical had come from the vault of his industrial clan. He considered it his golden handshake for the ten years of his life he had spent as an enforcer, ten years eating shit so the clan directorship could live like pre-Warming princes on their Market Harborough estate. They had decided his profession for him when he was twelve years old, after a battery of physical and psychological tests which every clan kid underwent to assess their potential. All very equitable and logical. Except, as he found later, directors' kids never qualified as enforcers, they went straight to executive grade.

The clan began to adapt him after his eighteenth birthday. They gave him implants, gave him Layia, and indentured him for fifteen years. He was proud at the time. Enforcers were the élite, with their coldly beautiful bodies and violence-hotwired minds, attracting any bedmate they wanted, earning only slightly less than the chairman.

He battled the odds, day in, day out, keeping the clan research teams secure, protecting the clan's markets, putting the squeeze on other clans' markets. And the odds, as he also found, were nigh on impossible to beat. Enforcers did not become executives, they didn't last that long. Not intact.

The Wine was his route out; it was worth half a million pounds sterling, gold-backed. If he could find a buyer. But he had been stupid. It was possible to offload items that hot in Peterborough, provided the city lord, Torreya, received her cut. In the ten years since she had inherited her father's empire, her sovereignty had become ominously pervasive; she ran both the street hustlers and the police, she controlled the council, the merchants answered to her.

But when Tenvis suggested there was no real need to involve her, Eason had thought about that extra percentage and said yes straight away. Stupid! Now he didn't even know if the enforcers at the pub belonged to Tenvis or Torreya. If they were hers he could never return.

He came back out on to the deck and leant on the taffrail, allowing himself to relax for the first time in a fortnight. He wasn't being followed and he had somewhere to hole up until Layia's wing healed.

No wonder enforcers never made executives, he thought sourly; the number of mistakes he had made during the last fourteen days was horrifying. He was acting like a hive ant whose controlling queen had died – not a bad analogy for a clan member.

The Fens Sea looked as though it had been polished smooth; the only disturbance came from Orphée's wake, quiet ripples which were swiftly reabsorbed. He could see the bottom a couple of yards below the boat, a flat black treacle of drowned peat. Long ribbons of kelp and mushroom-like bulbs of newgene seafruit rose up out of it, swaying in the languid currents.

Althaea sat on Orphée's prow, letting the breeze of their passage dry her hair, a sensual living figurehead. Carnea was standing amidships, staring at the horizon, straight-backed and resolute. Every inch the ship's mistress.

Eason settled down in the stern and speculated idly on which of them would be best in bed, although he would know soon enough. After all, he had to have something to alleviate the boredom of living on an island in the back of beyond. A mother-daughter combination would be fabulously erotic.

They moved into the archipelago three hours after leaving Peterborough. Die-hard Fenland families had started to plant the rings of newgene coral on Ranson Moor right after the Warming; now there were thousands of them.

The big inhabited islands were spaced a mile or so apart, leaving a broad network of channels to navigate through. Carnea guided Orphée around the innumerable spits and reefs without even reducing speed.

Eason gripped the gunwale tightly as vicious jags of coral flashed past the outriggers. Most of the islands he could see had spindly palms and coconut trees growing above the waterline; there were no beaches visible, just shelves of mud dotted by straggly bushes. Small fishing villages were sprawled on the seaward slopes, single-storey wooden houses, whitewashed planks glowing copper in the sinking sun.

'There it is,' Althaea called excitedly from the prow. She was on her feet, pointing ahead. 'Charmaine.' She gave Eason a shy smile.

The island had a lot more foliage than the others; its trees formed a veritable jungle, extending right down to the water's edge. Their trunks were woven together with a dense web of vines; grape-cluster cascades of vividly coloured flowers, fluoresced by the low sun, bobbed about like Chinese lanterns. There was no village, he couldn't even see any houses.

Orphée was heading for a jetty sticking out from the narrow skirt of mud shingle which passed as Charmaine's shore.

'What do you do here?' he asked Carnea.

'Scrape by,' she said, then relented. 'Those trees are all newgene citrus varieties. We used to supply all the nearby islands with fruit, it gave the community a sense of independence from the mainland. As a general rule vegetation has a hard time out here, even newgene plants. There's never enough soil, you see. But my great-grandfather started dredging up peat as soon as the coral rose above the water; it took him twenty years to establish a decent loam. I'm afraid I've allowed the groves to go wild since my husband died.'

'Why?'

She shrugged, uncoiling a mooring rope. 'I didn't have the heart to carry on. I'm just hanging on until Althaea finds herself someone. It's her island really. When she has a family of her own they can put it back on its feet.'

The house was set in a dishevelled clearing about a hundred yards from the jetty. It was a two-storey stone building with climbing roses scrambling around the ground-floor windows and a wooden balcony running along its front. Big precipitator leaves hung under the eaves, emerald valentines sucking drinking water out of the muggy air. When he got close, Eason could see the white paint was flaking, moss and weeds clogged the guttering, and the balcony was rotting away; several windows were boarded up.

His situation was looking better by the minute. Two women, a drunk and an isolated, run down island. He could stay here for a century and no one would ever find him.

As soon as they walked into the clearing birds exploded from the trees, filling the air with beating wings and a strident screeching. The flock was split between parrots and some weird blunt-headed thing which made him think of pterodactyls. Whatever they were, they were big, about eighteen inches long, with broad wings and whip-like tails; their colours were incredible – scarlet, gold, azure, jade.

Rousseau clamped his hands over his ears, belching wetly.

'What the hell are those?' Eason shouted over the din.

Althaea laughed. 'They're firedrakes. Aren't they beautiful?'

'They're what?'

'Firedrakes. It's a sort of cross between a bat, a lizard and a parrot.'

He gawped, using Layia's enhanced retinas to get a better look at one; and damn it, the thing did look like a lizard, with membranous wings where the forepaws should be.

'My father bred the original ones about forty years ago,' Carnea said. 'He was a grade-sixteen geneticist, one of eight in the whole country.'

'You could make a fortune selling them,' he said.

'Not really. They can't fly very far, they only live three years, there are a lot of sports, only a third of the eggs ever hatch and they're prone to disease. Father was going to improve them, but he never got round to it.'

'But they're ours,' Althaea said proudly. 'Nobody else has them. They help make Charmaine special.'

Eason walked into the ground-floor study the morning after he arrived. He was still kneading kinks out of his back; the bed in the fusty little rear bedroom they'd given him was incredibly hard. It was only for one night; Carnea had told him he would be living in the pickers' accommodation.

The study, like the rest of the house, had dull-red clay tile flooring and whitewashed plaster walls; several prints were hanging up. A big brass fan was spinning slowly on the ceiling.

Carnea was sitting behind a broad teak desk, wearing a sleeveless white blouse. The only objects on the polished wood surface in front of her were a computer slate, a blank grey rectangle a foot long and an inch thick, and a pack of cards with a fanciful design printed on the back – from what he could see it looked like a star map.

He sat in an austere high-backed chair facing her.

'About your duties,' she said. 'You can start by repairing the picker shacks. We have a carpentry shop with a full set of tools. Ross doesn't use them much these days. Are you any good with tools?'

'I couldn't build you a cabinet, but cutting roofing timbers to length is no trouble.'

'Good. After that I'd like you to sort out the garden.'

'Right.'

Carnea picked up the pack of cards and started to shuffle them absently. She had the dexterity of a professional croupier. 'We are getting a little bit too overgrown. Charmaine might look charmingly rustic, but the vines are becoming a nuisance.'

He nodded at one of the big prints on the wall. It was of three people: Carnea when she was younger, looking even more like Althaea, a bearded man in his late twenties and a young boy about ten years old. 'Is that your husband?'

The cards were merged with a sharp burring sound. 'Yes, that's Vanstone, and Krelage, our son. They died eighteen years ago. It was a boating accident. They were out on the edge of the archipelago when a hurricane blew up. They weren't found until a week later, there wasn't much left. The fish . . . '

'It must have been tough for you.'

'Yes. I loved him like nobody else. Ours was a genuine till death do us part marriage. If it hadn't been for Althaea I would probably have killed myself.'

He glanced up sharply, meeting a hard-set smile.

'Oh yes,' she said. 'It is possible to love somebody that much. Have you ever known that kind of love, Eason?'

'No.'

'I don't know whether to envy you or pity you for that lack. What I felt for Vanstone was like a tidal force. It ruled my life, intangible and unbreakable. Even now it hasn't let go, it never will. But I still have my hopes, for Charmaine, and Althaea.'

'She's a nice girl. She should do well with this island, it's a wonderful inheritance.'

'Yes, she has a beautiful future ahead of her. I read it in the cards.'

'Right.'

'Are you a believer in tarot, Eason?'

'I like to think I can choose my own destiny.'

'We all do. It's a fallacy. Our lives are lived all at once, consciousness is simply a window into time. That's how the cards work, or tea-leaves or palmistry, or crystals for that matter. Whatever branch of the art you use, it simply helps to focus the mind, allowing us to see what we will do in the future. And, thank God, Althaea isn't going to suffer like I have.'

He stirred uncomfortably, for once feeling slightly out of his depth. Bereavement and isolation could pry at a mind, especially over eighteen years.

'Would you like to know what your future has in store?' she asked. The pack of cards was offered to him. 'Cut them.'

'Maybe some other time.'

Rousseau walked him over to the shack, following a path through the gloomy avenues of trees at the back of the house. The old man seemed delighted with the prospect of male company on the island. Not least because his share of the work would be considerably lessened, probably to around about zero if he had his way, Eason guessed.

'I've lived here all my life,' he said. 'Even longer than Carnea. Her father, Nyewood, took me on as a picker when I was younger than you.' He looked up at the tangle of interlocking branches overhead with a desultory expression pulling at his flabby lips. 'Old Nyewood would hate to see what's happened to it. The island's success was all down to him, you know. Half of these trees are varieties he spliced together, improvements on commercial breeds. Why, I planted most of them myself.'

Eason grunted at the old man's rambling reminiscences. But at the same time, he did have a point. There was a lot of fruit forming on the boughs, oranges and lemons in this section, most of them inaccessible. The branches hadn't been pruned for a decade, they were far too tall; and the snarl of grass and scrub plants which made up the undergrowth was waist-high. It wouldn't take too much work to make the groves productive again.

'Why stay on, then?' Eason asked.

'For little Althaea, of course. Where would she be without me here to take care of things? I loved Vanstone when he was alive, such a fine man. So I do what I can for his daughter, for his sake. I have been like a father to her.'

'Right.' Nobody else would take on the old soak.

There were twelve shacks forming a semicircle in their own clearing. Rousseau called it a clearing; the grass came up to Eason's knees.

'My old shack, the best of them all,' Rousseau said, slapping the front door of number three.

Shack described it perfectly: two rooms and a shower cubicle, built out of bleached planking that had warped alarmingly, a roof of thick palm thatch which was moulting and a veranda along the front. There was no glass in the windows: they had shutters to hold back the elements.

'I fixed up the hinges and put in a new bed last week,' Rousseau said, his smile showing three missing teeth. 'Carnea, she told me to fix the roof as well. That woman expects miracles. Still, now you're here, I'll help you.'

Eason paused on the threshold, a gelid tingling running down his spine.

'What do you mean, last week?'

'Last Thursday it was, she told me. "Ross," she said, "get the shack fixed up, ready for the man to live in." It was a mess, you know. I've done a lot of work here.'

'Ready for *me* to live in?'

'Yes.' Rousseau shifted uncomfortably from foot to foot as Eason stared at him.

'Did she mention me by name?'

'No. How could she? Listen, I made sure the toilet works. You don't have to run back to the house every time.'

Eason reached out and grasped the front of Rousseau's vest. 'What did she say, exactly?'

Rousseau gave him a sickly grin, trying to prise his hand loose. Sweat broke out on his forehead when he found just how implacable that grip was.

'She said there would be a young man coming to stay with us. That's all, I swear. And I wasn't to tell anybody.'

Eason let go of his vest. 'Why not?'

'Because you would be on the run.'

After Eason finished cleaning out the shack he sat on the cot-style bed and pulled off his T-shirt. The sphincter muscle hidden in his left armpit dilated and the pear-shaped ampoule of nerve booster burped out. He packed it away in the bag and took out one of the Wine ampoules, pushing its neck into the star of raw flesh. Peristalsis took over and the ampoule was gobbled inwards.

Carnea worried him. How the hell could she know he would be coming out to Charmaine? And that he was on the run? He hadn't even met Tenvis a week ago, for Christ's sake.

It was no good terrorizing Rousseau; that drunken fart didn't know anything. But Carnea was going to explain in elaborate detail, and it would be the truth – an extravasation of Wine would make sure of that.

Wine was the enforcers' name for the neurochemical, deriving from Communion Wine. It was, in fact, a sorcerer's concoction cooked up by the clan's neurologists to educe a temporary empathic ability. A communion of sorts, a laying-on of hands, or any other form of close physical contact, which allowed dangerously stretched neurones to receive dusky images and tenuous strands of emotion from a subject's mind.

Eason couldn't quite pick out individual thoughts, but he could spot a lie instantly.

'I brought some meat for Layia,' Althaea said. She was standing in the doorway, lanky body diplomatically covered by a mauve summer dress. Her face crumpled miserably when he looked up in surprise.

He lowered his left arm. 'It's all right, come in. I'm just having a scratch.'

'I'm sorry. I didn't think. I always walk straight into mother's room.'

'No trouble.' He pulled on his T-shirt, and zipped up the bag.

She bent over to look at Layia, who had taken over the back of a cane chair as her perch. He had splinted the wing last night and used the affinity bond to place a prohibition on scratching it.

'You set her wing.' She grinned at him.

'Yes, she should be all right to fly in a month or so.' He ordered an extravasation of Wine and stood up.

Althaea was offering Layia small chunks of meat. The kestrel pecked at them daintily.

He reached out and touched her long bare arm. 'Why don't you show me round the island?'

He saw an eidolon mirage creep out of the planking, a room with white walls, dim holographic posters of rugged snow-capped mountains and a magical white Bavarian castle, a bed with a red-spotted counterpane, a big brown animate animal bear, whose bioware had long since expired, sitting on the pillow. Emotions overlapped: there was the skittishness at being in his presence, the delight of him touching her.

'Yes,' she stammered. 'All right.'

Charmaine's lagoon was six hundred yards across, with a broad beach of fine pink sand running the whole way round. Eason counted five tiny islands, each with a clump of trees festooned in vines. The water was clear and warm, and firedrakes glided between the islands and the main jungle.

It was breathtaking, he had to admit, a secret paradise.

'The sand is dead coral,' Althaea said as they walked along the beach. 'There's a grinder machine which turns it to powder. Mother said they used to process a whole batch of dead chunks every spring when father was alive. It took decades to make the beach.'

'It was worth it,' he said.

She gave him a cautious smile. 'The lagoon's chock-full of lobsters. It fills up through a vent hole, but there's a tidal turbine at the far end. They can't get past it, so they sit in there and breed. They're easy to catch.'

'You must have been very young when your father died.'

'It was before I was born.'

'And you've lived here all your life?'

'Yes. Mother says the family used to farm here before the Warming. The house we've got now is built out of stone salvaged from the old farmhouse.' She skipped up on an outcrop of yellow coral and gazed out across the lagoon. 'I know it must look terribly ramshackle to you, but I'm going to wake it up. I'm going to have a husband, and ten children, and we'll have pickers in the groves again, and boats will call every day to be loaded with fruit, and we'll have our own fishing smacks, and a new village, and big dances under the stars.' She stopped, drastically self-conscious again, hunching up her shoulders. 'You must think I'm so stupid, talking like that.'

'No, not at all. I wish I had dreams like yours.'

'What do you dream of?'

'I don't know. Somewhere small and quiet I can settle down. Nothing as grand as Charmaine.'

'But it could be an island?' She sounded hopeful.

'Yes. Could be.'

The Halo dominated the southern night sky as Eason walked across the lawn towards the house, a frosty contrail curving delicately from east to west, as bright as a star. A distended ring of pulverized asteroidal rubble which, if it had been completed, would have reflected away enough sunlight to put a brake on the Warming.

The Americans and Russians had abandoned it eighty years earlier due to lack of cash, lack of confidence, leaving it to decay along with all the other technophiliac travesties of the High Frontier dream.

He went into the silent house, taking the stairs two at a time. When he reached Carnea's bedroom door he turned the handle, ready to push until the lock tore out of the frame. But it wasn't locked.

Halolight shone through the open window, turning the world to a drab monochrome. Carnea was sitting cross-legged on the double bed, wearing a blue cotton nightshirt, the pendulum held out in front of her. She didn't show the slightest surprise at his presence.

Eason closed the door, aroused by the scene: woman waiting calmly on a bed. 'You have something to tell me.'

'I do?'

'How did you know I was coming? Nobody could know that. It was pure chance that I bumped into Althaea.'

'I read it in the cards.'

'You expect me to believe that crap?'

'How do you explain it, then?'

He crossed the room in three quick strides and gripped her arms. The pendulum bounced away noisily as she dropped it.

'That hurts,' she said tightly.

He increased the pressure until she gasped. Her pain tweaked his synapses, the Wine showing him her shock and fury. But no fright, he noted; he couldn't intimidate Carnea, her thoughts were too well ordered, glacial.

'How did you know I was coming?' he demanded.

'I read it in the cards,' she hissed back. 'I told you, from where we are, all life is predetermined.'

He studied her eyes, the wraith-like thoughts swirling behind them. She was telling the truth, or believed she was. Crazy bitch!

He shoved her back on the bed and glared down at her, angry at himself for the growing sense of impotence. All this astrology shit was too far outside his experience.

The nightshirt had ridden up her legs. He let his eyes linger on the long provocative expanse of exposed thigh.

'Take it off,' he said softly.

'Fuck off.'

He knelt on the bed beside her, smiling. 'You knew exactly what you were doing when you asked me out here. Didn't you? You knew I'd come up here. Or didn't the cards mention that?'

He stroked her chin, receiving another glimpse into that steely reserve, but this time there was a spark of guilt corroding the composure. 'Yes,' he said. 'You knew.' His hand slipped down inside the nightshirt to cup her left breast. He enjoyed the fullness he found, the warmth, his thumb rubbing the large nipple.

'Don't push your luck,' she said. 'Remember, the only way off this island is the *Orphée*, and she's affinity bonded to me. If you want to clear out ahead of whoever is hunting you, you do what you're told.'

'If that's what you want, then fine. I can always go see Althaea. How do tall handsome strangers fit into her horoscope today?' He let go of her and stood up.

'Bastard!'

'Part of my appeal.'

He waited until she started to unbutton the nightshirt, then tugged off his T-shirt and jeans.

Charmaine's daily routine was insidiously somnolent. Eason soon found himself lapsing into the same unhurried rhythm Rousseau used to approach any task. After all, there was nothing which needed doing urgently.

The old man showed him the outhouse which was fitted out as a carpentry shop. Its roof leaked, but the tools and bench saws were in good condition, and there was plenty of power from the tidal turbine. It took him three days to fix up the shack's frame properly. He had to junk a lot of the planking, cutting new wood from a stack of seasoned trunks. After that he began to survey the remaining shacks. Two of them had rotted beyond repair, but the others were salvageable. He started to measure up, surprised to find himself enjoying the prospect of restoring them.

He decided it was because the work he was doing on Charmaine was practical, the effect instantly visible. Not like the clan's cerebral chess-like stratagems, using himself and other enforcers as the pawns, researchers as the knights.

Althaea was inevitably attracted to him, bringing him an endless supply of drinks when he was working on the shacks, eager to hear stories of the mainland beyond Peterborough. The chilled fresh juice, the sweltering heat, Rousseau's continuing laziness, and her interest were good enough excuses to down tools.

Carnea would take *Orphée* out sailing every two or three days, visiting the neighbouring islands. They would pick a couple of crates full of fruit from the accessible trees around the lagoon to trade, returning with fish or cloth or flour. She told him they only visited Peterborough every couple of weeks, carrying a cargo of lobsters from the lagoon to sell at the harbour's market, and buying essentials only available in the city.

She spent most of her days working on the *Orphée*. A lot of effort went into keeping the boat seaworthy.

He kept returning to her at night, though he was beginning to wonder why. After a week he was still no closer to understanding her. Her body might have been in great condition, but she was lifeless in bed; appropriately, for she fantasized she was making love to a dead man. On the few occasions he had managed to bring her to a climax she had called out Vanstone's name.

On the tenth day he turned down an invitation to sail with the three of them on a circuit of the islands. Instead he spent the morning overhauling a mower tractor which he found in the cavernous shed used to garage Charmaine's neglected agricultural machinery. After he had stripped down and reassembled the gearbox, and the power cells had charged up from the tidal turbine, he got to work on the lawn, driving round and round the house, grass cuttings shooting out of the back like a green geyser.

When Althaea emerged from the trees late in the afternoon, she gawped at the lawn in astonishment, then whooped and hugged him. 'It looks wonderful,' she laughed. 'And you've found the lily pond!'

He had nearly driven straight into the damn thing; it was just a patch of green swamp, with a stature of Venus in the centre, concealed by reeds. If it hadn't been for the frogs fleeing the tractor's blades he would never have guessed what it was in time.

'Will you get the fountain working again? Please, Eason!'

'I'll have a look at it,' he said. Pressed against him, her lean body left an agreeable imprint through the thin fabric of her dress.

She took a step back, face radiant. 'Thank you.'

That night Eason jerked awake as Carnea's hand jabbed into his side.

'Get up,' she hissed urgently.

It was gone midnight; a storm had risen to batter the archipelago. Huge raindrops pelted the windowpanes; lightning flares illuminated the garden and its palisade of trees in a stark chiaroscuro. Thunder formed an almost continous grumble.

'They're here,' she said. 'They're docking at the jetty, right now.'

'Who's here?' His thoughts were still sluggish.

'I don't know their bloody names!'

'Then how do you know anyone's here?'

'*Orphée* has a set of dolphin-consanguineous echo receptors fitted under her hull.' She had closed her eyes. 'I can see the boat. It's small, like a rowing dinghy. Ah, they've hit the jetty. It's wobbling. They must be getting out.'

Enforcers! It couldn't be anyone else, not creeping up in the middle of the night. Eason's training took over: assess, plan, initiate. He cursed violently at being caught so simply; his plasma pulse pistol was in the false lining of his bag back at the shack; he didn't even have nerve booster loaded in his infuser. Fat lot of use Wine was going to be in combat. Ten days was all it had taken for Charmaine's cosy existence to soften him. 'How many of them?' he demanded.

'Three. The cards said three.'

'Oh, for fuck's sake.' Crazy bitch! 'Stay here. You'll be safe. They only want me.' He rolled out of bed and shoved the window open, climbing out on to the balcony, still naked.

At least the rain and wind would stop them from using a bird to scout, but it still didn't look good.

Eason scrambled down one of the balcony pillars, rust flakes scratching his palms and thighs. He raced across the lawn, desperate to reach the cover of the trees, slipping three times on the sodden grass. Thorns tore at his legs as he sprinted into the undergrowth. There was no sign of the intruders yet.

Layia was tripping out on his tension, clawing at the cane chair in the shack where he had left her.

He forced his way through the mass of clawing vegetation until he was ten yards from the path to the jetty, then started to climb the gnarled trunk of an orange tree. The branches were dense, unyielding, but he twisted and wriggled his way through them, feeling them snap and bend against his ribs, only stopping when he was actually above the path.

Thunder and lightning swamped his senses, although he could just make out a human silhouette edging tentatively along the sombre tunnel formed by the trees. A man in dark oilskins and a broad-rimmed hat, cradling some kind of rifle. What he couldn't understand was how they had found him. If they had followed him after the aborted meeting with Tenvis, then why wait until now? It didn't make any sense.

Someone else was floundering through the undergrowth parallel to the path, making enough noise to be heard above the thunder and incessant rain.

They couldn't possibly be enforcers. Not making that much racket.

The man on the path had almost reached him when there was a commotion away towards the sea. Someone screamed. It choked off rapidly, but not before Eason got an approximate fix.

'Whitley? Whitley, where the hell are you?'

That was the one Eason had heard blundering about, shouting at the top of his voice.

'Come on, let's get out of these bloody trees,' the one on the path called in answer. 'Now shut up, he'll hear us.'

'I can't fucking hear us! And what happened to Whitley?'

'I don't bloody know. Tripped, most likely. Now come on!'

The figure on the path started to advance again. Lightning sizzled as he walked under Eason, showing a man in his late forties, a craggy face and long dark beard, eyes screwed up against the driving rain.

Eason landed behind him as thunder shook the creaking trees. He focused, and punched. Powered by an adapted musculature, his fist slammed into the back of the man's neck, snapping the spinal cord instantly, shoving fractured vertebrae straight into his trachea, blocking even a reflex grunt from emerging.

The body pitched forward, squelching as it hit the muddy path. Eason snatched up the rifle, checking it in a glance. It was a shotgun, double-barrelled. He looked to see if the cartridges were loaded and plunged back into the undergrowth, crouching low as he closed the gap on the second intruder.

The man was leaning against a tree trunk at the edge of the lawn, peering through the branches at the house. Eason stood four yards behind him, pointed the shotgun at his legs, and fired.

'Who are you?'

'Jesus God, I can't feel my legs.'

Eason had his free hand clamped over the man's face, palm squashing his nose flat. The infuser was pumping a deluge of Wine into his arteries. Raw animal panic was surging up his arm from the man's mind. 'You wont feel your prick if you don't answer me, now who are you?'

'Fermoy.'

'The truth, well done. Now, what are you? Where do you come from?'

'I'm a shipwright, over on Carlton.'

'Where's Carlton?'

'An island, five miles away. God, my legs!'

'What are you doing here, Fermoy?'

'We came for the man. You.'

'Why?'

'You're wanted.'

'And you wanted a reward?'

'Yes.'

'Who were you going to give me to, Fermoy?'

'Torreya.'

'Why her?'

'You were running from Peterborough. We thought she must want you. You wouldn't be running otherwise.'

'Who told you I was running?'

'Ross.'

Eason stared down at him, teeth bared in rage. That drunken *shithead!* He had been safe on Charmaine, home dry. He made an effort to calm down. 'When did he tell you?'

'This morning. We were drinking. It came out. You know what he's like.'

'How many of you came?'

'Three, just three.'

'And how many people on Carlton know I'm here?'

'Only us.'

He jerked his hand away from Fermoy's face. The man looked up at him, blood streaming from his nose, dread and incomprehension scarring his features.

Eason turned his hand edge on and chopped down.

The third bounty hunter, Whitley, was easy to find. He lay in the centre of a broad circle of mangled undergrowth. Eason took a couple of cautious steps towards him, shotgun held ready.

A vivid lightning bolt burst overhead.

Whitley was wrapped from his neck downwards in what looked like a spiral of piping, a foot thick, jet black, glistening slickly. He was gurgling weakly, drooling blood. Eason squinted forward, every nerve shrieking in protest.

The snake's head reared up right in front of him. It was a demonic streamlined arrowhead two feet long, the jaw open to show fangs the size of fingers; a blood-red tongue as thick as his forearm shot out, vibrating eagerly.

'Jesus!' Eason yelled. Training or not, he lurched back in terror.

'Solange won't hurt you,' Carnea shouted above the storm.

She was standing behind him, her rain-soaked nightshirt clinging like a layer of blue skin.

'That *thing* is yours?'

'Solange? Yes. He's another of my father's designs. But I'm not sure he was supposed to grow this big; he eats rather a lot of firedrakes, you see.'

The real horror was the lightness of her tone. So matter-of-fact. Crazy bitch.

Eason took another couple of steps back. The snake had been on the island the whole time. She could have set it on him whenever she wanted; he would never have known, not until the very last instant when it came rustling out of the thick concealing undergrowth.

'Do you want to question this one?' Carnea asked, gesturing at Whitley.

'No.'

Her eyes fluttered shut.

Whitley started screaming again as the coils around him flexed sinuously. The sound was swallowed up by the crack of snapping bones, a sickeningly wet squelching. Eason looked away, jaw clenched.

'I'll take their boat out and scuttle it,' Carnea said. 'Everyone will think the storm capsized them. You can bury the bodies. Somewhere where Althaea won't find them, please.'

Eason had Layia with him when he and Rousseau went drinking the next night. She claimed her usual perch on his shoulder, head swivelling around, scanning the edge of the jungle. Her natural instincts alone would alert her if that brute of a snake was anywhere near. It wasn't.

He and Rousseau sat with their backs against a fallen tree trunk on the lagoon's beach as the gloaming closed in, passing a bottle of the old man's home-brewed spirits to and fro. Eason wasn't drinking any more, although he made it look like he was.

'She's a hard woman, that Carnea,' Rousseau slurred. 'Cracked up completely after Vanstone died. Never shown a single emotion since. Not one. Can't tell me that's natural.'

Eason grunted his interest and passed the bottle back. They had been drinking solidly for two and a half hours. A sheet of low clouds hid the stars and Halo. Balmy warmth and serenity were a profound contrast to the previous night.

'She loves Althaea,' Eason said. 'That's an emotion.'

Rousseau took a long swig, his eyelids drooping. 'Crap. Loves nobody else, not even her children.' He took another swig, the liquid running down his stubble. 'Gave one away. Ice woman. Never thanks me for what I do. Kept Charmaine going, I have. All for little Althaea, not her.' He started to slide over, the bottle slipping from his fingers.

Eason put out a hand to steady him. 'Gave one what away?'

Rousseau only mumbled, saliva bubbling from his mouth. His eyes had closed.

'Gave what away?' Eason shook him.

'Twins, they were,' Rousseau sighed. 'Beautiful twins.' Then every muscle went limp; he sprawled on to the sand as Eason let go.

Eason looked at him for a long moment. Pathetic, and utterly harmless. But he was a liability.

Layia let out a mournful cheep, the only outlet for Eason's sentiment as he put his hands under Rousseau's shoulders and dragged him down to the water's edge. The old man was so drunk he didn't even react to having his head immersed in the water. Eason held him under for two minutes, then waded out and started to sweep away the incriminating tracks in the sand.

They held the funeral two days later. A dozen people attended from the neighbouring islands, staid men and women in sturdy clothes gathered around the shallow grave. Althaea leant against her mother the whole time, sobbing softly. The ceremony was

conducted by Lucius, a forty-year-old deacon from the Church of
the Lord's Earth. He was a broad-shouldered, powerful man who
captained the *Anneka*, one of the cult's traders.

Eason knew the Church of the Lord's Earth was widespread
through the archipelago; Christian-based, with a doctrine which
was implacably opposed to spaceflight. The débâcle of the Halo
had given it a solid foundation and it had grown steadily ever
since.

Along with three men from the islands, he lowered the rough
coffin he had made into the hole while Lucius led the singing of a
hymn. It came to rest on the bedrock of coral four feet down.

After the mourners departed, Eason shovelled the rich loam
back in, two of the men helping him. Nobody questioned his
presence; he was the new labourer Carnea had taken on, that was
enough for them.

It started him thinking. He had only possessed the most
generalized notion for the future when he stole the clan's
neurochemical; sell it and get out, start over somewhere else. No
destination in mind, simply a place where he could live peaceably
and indulgently; the old wine, women and song ideal.

Looking around, he didn't think he could find a more arcadian
location than the archipelago to live. It was just the lifestyle which
was the problem, this vaguely sanctimonious poor but proud kick
which the islanders shared. That and a snake which even hell
would reject.

But changes could be made, or paid for, and snakes were not
immortal.

The wake was a mawkish, stilted ordeal. Conversation between
the islanders was limited to their fishing and the minutiae of large
family genealogies. Althaea sat in a corner of the lounge, her
mouth twitching in a kind of entreating helplessness if anyone
offered their condolences. Even Carnea allowed her relief to show
when it limped to its desultory conclusion.

'I've arranged with Lucius for some pickers to visit us in a
fortnight,' Carnea told Eason after they saw off the last of the boats.
'It's a group from Oliviera, that's a CLE parish island about eight
miles away. They usually come twice a year to pick whatever fruit
is ripe; some of it is handed round to other parishes, the remainder
is sold to a trader in Peterborough and we split the proceeds.'

'Couldn't you find a better partner than the Church of the Lord's
Earth?' he asked.

She cocked her head on one side and gave him a derisive look.
'Vanstone used to be a member of the CLE until he met me,' she said.

'Right.' He didn't know what his status with her was any more, not that he had been all too certain to start with. But he hadn't bedded her for the last three nights; thoughts of that damn snake were just too bloody inhibiting.

'I don't accept their doctrine,' she said. 'But they make decent neighbours, and there are several parishioners Althaea's age. She'll enjoy their company and she deserves something to cheer her up right now.'

Halolight was an icy silver radiance that evening, tinting Charmaine's trees and foliage a dusky grey. Eason found Althaea arranging a garland of scarlet flowers on Rousseau's grave, a quiet zephyr twirling her loose mane of hair. The dark blouse and skirt she had worn for the funeral seemed to soak up what little light there was, partially occluding her with shadows.

She stood up slowly when he arrived, making no attempt to hide her dejection. 'He wasn't a bad man,' she said. Her voice was husky from crying.

'I know he wasn't.'

'I suppose something like this was bound to happen.'

'Don't dwell on it. He really loved you. The last thing he'd want would be for you to be unhappy.'

'Yes.'

He touched her shoulder as his implant extravasated a dose of Wine. The thoughts he found were so drab and wretched they were virtually unrecognizable. She had been completely numbed by the tragedy.

He kissed her brow, and began to undo the buttons on her blouse.

'Don't,' she said. But even that was an effort for her.

'Shush,' he soothed her, and carried on.

She simply stood there with her shoulders slumped, as he knew she would. He could see there was no spirit in her to protest; what he was doing barely scratched the surface of consciousness.

He pulled back the front of her blouse and looked at her breasts, then led her back through the unruly trees to his shack.

Althaea was a sublime conquest – youthful, lithe, obedient. The danger of discovery added to the intensity of his excitement. Layia was banished to the shack's roof to act as snake sentry. But Solange was nowhere to be seen, not on that night nor any which followed.

Making love to Althaea gave him the satisfaction of thwarting Carnea, her cold indifference, replacing her with her own daughter. Sweet revenge indeed. She must have known, lying alone in her own bed as Althaea was corrupted in his.

Wine allowed him to become the daemon lover which lurked in

Althaea's subterranean fantasies, frightening and thrilling her with his strength, the skill with which he played her. She would slip away from the house each night, returning to the spicy warmth and shadows that filled his bedroom. Wine showed him the sensitive filigree of nerves hidden beneath her skin, the special raw clustered endings which would make her cry out loud when his fingers and tongue commanded. He would rarely spend himself, content to taste and savour the multiple orgasms he provoked in her as she lay on his cot through the long dark hours, a pleasure parasite.

The parishioners from Oliviera were a chirpy, energetic bunch. There were twenty of them, trooping down the jetty from *Anneka*'s deck, teenagers and adolescents, loaded up with backpacks and wicker baskets. After Charmaine's usual solitude they were like an invading army.

Eason had prepared a section of the island for them, renovating a rotary scythe unit which fitted to the front of the mower tractor. He and Althaea had taken it in turns to drive the vehicle through the orange trees which were fruiting, blades hacking at the thick tangle of vines and low bushes, terrorizing the parrots and firedrakes. Now they were left with broad avenues of shredded stems, the frayed ends of limp vines swinging from arching branches. That one section, a hundred and fifty yards long, stretching right across the saddle of coral between the lagoon and the mud shingle shore, was almost back to being a grove instead of a wilderness. It was also a zone where Solange couldn't skulk about unseen.

'We'll need another trader boat to cope with the load,' Lucius said after they'd filled the *Anneka*'s outrigger holds by the afternoon of the first day. 'We don't normally get so much fruit. You've done a good job improving things here, Eason.'

He tipped his straw hat back and smiled. 'Thank you. Can you get hold of another boat?'

'I'll put in at the cathedral island this evening, ask the bishop to assign us a second. It shouldn't be a problem.'

At night the pickers gathered on the lawn. Carnea had set up a long open-range charcoal grill. They ate lobsters and thick slices of pork, washed down with juice and wine. After the meal they sang as the Halo glimmered high above, and the fountain sent a foaming white jet twenty feet up into the air.

Althaea was in her element as she moved between the groups, her face animated in a way he had never seen before.

Still later, when they had stolen away to make love in the

jungle, he lay back on his blanket and watched her undressing, skin stippled by Halolight filtering through the thick canopy of leaves, his resolve crystallized. He was going to stay.

It was Layia who spotted them, two figures sitting in the shade of an orange tree during the lunch break. Althaea and one of the parishioners, a lad in his teens.

Layia hovered silently above them, wings flickering in a steady rhythm. They were talking avidly, passing a chillflask to and fro. Her easiness with the lad irritated Eason. But he made a conscious effort to keep his feelings in check. The last thing he wanted was a scene which would draw attention and comment.

When Layia focused on the lad's face, Eason could see a disturbing amount of adoration written there. But there was something about his features which was familiar: he had a broad face, strong jaw, longish blond hair, clear blue eyes – a real charmer. Faces were an enforcer's business, and Eason had seen that face recently, yet he couldn't even point in the direction Oliviera lay.

It was Althaea who introduced him to the lad. His name was Mullen, he was seventeen, polite and respectful, if slightly over-eager. It was an engaging combination. Eason found himself warming to him.

The three of them sat together that night, Eason and Althaea and Mullen, biting into thick slices of pineapple coated in a tart fiery sauce, drinking a sweet white Wessex wine.

Carnea sat on the other side of the grill, her outline wavering in the heat shimmer given off by the glowing charcoal. Her gaze was locked on them.

'So how many times have you come here to pick?' Eason asked.

Mullen tore his attention away from Althaea. 'This is my first time. It's wonderful. I've never seen a firedrake before.'

'Where were you living before Oliviera?'

'Nowhere. I've always lived there, it's my home. This is the first time I've been anywhere except for other CLE parish islands. And they're all pretty much the same.'

'You mean you've never been on the mainland?' he asked, surprised.

'Not yet, no. I'm probably going to go next year, when I'm eighteen.'

'You've got a treat in store,' Althaea said. 'Peterborough's a riot, but just make sure you count your fingers after you shake hands.'

'Really?' Mullen switched his entire attention back to her.

Eason felt lonely, out of it. The truth was, their conversation had been incredibly boring all evening. They talked about nothing – the antics of the firedrakes, weather, which fish they liked best, how the picking was progressing. And every word was treated as though it had been spoken by some divine prophet.

When he looked around, Carnea was still staring at him, her face sculpted, immobile. He couldn't think of anything he'd done to annoy her.

He allowed Mullen and Althaea to babble on for another ten minutes, then plucked at her shirt sleeve. 'Come on.'

She glanced at him, frowning, as he rose to his feet, slapping sand and grass from his jeans. 'Where?'

He let an impish grin play over his lips and picked up their blanket. Althaea blushed, her own demure smile beginning.

'Goodnight,' Eason said affably to the lad, and steered Althaea towards the black picket of trees. He liked Mullen, but the boy had to understand exactly who she belonged to.

Layia was perched on the balcony rail, looking down at the pool of tangerine light which the charcoal spilt over the lawn. The kestrel showed him Mullen covering his face with his hands, shoulder muscles knotted. And Carnea, who hadn't been staring at him after all, because her eyes never moved when he and Althaea departed. She was watching Mullen.

When the lad's hands slipped back down to reveal a crestfallen expression, the corners of her mouth lifted into a serene smile.

Eason stood on the end of the jetty, his arm around Althaea as they waved goodbye to the *Anneka*. The parishioners were leaning over the gunwale, waving back, shouting farewells which were scrambled by the wavelets lapping on the mud shingle.

Carnea started walking back to the house. Eason turned to follow and gave Althaea a reassuring hug, noting a certain wistfulness in her eyes. 'Don't worry, I'm sure your boyfriend will stay in touch. He's madly in love with you after all.' He grinned broadly to show he understood.

Althaea shot him a look of pure venom, then her face became that same blank mask which defended Carnea from the world.

'Hey, listen–' he began.

But she shook herself free and ran off down the jetty. He stared after her in consternation.

'What did I say?'

Carnea arched her eyebrow. 'It's not what you say, it's what you are.'

'You make me out as some kind of ogre,' he snapped, suddenly exasperated with her, the tirade of oblique remarks. Even screwing her daughter hadn't chastened her. Maybe Rousseau had been right after all.

'In medieval times that's exactly what you would be.'

'Name one thing I've done to hurt her.'

'If the cards had shown you hurting her, I would never have allowed you to set foot on Charmaine.'

'Cards!' Crazy bitch.

She shrugged and sauntered off down the path to the house.

He slept alone that night, for the first time in three weeks. At midnight he sent Layia over to the house to hover stealthily outside Althaea's window. The curtains were open, but there was no light on. Layia's enhanced retinas showed him Althaea curled up on top of her bed, arms around the ancient bear, staring at the ceiling. She had been crying.

He called Layia away, guilty at intruding, still not knowing what it was he'd done.

The next morning she gave him a timid smile, and he glossed over any awkwardness with an enthusiastic account of how he planned to start clearing all the old service tracks with the mower tractor. That night he welcomed her back to his bed, but there was a reserve in her mind. The Wine revealed it to him, a dark private nebula at the centre of her thoughts which, no matter how exquisite their lovemaking was, how much ecstasy he brought her, could not be banished.

Carnea sat behind her desk in the study, dealing from her pack of tarot cards. She was aligning them in the shape of a cross, each one pushed firmly down on the wooden surface with a distinct *snick*.

'I'd like to live here permanently,' Eason said.

'You wouldn't enjoy it, not full-time,' she said. 'Oh, granted you're riding a crest with all these improvements you're making right now. It's all new and thrilling to you. But forty years of hard labour? I don't think so.'

'I wasn't proposing to do it all myself. I'm offering to buy in. I'm not poor.'

'A dowry. How quaint.' The arms of the cross were laid down methodically, five cards on each side. 'The man Althaea chooses won't have to buy his way in. I'll greet him with open arms. He will have Charmaine because she has Charmaine. It's that simple, Eason. Have you asked her if she wants to share it with you?'

'No,' he admitted. That piece of herself she held back was

starting to haunt him. It meant she wasn't entirely his any more. He didn't know how to deal with that. In some respects she was as bad as her mother.

'Good,' Carnea said. 'I don't think now is quite the right time for trite speeches of undying love.'

The sly mockery infuriated him. He leant over the desk and caught her wrist as the last card was slapped down. His infuser pumped a dose of Wine straight into his bloodstream.

Carnea didn't flinch at the pressure he exerted. He found her chimerical thoughts: surprise at his action, but no fear.

'Maybe you're jealous,' he said harshly.

A burst of shock was swiftly overcome with indignation. 'Of you? Good God, no.' And, as always, her heart longed for Vanstone.

He bit back his furious retort. Mother and daughter were so bloody alien to him, both of them defying any conventional category.

'Would you mind letting me go now, please?' Carnea asked grimly.

He released her, slouching back in his own chair. 'The money would make an incredible difference,' he said, refusing to give up. 'We could buy some more tractors, clean out the avenues, hire some labourers to strip those damn vines out of the trees. Then there's the house to fix up properly.'

'That's the short cut, Eason, the easy option. You want to be a manager, the grand plantation owner living in his mansion while others bring the crops in. That's not the way to do it. Life is about cycles; you can't fight what nature has ordained. And now we have come round to the time when Althaea is given Charmaine, just as I was given it all those years ago. I haven't done very well with it, but Althaea and her husband will. They'll rebuild Charmaine slowly. Every day there will be some new accomplishment for them to rejoice about. Their whole life is going to be rich with genuine satisfaction, not this cheaply bought gratitude you offer.'

'Then I'll give the bloody money away. She can have me just the way I am, a destitute drifter.'

Carnea's mask of indifference cracked for the very first time. She gave him a tired smile, compassion lurking in the flecked emerald irises. 'It won't make any difference,' she said weakly. 'Not to my answer, or hers.'

'I don't get it, I really don't. You brought me here, you and that monstrosity helped snuff the bounty hunters, you screwed with me, you don't mind me screwing your daughter. Now you tell me you don't want me here.'

'You are welcome to stay here as long as you like. But neither Althaea nor Charmaine is ever going to belong to you.'

'Why not?' he shouted.

Wordlessly she turned over the central card in the cross. The picture was elaborate and arcane, a hallucinogenic nightmare perfectly realized. It was death.

The clinic belonged to Torreya. It was in Peterborough's Bretton district, a three-storey post-Warming building, its tiered balconies circling a brick-paved courtyard. Eason sat in a comfortably furnished reception room on the second floor, looking out across the central well.

An enforcer had been assigned to him; Keverne, somewhere in his late twenties, whose implant eyeballs were completely black. Eason guessed they were capable of infra-red as well as low-light vision, absorbing every stray photon. It also meant he could never quite tell whether or not Keverne was looking at him.

Eason wasn't used to enforcers in executive roles. There were none in his clan, it was too big a concentration of power. Either Torreya had a lot more trust than clan directors, or her control over individuals was more extensive than even rumour allowed for.

Eason took two Wine ampoules from his jacket pocket and placed them on the table between them. He had decided the front-door approach was the only way to get rid of the Wine. It was a gamble, the greatest he'd ever made, but he had to know, had to get it *settled*. If it was Torreya who had sent the enforcers to the pub in Millfield, he could only ever use the archipelago to hide in, he could never hope to live there as he wanted, not as the lord of the isle. Torreya would notice him eventually if he did, and she was not one to forget.

Death. That's what the card had shown. And though he hated to admit it, each one of Carnea's prophesies had come disturbingly true.

It was the card which had finally goaded him into the clinic. He could not allow that crazy bitch to influence his actions, fill him with gnawing doubts, making him frightened to walk under an open sky for fear of lightning. She would end up ruling him.

But for all his determination he had to call on a deep reserve of discipline to banish the quaver in his voice as he spoke. 'I have two hundred and ninety on offer,' he told Keverne.

Keverne picked up one of the ampoules and examined the clan's seal. 'Ah yes, we were wondering when these would return to us. It was most impertinent of Tenvis to try and set up a deal outside of our auspices. Astute of you to come directly to us this time. How much do you want for them?'

Torreya knew, but she was still offering him a deal! They couldn't have been her enforcers. He almost grinned. Carnea and her cards had been wrong. 'A course of neural-expansion hormones, and three hundred thousand sterling.'

'Naturally, we are most interested in acquiring this empathic capability for ourselves,' Keverne said. 'So I can offer you the hormone course, plus fifty thousand.'

The hormone course cost a hundred and fifty thousand. Which meant, he calculated, they were offering him forty per cent of the Wine's true value. He wasn't being let off scot-free for attempting to deal with Tenvis, after all. 'One hundred.'

'Seventy-five.'

'Agreed.' It would be more than enough to buy new equipment for the groves, with plenty left over to furnish the house – starting with a double bed.

The exchange took place in a harbourside tavern less than an hour later. Eason wasn't expecting trouble, but he had his nerve booster ampoule loaded just in case. There was none of the expected sense of *déjà vu* as he sat at the rough wooden table while the ever-vigilant Layia spiralled over the district's rooftops, scanning the streets. Instead, he felt resentful at the clandestine operation; it seemed strange after six weeks of cutting timber and repairing machinery, almost as though he was backsliding.

Keverne appeared at the appointed time, accompanied by two more enforcers, whose excessive muscle-grafting parodied human form. Their respective packages were swapped in the shadowy privacy of a booth at the rear, then Eason was out. Out of the tavern, out of his own past. Moving fast. Not running, but shifting with casual agility, nerve booster singing sweetly along his spine.

He was back on the *Orphée* ten minutes later. Home and dry. He laughed as he came down off the nerve booster and picked Althaea up, spinning her round, kissing her exuberantly. She picked up his mood and hugged him back, closer than she had been for a week.

Once they were clear of the harbour, he went into the little cabin and extracted his nerve-booster ampoule, then pulled out the flat, hand-sized black lacquered box containing the neural-expander hormone ampoules. There were seven of them nestling in the contoured foam, each designed to be extravasated over twenty-four hours. He took out the first and pushed it up into the vacant O of the sphincter.

It was his clan and their dictatorial adaptation of his body which had made him what he was. Now he was going to reverse the trend, or at least counter it.

Learning how to expand the human intellect had taken twenty years of solid research; the goal was permanent access to the brain's innate savant ability. People had never realized the full potential of their neuronic structure before; a paltry fifteen to twenty per cent was the best everyday life occupied. But a medical industrial clan based in Birmingham had perfected the treatment three years previously.

Cost prevented it from becoming widespread, but several clans thought it worthwhile enough to pay for their premier executives to be expanded. And he knew his own clan's researchers had been petitioning for applications when he left, the prospect of super-technology gadgets dangled enticingly before the finance director. Then there were the rumours of city lords undergoing the course, turning themselves into political Napoleons, able to strengthen their grasp without having to add a single new enforcer to their ranks.

The hormones in the ampoule acted as synaptic stimulants, marshalling every cell in that fertile acreage of unused grey matter into full-time employment. His thought-processing ability would be increased by roughly a factor of three, with an even larger jump in memory capacity. From now on rationality would rule, not just training-installed instinct; he was moving up into executive territory, the first step into his new life. Charmaine had stopped being a hiatus. Carnea was now nothing more than an annoying irrelevance, one he could ignore with impunity. She was deranged, reading portents in the sky. Althaea belonged to him, and through her Charmaine. *Fait accompli.* If Carnea objected...well, there had already been one boating accident in the family.

It was for the best. He could do wonders with Charmaine; a smart, tough lord with plenty of money to invest was exactly what it needed. In a few years the old place would be up and jumping.

He opened the hatch and climbed out on to the deck. Humidity and silence tightened around him. Carnea was leaning against the mast, smiling dreamily. Althaea was lying on the cabin roof, propped up on her elbows, shirt open to let the air circulate over her perspiring skin.

He walked over to the gunwale and threw the nerve-booster ampoule as far as he could. It landed with a dull *plop,* sending out a few insipid ripples. Layia hovered inquisitively above the epicentre until they dispersed, then darted back to the *Orphée* and the meagre shade cast by the membrane sail.

The next week was hell. Nausea and dizziness were his constant companions as the hormones percolated through his brain, leaving him lethargic and crabby. When the rains came, he welcomed them, spending two days alternately dozing and shaking feverishly on the shack's cot.

Althaea was convinced he had come down with a virus, but he managed to talk her out of sending for a doctor from the CLE's cathedral island. They couldn't make love, of course, although she slept in the shack with him each night. He contented himself with thoughts of how high his brain would be able to take him when the course was complete, soaring like an eagle among Himalayan nirvana peaks.

On the eighth day he woke to a grey dawn light slipping through chinks in the shack's shutters. Althaea was curled up in a blanket on a nest of cushions.

His perception of the dusty wooden room was sharper than it had been in the past. It was as if he had suddenly gained a pair of prefect retinal implants after years of stumbling through life with blurred vision.

Memories had acquired the same clarity as real-time events, a savagely bright montage of images and feelings dancing behind his eyes. There was his mortification as Solange began to constrict around Whitley, the ruthless delight when he made love to Althaea for the first time. He could call up a section of Charmaine he had walked through a fortnight or a month ago, each minute detail unique and beautiful, as though it had been painted by da Vinci himself: trees, bushes, vines, mud-dusted blades of grass on the verge above the shore, all superbly textured.

There was more, beyond the recent past. He could visualize a host of places and faces from childhood, adolescence; people he hadn't thought of in over a decade, the way they laughed, their inflections and peculiarities. He had regained his entire life, the good as well as the bad.

And right there in the giddy centre of all his wonder and astonishment was the single irrevocable conclusion which his hyperactive grey cells had arrived at: he knew exactly who Mullen was.

The door of the study hit the wall with a loud *whack*. Eason strode over to the print on the wall and looked up at it. Carnea, Krelage and Vanstone, evading entropy's encroachment, a smiling family with their arms around each other, united by love, the sheer joy of living. Vanstone in his late twenties, with his beard, and his blond hair, and his clear blue eyes. Mullen. As Althaea was Carnea.

He heard the soft slap of bare feet on stone tiles and turned. Carnea stood in the doorway, dressed in a faded purple towelling robe.

'What have you done here?' he demanded.

Her glacial expression never wavered.

He walked towards her, infuser throbbing as it pumped out a dose of Wine. 'What are they, Althaea and Mullen?' His hands closed around her head, clamping down hard.

A deluge of light and sound and foreign emotions seared into his cortex, fantastically lucid.

It was her psyche he had broken open. His expansion had enhanced the Wine-induced empathy as it did every other cephalic function.

Iridescent phantasms swarmed around him, the wispy recollections of infancy, blobs of primary colour he could barely identify as humans, a world peopled by giants. Everything was extremes; heat and cold, starvation and fullness, stench and perfume, tear-rage and cooing-joy.

Childhood was unmistakable, vast strata of brightness and exhilaration. Long golden years when the world was always kind, and everyone was a friend. There were parties and sweets, presents and gorgeous dresses, smiles and shrieking laughter. Through her eyes he saw Charmaine in its prime, the way he always dreamed he could make it. She would run along endless avenues of lovingly maintained trees, feet sinking into the lush carpet of cropped grass, the air clogged with snowstorms of blossom.

Vanstone dominated her adolescence, his presence entwined snugly with every thought. From the moment he stepped ashore off the CLE trader boat she never looked at anyone else. Her lover from one of the picker families was discarded without hesitation or regret, and they were married in a glorious day-long carnival on the lagoon's beach, in front of the families from all the neighbouring islands.

Eason raced through it all, instinctively hunting out the stains of darker emotion, the sadness and longing which diseased her late twenties right up to the present day. He found the mind-shattering pain of loss when Vanstone and Krelage were drowned. The vagrant months of mourning which followed. The thoughts of suicide, of being once again with her only love. And finally the resolve: what they had kindled in each other was so special it should not, must not, be allowed to die.

Eason jerked his hands away from her, stupefied. 'My God, you cloned Vanstone.' He stumbled to a halt, reliving every nuance of the arguments she had with her father eighteen years ago, pulling them out of her memories – his memories. He remembered her, all of her, everything he had perceived through the empathic link. 'And yourself. Both of you were cloned.'

'Yes. Perfect clones were a challenge even to my father. But he triumphed in the end. He engendered them in his laboratory and I nurtured them in my womb; a second little me, a second little Vanstone, growing together even then. And when they were born I kept Althaea and gave Mullen to the CLE to raise. The cult is ever-hungry for recruits no matter what age.'

'You really think she's going to fall in love with him, don't you?' he asked, aghast.

'She already has, she couldn't do anything else. The love between us cannot be broken, it's too strong, too beautiful. And this time round there will be no intervention by fate. I read it in the cards; this time they are going to die of old age.'

'You used me. You had a lover before Vanstone. That's why you let me come here, to make the conditions as close as possible to the way they were for you.'

'Of course, as you used us to escape whatever it was you were fleeing. Althaea had to learn the difference between a meaningless sexual infatuation and the true love which only Mullen can provide.'

'Crazy bitch! You can't dictate her life like this.'

'But it's *my* life, Eason. And you *know* she doesn't belong to you. You saw the effect Mullen had on her, and she on him. He'll be back, just like my Vanstone came back.' She smiled, distant with recollection. 'So brave he was, sneaking away from the CLE and its rigid discipline, all because he couldn't forget me.'

The memory was irrepressible, that morning thirty years ago when she'd seen the stolen rowing boat stuck in Charmaine's mud shingle. A terrified, elated Vanstone pleading with her father not to send him back.

'It won't happen this time,' he shouted at her. 'I won't let it happen. Althaea is mine.'

Carnea started to laugh. He snarled at her, helpless against her mockery, then he ran from the study.

There was only a vague suggestion of the Halo left in the pale dawn-washed sky as he sprinted across the clearing to his shack.

Althaea was standing on the veranda, stretching the sleep from her limbs. She gave him a smile which soon faded when his expression registered.

'What is it?' she asked.

He stood in front of her, breathing heavily from the run. 'Do you love him?'

She blinked in surprise. 'Who?'

'Mullen. Do you love him?'

'Eason, what on earth is–'

He let out a strangled cry, and summoned up a massive extravasation from the infuser. The Wine squirted into his brain, scorching its way along the capillaries. His immediate universe became alive with dancing fireflies, pinprick flares of light, spiralling ever faster. And somewhere nearby Althaea was squealing in alarm.

Her memories burst into the chaos. A clear cool stream of consciousness.

She had seen Mullen as he was stacking baskets of oranges. A godling who was endearingly awkward when she spoke to him, who had nothing much to say, but who was desperate to talk to her. Who laughed so easily, and looked so fine. Whose face seemed to eclipse more and more of her waking thoughts.

Eason lurched forward through the cascade of impressions, into the now.

She didn't want to hurt him. She didn't know how to tell him, now that she loved another. Because he had been everything she thought she wanted from a man, the cool resolve, the physical delirium he brought, and even his imperfect past. It made him fascinating, a rich exotic tang in her bland life. He deserved better than being cast aside for someone she barely knew, someone utterly unforgettable. It was so stupid, a girlish romanticism, but she couldn't help it.

And hidden at the core of that soulful nebula of emotion he found the barrier, an event horizon cloaking the soul, oozing real-time sensations into the vault of personality.

He pressed against it, desperate to escape the harrowing bombardment of rejection. Breakthrough. He was abruptly freefalling through another set of memories. Future memories.

'We live our whole life at once,' Carnea had told him. 'Consciousness is just a window into time.' Crazy bitch with her dumb gypsy cards. Her faith in spirituality acting as a religion substitute. Or so he'd always thought.

Now, whenever now was, he experienced an emotion of pure

blinding awe, a small child lost in a cathedral of ever-shifting rainbows.

His mind began to pick out themes from the wealth of memories, weaving them into a coherent picture. He saw Althaea as a twenty-five-year-old, at thirty, at fifty, a wizened silver-haired crone, ninety-four years old. She lay in bed, joints stiff, looking out of the window at a Charmaine she had given her life to: the neat ordered ranks of trees, the rooftops of the fishing village, a crowd of people busy setting up tables in the garden for a party that evening, children laughing, adults singing. She was surrounded and adored by children, grandchildren, and even six great-grandchildren. Her eyes closed in perfect contentment.

The death-bed glimpse repelled him. He slipped back down into her near future.

Mullen would turn up ten days from now, paddling a dinghy all the way from Oliviera. A month after that they would marry, hot pink sand of the lagoon beach burning her feet all through the open-air ceremony. She was wrong about the children though, she only had seven, not ten. The first was a boy, and they called him Krelage to make her mother happy.

He could feel them in her womb, kicking softly against her belly; the pain and glory she endured at birth, blood and fluid voiding between her legs, a grotesque squeezing inside and out. Mullen's gentle proud smile lighting up her whole world.

He fled in torment, like he always did, retreating back to the only place left to him. His own childhood, the blissful sanctity of innocent youth, which was really what he had been chasing all along.

Familiar childhood summer days embraced him: times when it never rained and the sun shone all day long, running across endless green fields with his dog and his kite and his friends, laughter and smiles filling his head until it threatened to burst.

Overhead, the future began to eclipse the sun, a black organic membrane contracting like an iris. Eason stood alone on the darkened field, kissed by starlight, his kite forgotten at his feet. He looked up at the hole in space above him. He wanted to know what lay in store behind it.

His consciousness washed ashore in the real world. He remembered he would be curled up in the dirt outside his shack. Althaea would be leaning over him with concern.

He opened his eyes to see a section of sky, a slice of the shack's roof, and Althaea's face. He remembered the little groans of fright and anxiety she emitted even as they fell on his ears, each one slotting perfectly into the sequence.

Every detail his perfectly eidetic neurones had absorbed was yammering for attention, a kaleidoscopic barrage of vivid images and Babel's caterwauling. Three lives, a hundred and eighty years of human experience crammed into his skull, bloating him, leaving him no room to think, no freedom to be himself. His own life was the worst: past, present and future lined up, every word heard and uttered, every sight, every movement, every spike of pain, locked immutably into time; happened, happening, and waiting to happen. He simply could not escape.

Althaea was about to ask him what was wrong.

'Eason, please, Eason, say something. Just tell me what's the matter. Please.'

The gulping sob she finished with rattled through his mind, a double echo on either side of reality. He anticipated it, he heard it, he remembered it.

There was an agonizing week ahead of him. The bewildered psychiatrist at the CLE medical centre, the tranquillizers. His own pitiful manic belief that he could triumph, that sheer self-determination would be enough to make him forget his future.

It would ultimately end when he spread his fingers wide and pressed them to his head, triggering the electroplaque cells' discharge, his eyes wide with glee.

He remembered the demented scream, bellow after bellow which left his throat raw and knotted. The scream which never actually ended for the whole week.

He jerked his head around to catch a last unencumbered look at her seraphic face. Somewhere in the hurricane of memories there was a thread of love and enchantment, the only one he had ever really known. But it was woefully faint amid the unceasing clamour.

His tears came first, then the tortured, excruciating wail broke free.

GAP-SICKNESS
Graham Joyce

When the legislation was enacted, and everyone who was diagnosed Gap-sick had their licences revoked, I started to make a lot of money. It was a great time for forgers, and a particularly good time for me. I'd learned the counterfeiting trade inside out from my husband before he was sent down. He got ten years, and I inherited his contacts, his commissions and all of his equipment.

Do I miss him? Since the advent of Gap-sickness I've stopped lying. No, I don't miss him. I did love him, but he lied to me, he cheated on me and he abused my kindness. It's only now I realize that the biggest forgery he ever made was our wedding certificate; and since they slammed the doors on him I've been having a good time.

Mostly.

Let me be truthful, if only because I don't want to get caught with a falsehood on my lips. No, I'm not Gap-sick myself, but I'm smart enough to know it could come at any moment. The reason I say 'mostly' is because I was having a good time until I allowed myself to fall in love with Gordon. Being in love with any man can of course be one kind of hell; but nursing a lover with Gap-sickness is another thing entirely.

Gordon first came to me for a licence. Don't they all?

'You Caroline Ward?'

'No. Goodbye.'

I was in the Cooler with the girls. I picked up my Blue Lady cocktail complete with pink paper umbrella and left him standing at the bar. I was worried that he'd found me so easily – a bad sign. He didn't look like the law but I never work without an introduction, final.

'Why do you get all the come-ons?' sexy Sadie wanted to know. Unlike the other girls, she knew my trade, and sometimes worked for me.

'It's not a come-on. He wants the celluloid.'

Sadie turned towards him and made eyes. 'He looks lost.'

'Don't encourage him.'

Tell a bee not to make honey. Sadie had been diagnosed Gap-sick almost two years. At first it had made her promiscuous. Some people become horny, others completely celibate. There are as many reactions as there are people. Only I knew Sadie's later experiences had made her utterly celibate. Now she played the raging nymphet to cover her complete loss of libido, and I usually played along with her.

She made a low, lupine growl in the back of her throat as she looked him over.

'Down, girl,' I said. To be honest, I wasn't interested either. I'd had a busy day stamping out the celluloid, and the fumes from the adhesives had made me slightly giddy.

Gordon – not that I knew his name at the time – turned away from her gaze and ordered a beer. True, he did look shy. A kind of loner. Tall, blond, bestubbled, a raincoat hanging aggressively open.

'All right,' I said to Sadie, because her judgement is twenty-twenty, 'tell me what you see.'

But Sadie was gone. Her eyes told me that. They were like pellets of aspic. I watched Gordon twitch nervously at the bar until she came back a few minutes later.

'Early stages of Gap,' she said, 'probably no more than three or four weeks. Look how quickly he swigs from the bottle, hasn't thought about using a glass. Hunched against the bar in case it happens, wants to pass himself off as a bar-fly. Gloves. I'd say he's given up smoking and it's driving him crazy. And, shame this, he's had one bad experience and he's been celibate since.'

'You can't tell that by looking?'

'The more I look, the more I see, kid. Was I gone?'

'Yep. Only a few minutes.'

'He's for real. You can trade.'

'Not without an introduction, final.'

'That's easily fixed.'

'No,' I protested. Why am I such a soft touch? I tried to grab her arm but she got up and *shimmied* – she's a minx but I love her – to the bar. Then she simply picked up his beer and propelled him over to us, making lustful faces behind his back as she pressed him into a seat. Finally she introduced us.

'You must be joking!' he said when I told him how much. 'It's only a computer-sensitive bit of plastic, for

God's sake!'

'I'm famous for never joking. You obviously don't appreciate the penalties these days. Ten years for forging; fourteen for selling; life if you're implicated in a Gap accident, however minor. That's the going rate.'

I could see it was going to take just about all he'd got. He looked at me and I had to stop that weak feeling in my knees. I'm basically too damned maternal to be a good businesswoman, but I told him to take it or leave it.

He had to have it, didn't he? He was a light-aircraft pilot, that was his job, flying business executives on the short hop. He just couldn't get it into his head that the Gap had made those days over.

'Forget it, boy. You're grounded!'

'You don't know anything about it.' He'd developed a pout, childlike and endearing. 'Flying is just two bursts of intense activity either end of a journey. The rest of the time no one would even know if you were gapped. I mean, it's not like driving a car.'

I'd heard that argument advanced before, but about driving. Obviously the authorities didn't agree. You can't get more than 10 miles on the road without the celluloid for the automated checkpoints. It must drive them crazy that a backyard set-up like mine can short-circuit their sophisticated, international computerized network. Because that's how I operate. I stamp out all the celluloid myself, pay only a couple of couriers – and I keep my husband's pistol loaded.

But living with a gun is a lonely thing. I looked into this man's lynx-eyes and I felt that trickling sensation deep inside, like meltwater, reminding me of the first time I met my husband. I wanted to help him, so I made a suggestion. There was some work he could do for me, short errands he could run, plus courier jobs to discount the charge for that small strip of celluloid. The plastics and the chemical adhesives necessary for the counterfeits were giving me migraines, I rationalized, and I need someone to help me work with them. Meanwhile, he still needed that licence in order to eat. He took a swig of beer and nodded sulky assent before leaving.

Sadie was grinning at me. 'You old tart,' she said.

I was going to say something back to her, but she was gone again.

You've guessed the rest. It so happened I lost one of my operatives, and Gordon had a lot of useful contacts. He gave up piloting and came to work for me; and before I'd let him into my business, I'd let him into my bed. Sadie had been correct in her analysis: somewhere along the line he'd been shaken by a bad experience, and he'd gone in for complete sexual abstinence for a while. But at twenty-nine he was only a few years younger than me and, anyway, a couple of bottles of champagne one night made him forget all about Gap-sickness.

Gap-sickness, otherwise known as Dwight's Syndrome or diakopic encephalitis was first diagnosed about ten years ago. Though the disease is not contagious, some 15 per cent of the adult population have since been diagnosed Gap-sick. The pathogenic bacteria have been identified, although conditions for replication are still the subject of research. Current theory suggests that the affliction is stress-related.

Gordon's symptoms at that stage were the same as everyone else's. He'd be talking perfectly normally and then he was 'gone'. Paralysed. A living statue. Or in the middle of some activity he would freeze. No warning, no signs. Just that sudden unblinking immobility, and you would have to wait, maybe half a minute, maybe two minutes, before he would come back to you.

The first time I saw it happen to him he was drying the dishes after a meal. Perfectly innocuous, mimicking a New Zealand client we'd had in that day. Then this sudden suspension in time, and he was frozen in place holding a tea-towel and a plate. I never saw him mimic anyone after that.

The second time we were walking in the park. I'd found a tennis ball and I tossed it to him. He'd put his hand up to catch it and froze. The ball had sailed over his outstretched hand and bounced off his face.

Gap-sick people don't immediately know they've been 'away'. They try to continue with the interrupted conversation or activity as if nothing has happened. Then a deep resonance or echo creeps up on them and they know it. Being around the Gap-sick is spooky. There they are in the flesh but turned to stone, and where have their minds gone? Then they unfreeze, apparently with no harm done. And you never get used to it. As the fits of paralysis get longer and more frequent, you simply adjust.

At first Gordon was embarrassed; and never more so
than after the time it happened while we were making love.
He was inside me and I was pinned under his corpse-like
weight. I had to count off the moments of undignified
silence until he came back. He was mortified.

'The humiliation! I can't stand it, Caroline!'

'Was this why you became celibate before?'

'Yes, but it was worse. You can't understand it. It's not
the way it catches you that drives you crazy, it's the way it
might catch you!'

No, I didn't understand, but I tried to help, and there
was always Sadie around to talk things through with him.
She's had longer to come to terms with the problem. It had
almost destroyed her; she'd taken up a habit to deal with it,
and to pay for that habit she was ready to go out on the
streets. I like to think I saved her from that.

Gap-sick people live in a state of permanent danger. It's
not hard to imagine why. After a series of motorway
smashes, the government revoked the licences of all Gap-
sick drivers. And pilots. And navigators. We would joke that
all kinds of activities are just not sensible for those afflicted.
Roller-skating. Downhill skiing. Bull-running at Pamplona.

But the danger is not always of their own making. Many
of the early cases were victims of muggings and rape. While
in a state of paralysis they were quickly relieved of their
wallets or divested of their clothes in some public place. The
rich ones responded by hiring minders; the poor depended
on family and friends, or like Sadie found working
arrangements in which they were protected.

Yet it's never the fear of being molested or abused that
haunts the sufferer of Gap-sickness. It is the terror of *the
character of the moment* of frozen immobility.

'It's whatever is on your mind at that precise moment,'
Gordon confided to me. Even as early as then a certain light
had crept into his eyes. Here he was, an airborne cabbie
coming on at me like some kind of mystic. 'You're trapped
with whatever momentary sentiment is foremost in your
mind. If you're caught with a depressive thought, or one
that's grudging, lying, envious, petty, then you're *locked
down* with it for the duration of the paralysis.

'At first this is only unpleasant. Maybe thirty seconds
stuck with a feeling of malice, with only a dim sense of time
passing. You come out of it with a nasty taste in your

mouth, and this echo of what was there all that time. Like a photograph of you caught doing something embarrassing waved under your nose. That's it: a psyche-dimensional snapshot of where you're at at a given moment. A self-dissection. Then, as the sickness becomes worse, you get to dread being caught for three minutes or even thirty minutes with such a feeling.'

I remember thinking: if this goes on, he's going to turn into a moral being, and then where will we be? 'But what about the good thoughts? Surely it works both ways?'

'But that's just it! Most of our day isn't spent with positive thoughts. Oh yes, if you're lucky enough to be locked down with a loving impulse ...' He had a habit of trailing off his words. I could tell he was suffering over these thoughts. Philosophizing was new to him, a common side-effect of the Gap. 'And even lust is wonderful, a spicy, erotic hot wind. But most of it, most of the day, doesn't consist of happy thoughts. When we're not being petty, or trivial, we're being empty, or ignorant, or half-asleep, and to suddenly be made to realize it is hell!'

Sadie had come in and was listening to all this with a special intensity. She knew what he was talking about. 'That's right. You catch yourself forcing charitable thoughts towards people you can't stand: geeks, bores, egoists, thugs. You try to find ways of looking kindly on them. All so you don't get shafted by your own mean spirit.'

She patted his hand. It was simply a compassionate gesture designed to help him out of his despair; after all, she was *there* with him.

As far as I understood it, each 'gap' came as a rude awakening. Then you were returned to what they called the daydreaming of ordinary life. Sadie likened it to a car smash she'd once experienced, long before she'd contracted the disease. 'There I was, miles away, driving with the radio turned up loud and then bang! Suddenly I'd come to a dead stop and I was surrounded by a heap of twisted, smoking metal. That's how it feels every time.'

'Seems to me there's nothing you can do about it.' I tried to sound sympathetic, but they were leaving me behind with all this talk.

'You're wrong,' he said. 'We're going to have to use it – I mean the twisted metal – to build a bridge.'

'A bridge to where?'

'To heaven.' And he gazed at me with such a sudden intensity I was forced to look away, at Sadie. But she was too busy staring at *him*.

Gap philosophy and religion had emerged out of nowhere, and Gordon became a real enthusiast. Weird movements sprang up, recruiting members exclusively from the Gap sick. He and Sadie began attending meetings and gatherings, returning to babble ideas I couldn't understand. One weekend they went off together to a Gap rally, and returned sporting badges which said HONOUR THE GAP.

Sadie tried to explain it all to me. She'd stopped pretending to be permanently horny and her eyes were filled with the irritating light of the newly converted. 'See, Caroline? It's linked to the moment of death! That's the meaning of heaven and hell. Eternity spent in the company of the very last thought which was on your mind at the moment of your death. Now what we must do is … you're not listening!'

'I am listening.' I was. It was just that I'd heard it six times already from one or other of them.

'What we have to do is treat each moment as if it is the last one we will have imprinted on our soul for ever. Imagine if it was some paltry or unworthy thing! Could you tolerate that?'

You had to admire them. They had turned their illness into a virtue. But there was something about this sudden rush of piety that made me feel slightly queasy. It wasn't until I saw them actually *inducing* the affliction that I realized what was going on. They were no longer victims of the strange, sudden paralysis; they had learnt techniques for bringing it on themselves at chosen moments. I challenged them about it.

'It's as if you're being told by an inner voice to WAKE UP!' Sadie was full of it. 'Simple pleasures. Drawing out the moment. To appreciate things, like the instant you slip into a hot bath.'

'Or savour a delicious meal. Or when an exciting wine trickles on the palate.' Gordon.

'Or freezing the moment when you're laughing together, letting it echo back inside you.' Sadie.

Laughing together. Oh yes, then the big one. 'Orgasm,' said Gordon. 'Suspending the exact instant of orgasm is the most incredible feeling in the world. It's like falling through time.'

'Like riding on the back of a giant-winged white bird,' said Sadie.

I had a bad thought. One which I didn't like to be saddled with for the split second of its occurrence, never mind the duration of a Gap. Surely they wouldn't. Hadn't I plucked Sadie from the streets? Hadn't I given Gordon everything I had? Nothing but love and kindness to both of them? Was there another kind of gap, a moral gap, where our respective understandings of loyalty and friendship could be spaced so far apart? I put the idea out of my head.

Then I was away for a couple of days, before returning unexpectedly early.

As soon as my key touched the lock to my apartment I sensed the moment. There was no scuffling or hiding or hastening to explain. How could they, when they'd frozen themselves in the moment of their mutual orgasm? This was more than any ordinary *flagrante delicto*. There they were, naked on my bed. He was on top of her, and her legs were clasped behind his arched back. They were locked in the act, faces contorted in ecstasy, falling through time, the perspiration still drying on their bodies. I'd caught them riding their white, winged bird.

I had no way of knowing how long they had been that way, or how long the condition would last. Their open eyes were fixed on each other, and although those eyes were like frozen chips of ice, something was still passing between. What sentiment were they honouring for each other? Did betrayal figure in this transcending of the Gap?

As I stood over them, I suffered a wave of sadness. How beautiful they looked, how unearthly. Rodin couldn't have captured it. Their abstract love seemed to pulse from them, the only moving thing in the room, and for a moment I was filled with the generosity of forgiveness and acceptance. I thought of everything they'd said, and perhaps it was true, perhaps I could have happily died with that thought in mind.

But in a single, venomous heartbeat the sentiment expired, to be replaced by a proper rage of jealousy and hatred. I went and fetched my pistol. I loaded it and levelled it at them, hands trembling wildly, perfectly prepared to blast them into eternity.

Something stopped me. I brought to mind the appalling truth of their philosophy of the moment of death. Did I really have the power to send them winging to heaven? Or crashing, in flames, to hell?

I went to my workshop and fetched an industrial-strength bonding agent. I used the instant adhesive to seal their lips, before bonding their genitals. When they 'came back' to find me gazing at them, there was going to be no sudden scramble for clothes, no desperately inadequate apologies. Then I sat down on the chair and cocked the pistol.

That was five minutes, or an eternity, ago. The moment they return to consciousness, I'm going to kill just one of them; Sadie or Gordon, I haven't decided. I want both of them to appreciate the act. One of them is going to find themselves bonded to a bloody corpse, and I'll take the responsibility in hell if their Gap-philosophy proves to be true.

But what hurts most as the seconds tick away is that there was a moment back there when I could have forgiven them. An instant of compassionate generosity, offered to me for a few seconds, which I failed to take. I'd really prefer not to have had the choice; then I could believe it's my unavoidable destiny to do the contemptible thing in carrying out this execution.

Because when they do come to, there's going to be one almighty Gap.

Friendship Bridge
Brian W. Aldiss

Someone he did not know was with him. They passed a place where light bulbs were made. He accepted all this. And this square was named after an enemy he could not recall. Everything was wooden.

He – or it was someone like him – was climbing wooden stairs. Laughter from an upper room. When he got there, after enormous effort, a madman with his hair alight was waiting to cut his head off. To remove it slice by slice.

And he seemed to want to have it done to him.

The noise was awful, as of cracking bone ...

1. THE SPEECH

The sound of firing in the Prospekt Svobody roused Burnell. He sat on the side of his bed, shaking, trying to compose himself. When the shots ceased, and the sound of running feet, he got up and went over to the window. Outside lay the avenue, lined with acacias, bathed in the acidic light of another Central Asian day. He could see no bodies. Perhaps the army had been celebrating an imagined victory.

Burnell spent some while soaking his face and regarding it disapprovingly in the mirror. Then he washed, rebandaged his leg and turned out his suitcase looking for a clean shirt. His dirty one he threw over a chair in distaste. He struggled into the ill-fitting suit which a Shi'ite tailor had run up for him. Before leaving the room he locked his suitcase.

The elevators of the Hotel Ashkhabad had ceased working, possibly during the war with Uzbekistan. The war with Uzbekistan could be blamed for many discomforts. A notice on the elevator gates said: PLEASE DESCEND TOMORROW. Burnell took the unswept staircase down to the foyer. A number of men in shaggy hats, some of them with light machine-guns hitched over their shoulders, stood about smoking. There was this to be said for Burnell's locally made suit; he appeared less foreign in it, and less an object of suspicion.

Since the dining room of the hotel did not open before two p.m., Burnell went out into the street to his favourite café. Heat was already beginning to bite and the smog to thicken. He liked the tree-lined streets about the centre of the city; he had been in worse places.

The Koreans had established a fast-food restaurant called Tony's. Entering, Burnell found himself a seat by the window, where he ordered coffee and yoghurt. By local standards, Tony's was both clean and elegant. At eight in the morning, it was already full of customers, all male, who appeared to have settled in comfortably for the day. The yoghurt was excellent.

Unsmiling but polite, the Koreans moved among the tables. Joseph Stalin had exiled their grandfathers here in the 1950s.

Sympathy with countries trying to live down their abysmal past and come to terms with an uncertain present was part of Burnell's survival kit in troubled parts of the world. He nevertheless disliked appointments that were not kept and contacts who never turned up. He prepared himself now, as he crunched a sweet, hard biscuit with his coffee, to meet one such contact three days later than arranged.

Through the throng, a broad-built man with a powerful face was bearing down on Burnell. Abed Assaad drew up a chair from another table and seated himself opposite Burnell.

Roy Burnell was slenderly built, in his early forties; he felt himself fragile against this mountainous man, whose head sat like a boulder on his frame. He smiled and greeted Burnell, enquiring after his wound.

'Which wound?' Burnell asked.

Assaad said, 'The leg, isn't it, no?'

'I thought you meant . . . Never mind.' Hastily, Burnell brought from his breast-pocket the crumpled business card he had found awaiting him in his pigeonhole in the hotel. He smoothed it.

It read:

Dr Abed Assaad
Curator-in-Chief
Archaeological Intensities Museum
1 Khiva Street
Ashkhabad
Turkmenistan Soviet Union

Seeing it, Assaad said, 'Is my old card. You see a misprint there, unfortunately. Also this nation naturally does not longer belong to the Soviet Union since the days of Boris Yeltsin.'

Burnell nodded. He added, compressing his lips, that his arrangements for this visit to Ashkhabad had been made in Frankfurt. It was understood that Dr Assaad or a deputy would meet him at Ashkhabad airport. No one had come. Nor had his hotel been booked, as promised.

Burnell had had to make his own arrangements, with some rather unofficial assistance from Murray-Johnson at the British Consulate. He had been in the city for three days, frustrated at every turn when it came to meeting qualified people. His work was almost done and only now had Dr Assaad appeared.

Dr Assaad nodded his head as he listened to Burnell's complaints, commenting only that the city was full of tourists, each with various demands. As he did so, he retrieved his card and tucked it into the breastpocket of his grey jacket.

'You received my letter, Dr Assaad?'

By way of answer, Assaad summoned a waiter and ordered two glasses of wine. He also suggested cake, but Burnell refused.

'Cake is good when not stale. But maybe too sweet for your British taste, possibly? I am sorry not to meet at the aeroport. Frankfurt is one place and Ashkhabad another. What cities have you seen?'

Burnell said that Murray-Johnson and a Unesco representative had driven him to Mary, with its five walled cities, but his parent body, World Cultural Heritage, had already registered the site.

With a non-committal shrug, Assaad said, 'I know Mr Murray-Johnson, naturally. Maybe he understands the problems of a new nation like Turkmenistan, maybe not. Possibly not. Since we have democracy, there are problems at all levels with bureaucracy. Is difficulty with organizations, you understand? New times, new problems.'

'I understand the same people are in power under President Diyanizov since the coup as were before.'

Assaad swept this statement away with a broad gesture. He hunched himself over the table, so that his powerful chest made a considerable approach towards Burnell. In a low voice, he said, 'Careful what names you mention. Get to know the immense changes which – what is it? – yes, convulse Central

Asia. Get to know me better, Mr Burnell. You will find a good man in a sea of imbeciles, unhappily. Don't take offence. New avenues are difficult to open. Much has been closed down since the war. I tell you, confidentially. The Archaeological Antiquities Museum is closed down. Even worst, is now a school for sons of mullahs, you understand? I have no job, though I do it still, as I can. Otherwise, I have to trade to support myself and my wife, indefinitely . . .'

He slumped back in his chair and smiled as if he was the happiest man in the world. When the waiter brought two small glasses of thin yellow liquid, he drained his glass at once. Burnell took his more slowly.

'Maybe too much sweet for the British taste, understandably?'

'So who looks after the local antiquities now? Isn't there a government department any longer?'

'Of course, of course. It pulls things down, not up. We can get no money from World Bank for reconstruction. Of course nothing from Moscow. Maybe we walk in the park where we can speak? Is not too hot for you?'

'Not too hot for British taste, no,' said Burnell with a smile.

Assaad smiled and winked as he handed a wad of folding money to the waiter. 'I like humour. There's quite a lot, eh?'

Pushing through the swing-doors into the avenue, they found the dry heat awaiting them. Assaad said in a hurried voice, 'You mention the president's name in there, so you make me nervous. Listeners may consider we plot.'

The park had been a pleasant place, abutting an immense building which was once the local KGB headquarters. A burnt-out gun-carrier stood among splintered trees, a reminder of the recent coup. Small boys played on it, shooting each other in friendly fashion.

Old men, bent and solitary, walked among birches. Their woollen clothes were grey with age. Their hands were clasped behind their backs.

'People listen in cafés,' said Assaad, matching his stride to Burnell's. 'Not many men speak English here, but they are suspicious, unavoidably. All nations in Central Asia search a new cultural identity, rightly. It makes them suspicious.'

'Your English is good.'

As they passed a melon-seller, Assaad frowned at the man as if he embodied all the country's vices.

'I am among the savages, Mr Burnell, frankly. It's a refreshment to hear your English spoken as only an Englishman can. Killing is the local occupation. Turkmeni tribes are peaceful nice people, but when the money and jobs run out, then kill, kill . . . Ten thousand men were killed here last February in the riots. Still there's shooting. We have no justice. Criminality on every level – tribal rivalries, once suppressed. Propaganda from the government. The water's bad. Medicine short. Epidemics rising. And I can nowhere find *The Hand of Ethelberta*.'

'Sorry? Who's Ethelberta?'

Assaad looked pained. He halted and scrutinized Burnell's face. 'You naturally know *The Hand of Ethelberta*? By your great novelist Thomas Hardy. It is the one of his best novels, understandably. Here, no such item can be found. Publishers in London and Paris are far distant. Not to be discovered in all the stalls of the grand bazaar. Maybe the mullahs pronounce it blasphemous. Do you say *The Hand of Ethelberta* is blasphemous? For over three years I have searched it.'

'You read much English literature, Dr Assaad?'

He threw up his hands, as if wishing not to delve deeper into the miseries of life. 'Well, it's the case that we all have hidden agendas in our lives. You also, I believe, Mr Burnell?' He gave a sideways glance at Burnell.

Burnell was not as yet willing to confide in his new acquaintance. He was due to meet Murray-Johnson again, and could check on Assaad's credentials. His answer was evasive.

After a brief silence, Assaad said with a sigh, 'Anyhow, I must assist you if I can do it. That's the point. That's my wish, intensely, to make you welcome in this city. Life is not simple here for foreigners.

'You write from Frankfurt that in the name of Culture you must visit the old mosque, 6 kilometres from here, the mosque of Mustapha Pasha. Is of great historic interest, very very beautiful. The dome of azure rises on parapets. In the front is a porch, supported by six slender marble columns. And on top of the porch, very unusually, is four small cupolas. The mosque is well built of worked sandstone, a rarity hereabouts, and of bricks in double rows. The date is from end fifteenth century and is famous in architecture.

'I shall drive you to see it in my brother's car, since he owes me a favour.'

The offer had come too late. Burnell had hired a taxi and driven out to the mosque the previous day. Hence his annoyance with Dr Assaad. He had found the mosque much decayed and hideously restored. The old mihrab, from which the Koran was read, proved to be a shoddy new construction. Most of the original interior tilework of the mosque was missing. Nothing remained that his parent organization, World Cultural Heritage, would wish to record. He said as much to Assaad, adding, 'It's not worth a prayer, never mind a visit.'

'Ah, your English humour! "Not worth a prayer, never mind a visit . . ." "Not worth a prayer . . ." Very very good. Anyhow, I agree, it's an ugly structure, entirely. It was built by a Jew.'

Burnell, always alert for anti-Semitism, bridled at this and rattled off a lecture about the enlightened Rabbi Moshe Gourits, who, to celebrate his cordial relationship with his Muslim neighbours, had financed the building of the mosque in 1491.

Bringing learning to bear, Assaad asserted, 'The Jew built in 1498, excuse me, by the Christian calendar. A bad year. Torquemada died and Savonarola was burnt.'

'The matter with the mosque,' Burnell said, 'is not that it was built by a Jew, but that it has been restored by Communists.'

Assaad gave him a melancholy look. 'I am a Syrian by birth, although many year pass since I see my native land. Forgive my simplicity. Jews and Syrians . . .' He drew a finger across his throat and hung out his tongue. Then he treated Burnell to a smile of wide and untrustworthy charm.

Feeling he had been unjust, feeling, as he so often did on his travels, that he would never understand other people, Burnell said, 'It is hot. Excuse me. Possibly there is some other memorable structure I should inspect which is not in the Frankfurt files?'

Assaad winked again, and held aloft a celebratory finger, perhaps as a token that he had won over this stiff and difficult Englishman. 'Tomorrow I come early to your hotel in my brother's car and I take you to inspect the Friendship Bridge.

'It's as you would say it, "Worth a prayer, never mind a visit".'

Burnell had procured a vintage postcard of the railway station. On it he wrote a few lines to his ex-wife in California, posting it before Dr Assaad arrived in an old Volkswagen Golf.

The nightmares had visited him again during a sleepless night. His leg pained him and he felt feverish.

Would Stephanie tear up the card, supposing it ever arrived in Los Angeles? Ashkhabad was further from Moscow than Moscow was from London. Even in the new twenty-first-century world, it remained a remote place, one hardly considered by the outside world until the disintegration of the Soviet Union in the 1990s. What would Los Angeles make of it? These cards he sent her from the distant places to which his profession took him had once been mute pleas to Stephanie to think of him, possibly even to love him again. Hope, much like the view of Ashkhabad railway station, had faded with the years. Now his cards were little more than boasts, pathetic even to himself. Dearest Stephanie, Ashkhabad is a pleasant modern city, situated on the world's longest irrigation canal. Look, I'm here, and enjoying myself. Moderately.

But there was another reason for his being somewhere east of the Caspian, apart from his quest for buildings which World Cultural Heritage might consider worth recording and preserving.

This he explained to Dr Assaad as they drove in the oven of the car away from the hotel.

Burnell's life had been disrupted, like a plate dropped on a tile floor. He was still trying to put the pieces together.

Roy Edward Burnell was a specialist in ecclesiastical architecture, just commencing commissioned work in Frankfurt, headquarters of the largely Germanic EC. He had stumbled into the Antonescu Clinic in Budapest. The Clinic had pillaged his memories, only parts of which he had been able to regain. Some of his most private moments had been sold round the world on the black market to the false-memory addicts of Nostovision.

'I need your help, Dr Assaad,' he said. 'You see, I believe a fragment of my memory which I vitally need is here – here in Ashkhabad. I have been led to believe that President Diyanizov has it.'

He started to explain how he had managed to buy back stretches of his memory in Budapest. The parts, if retrieved, could be reinserted in his brain. But Dr Assaad was not listening. He sounded his horn to drive pedestrians from the middle of the crowded street. The roadway was choked with vehicles, all hooting.

'It was in Budapest . . . A small nameless square off Fo Street,' Burnell found himself saying. 'Next to the Ministry of Light Industry. And to think I went there voluntarily . . . A new form of mental vandalism...' He pressed a hand to his face, close to where emptiness had its throne.

'Hang up a moment,' said Assaad. Then more angrily, 'Curses!' He stopped the car abruptly. People were jostling past the vehicle, swarming ahead to where a posse of armed police controlled a barricade.

'*Merde*,' said Assaad. 'I should have drove the other way. Now we're stuck, obviously. In the main square, the President's chief general, General Makhkamov, will address the people today. I forgot it . . . We cannot escape. It would look hostile. We leave the car and go to listen to Makhkamov.'

'Is it safe?'

'For us or for the car? Come. Men must listen to lies occasionally. It's duty.' After parking his brother's car under a tree, Assaad removed the spark plugs from the engine and locked all the doors.

A crowd was gathering outside the main mosque. Looking about, Burnell saw a handful of veiled women, standing close together in the shade of a tree. All the rest were men and boys, mostly wearing suits, with keffiyehs slung round their heads.

Women! The element of Muslim society which Burnell found most dispiriting was their seclusion. When women were to be seen, most went shrouded in *chadors* from head to foot. He missed their presence in shops, in restaurants, on the street. He had visited a brothel but felt more compassion than lust for the girls imprisoned there. The lean hags of Tartary held little appeal.

Yesterday, a woman driving a car had waved a greeting to him. He had been too surprised to return the wave. Later he realized she must have been on the staff of a European embassy. He still carried an impression of her smile, her hair blowing free, her naked wrist, unbraceleted.

'You see,' Assaad said into Burnell's ear, 'President Diyanizov stands for the development of Turkmenistan as a modern secular state after the Turkish pattern. This General Makhkamov supports him. Both men are of the same tribe. But the mullahs wish to follow Iran into a fundamentalist Islamic pattern, which will mean a closed society and many difficulties for us Unbelievers. So the General Makhkamov may say something interesting. We may learn which way the struggle goes, hopefully.'

He added, 'One problem is, here we are closer to Iran than Turkey. And more close still to nowhere . . .'

The sun shone. In the main, the crowd stood silent. Burnell could see no foreigners apart from himself. On the outskirts of the gathering stood a more rural kind of man, dark of visage, turbaned, some with dogs and small hairy goats on strings. Beyond them, lining the square, were tanks with their guns pointing inwards. All waited with a patience Burnell tried hard to feel in himself.

A band played distantly, its notes bleached in the fierce sunlight.

General Makhkamov was a sturdy man, small of stature, with dark piercing eyes which searched the crowd before he ascended a podium to speak. He was in uniform, shaven, moustached, with a row of medals on his chest and a military strut. Burnell had seen such men before; in his experience they did not last long. But there was an unending supply of them.

Assaad translated some of Makhkamov's speech into Burnell's right ear.

'"Those of you who fought in the war against a cruel enemy, you will be rewarded. Those cowards who stayed at home will get nothing when the time comes . . . Our brave heroes, all those who took up arms, all those prepared to die for our nation, all those who stood fast against an evil foe and trod the path of Allah and legality, all those who bathed themselves in the gore of the invader – they all shall come to high office . . . We shall see it happen . . . We shall become a great nation in world affairs, guarding our independence under a just God . . . Your scars, your medals, your courage, your loyalty, shall gain you power. And we shall be ruled by brave and honourable men . . ."'

Assaad turned away in disgust when the speech and prayers were over. He remarked to Burnell as they got back into the car, 'Oh, to live in a country where cowards are allowed to rule . . .'

'People always rant like that after a war. Nothing ever gets done. So what are the indications? Which will prevail? The secular state or the Islamic one?'

Flinging the car violently into gear, Assaad backed through the dispersing crowd, hooting continually. 'Muddles, Mr Burnell. Nothing clear. You see, it's not just the religious question. Also are tribes competing – Ersaris, Yomuds, Goklans, two sort of Tekkes . . . Not bad people, pretty easy-going, unlike my own countrymen, I'm afraid to say it. What are you to do?'

He shrugged his ample shoulders, smiled, shouted a curse at a cyclist he had just missed.

'You don't plan to go back to Syria or to the West?'

'The West I hate, honestly. Not her books but her ambitions. Is the cause of many troubles. Russia always makes mistakes in looking to the West, in envy or in admiration. But I hate Russia more and more. And Turkmenistan most.' He laughed, removed his hands from the wheel to exclaim, 'All men here believe Genghis Khan's blood runs still in their veins. What a life, is it! And my wife is Goklan tribe, wishing never to eat the bread of a different nation . . . Syria I don't like. Do you like your own country, the country of Thomas Hardy?'

'Yes, I suppose so. It's much changed.'

They were moving through suburbs now. Pleasant trees grew here and there, mitigating the utilitarian aspect of the streets.

'Then why you are come to such a place as this?'

'As I was trying to explain, I believe President Diyanizov has a vital fragment of my memory. I want it restored to me. Can you secure me an audience with him? Frankfurt was unhelpful in that respect.'

'What you want back your memory for? It makes only trouble. You see this fine little General Makhkamov, who never met a live enemy on the battlefield, he stirs up memory in his people. They hold thousand-year-old grudges against the people in the north. Isn't that mad, I'd say! Memory is the curse of nations. Best to be free of all memory.'

'So you can't help?'

'Maybe tomorrow. Be in no hurry. Old Goklan saying is, "Sit on your horse and see the grass grow . . ." Today we visit the bridge.'

Sweating in the heat, Burnell, who hated asking favours, pursued the question. 'Dr Assaad, this fragment of my memory – well, I've been informed by a dealer that it was sold to President Diyanizov. One of a very limited number of prints. If I could get hold of it, I could have it reinserted. It's one of a crucial period of my life. Without it – I can't explain. I'm a prey to nightmares. I never feel complete.'

The thin traffic ahead was slowing. They were approaching a crossroads. A motorcyclist roared up and down the road, signalling vehicles to stop. Assaad muttered to himself and wound down his window. Imitating the action, Burnell thrust his head into the heat, tasting the bitter tang of unburnt diesel. A tank was manoeuvring into position ahead in a haze of exhaust, establishing a roadblock. Armed guards unbaled razor wire across the road, directed by an officer, while a guardpost with the national flag was being set up.

Two soldiers were moving away pedestrians. A woman shouted harshly at them, gesticulating while her child screamed. Cars backed and revved down a side road, directed by a policeman holding an incongruous pink parasol.

'What's up?' Burnell asked, thinking even as he did so that the question was foolish. Assaad did not answer. He switched off his engine and sat waiting while an officer on a motorbike approached the car. The officer thrust his face through the window, looked about suspiciously and demanded their papers. Burnell and Assaad handed them over, the latter conversing in a mild way, his face full of smiles.

The officer scrutinized Burnell's EC passport and WCH credentials, returning them with a few courteous-sounding remarks.

'He says you are not to look so worried,' Assaad translated. 'As a foreign visitor from the West, you are welcome here, and will not be harmed. He wishes to announce he follows English football.'

More conversation passed between Assaad and the officer until Assaad was ordered to turn the car round and head back to town. The officer gave them a salute and a smile as they moved off, before turning to the next vehicle to arrive.

'I happen to know where he lives,' Assaad remarked, 'and once sold his brother some carpets at a good price, financially. We cannot leave the city today. It seems that after we left the main square, Academy Square, some naughty fellow shot at the General Makhkamov whom we listened to. Now they seek this naughty fellow, and have closed the city . . . It's just a game these people play.'

'So, it's tomorrow we must visit the Friendship Bridge.'

2. THE BULLET

Robert Murray-Johnson was a red-haired man with a square jaw and an air of good humour. Burnell had already discovered that this good humour concealed an agreeable vein of misanthropy, which found ample to feed on in the Turkmeni capital to which Murray-Johnson had been posted.

He collected Burnell from the Hotel Ashkhabad just as night was falling and the intense heat of the day promising to abate. The back of his small car was loaded with tennis racquets and sports gear.

'You're sure you want to do this, Roy?' Without pausing for an answer, he went on, 'Your friend Dr Assaad came to see me as soon as he dropped you this morning. He knows his way round the city okay, poor bugger. His survival depends on it. We do him a favour, stretch a point now and then. After all, Syria is rather popular in Britain just now, can't think why. Seems Britain's popular in Syria too – again, can't think why.'

'They read Thomas Hardy.'

As he steered into the heavy evening traffic, past the camel-coloured Russian tour buses lined up outside the hotel, Murray-Johnson explained that it was impossible for any foreigner, apart from heads of state, to have audience with the President. Certainly, no matter as personal as a stolen memory could be broached, even through intermediaries.

However, Dr Assaad knew someone who owed him a favour who kept a Nostovision shop in the back streets of Ashkhabad. NV had been banned in most of Central Asia because of its high pornographic content; but, as with most things – said Murray-Johnson with a sly smile – there was a way round that. Assaad had arranged that they could look the stock over.

Chinese-built trams rattled along the centre of the avenue as they eased their way down the long Ulitza Engleska. Murray-Johnson cheerfully put a gloss on the street name by explaining to Burnell that the British Army had defeated the Red Army near Ashkhabad in 1918, and occupied the area. As they passed a busy market, where the fruit stalls outside its portals were illuminated by small kerosene lamps, the street grew more drab.

'About here,' Murray-Johnson muttered. 'Dog's Piss Alley . . .'

He turned down a side street, to pull up next to a ramshackle *chaykhana* from which loud music boomed. The day had turned as purple as a bruise. Assuring Burnell he had been here many times before, he led the way down an alley beside the teahouse, and banged on the door of a large building constructed of breeze blocks. Fruit bats poured from an enormous quercus tree overshadowing the building. The door was promptly unlocked from inside and Burnell and Murray-Johnson were admitted.

A beefy man standing inside held out his hand. Murray-Johnson passed over some cash.

They had entered a large store. Racks filled with diverse goods formed narrow aisles. Murray-Johnson moved down the aisles without hesitation. In a glass-fronted office on the far side sat a small wizened man with oriental features, introduced to Burnell as Mr Khan.

Mr Khan put aside a cigarette, coughed, and led them to the Nostovision department. NV bullets were piled everywhere, each in its plastic pack. Large signs above the racks indicated categories: MURDER, LOVE, SEX, ADVENTURE, CHILDHOOD, and so on. All the stock was second- and third-hand.

Here were stored true memories, some legitimately obtained – for many people were ready to sell exceptional parts of their life memories to NV studios – and some stolen, as Burnell's had been in Budapest. These thousands of memories represented fragments of real lives – happy, sad, crazy. Memories of mad people had enjoyed a vogue in the West a year earlier.

Khan shuffled among his wares in silk slippers, pointing vaguely here and there, explaining in broken German. While the legitimate bullets were labelled correctly, stolen memories were deliberately mislabelled, as a provision against prosecution. Seeing Burnell's expression of despair, Khan winked, raised a knowing finger and took him to a side table.

Following Murray-Johnson's instructions, the storekeeper had set aside six NV bullets sorted from his stock. All their plastic cases bore the legend *'Fabriqué en San Marino'*. This, Khan assured them, meant the bullets originated in an illegal studio in Budapest. It was the studio's way of covering its tracks.

'Do you buy these from the President when he's finished with them?' Burnell asked.

Half-closing his rheumy eyes, Khan gave him a sidelong glance and said, 'Mein herr, I am a poor trader, ask no more. *Die Welt zerfällt in Tatsachen*. But there are no facts here, illusions only.'

'What's he on about?' Murray-Johnson asked.

'Believe it or not, I think he's quoting Wittgenstein: "The world divides into facts" . . . Let's have a look at these bullets.'

He sorted through the cases, conscious that hope was making his heart beat faster. Their titles suggested an arbitrary knowledge of the English language: 'Not in the Tree Ran any Lake', 'In the Hat Warfare a Sky Tooth Jumper', 'Animals Sequestered with a Green', and others, equally oblique.

Four of the familiar Nostovision receivers stood against one wall. Burnell seated himself in one of the chairs and adjusted the plastic helmet over his head before switching on. He inserted one of the bullets into the system unit and touched a couple of keys.

His eyes closed. Almost at once, he lost a clear perception of his surroundings – an instance of how quickly short-term memory decayed. Peculiar lassitude overcame him. In what felt like the fibre of his being, electric current was stimulating the amacrine cells of his brain. Next second, the synaptic transfer was made: the memory data stored in the bullet flooded his cortex with mnemons.

The interior of the hut was dim. Its details had not registered. The floor – he could see that clearly enough – was bare earth. An animal of some kind was there. A bed of a sort with a blanket on filled one side of the room. A barefoot woman crouched by the bed. Some details were sharp: the big blue flowers on her dress, crawling round the outline of a buttock, ascending across the broad back to the neck. She wept into her large hands, spatulate fingers pressed to forehead.

Burnell too was making noises, sobs part-stifled. He moved nearer to the woman, putting a gnarled hand on her shoulder. Hand and shoulder smudged into dimness, lost by the distortions of a tear.

He looked down as she did at a child lying on the blanket. He knew it had died of a variety of ills, mainly pneumonia, brought on by near-starvation. It was a boy. The boy's lips were drawn back, revealing pale gums in a horrifying grimace. Burnell reached out and closed the mouth and eyes. The woman rose, beginning to shriek, beating her head with clenched fists in her pain.

Feeling his own weakness, Burnell stooped, tenderly lifting the dead child. Probably he was the father of the weeping woman; probably she was the mother of the boy. He had other people in his mind, dark, concerned, slow-moving.

Slow-moving himself, he carried the boy from the shack. The woman remained behind, standing against a wall. Again the blue flowers on the dress, drooping.

The world outside was dung-coloured. He felt the sun at zenith weighing on his shoulders, a familiar burden. Other people arrived, walking as if in a fog. They spoke an incomprehensible language – yet Burnell understood it. They shared his grief. All suffered alike. A sense of community was strong.

He settled himself under a tree, easing himself down against its slender trunk, still clutching the dead child. The boy was as light as a toy in his arms. Cross-legged in the shade, he also wept. Old men squatted by him, prodding grey fingers abstractedly in the dust.

Burnell said to them, 'We have not long before we follow him.'

A leaf fell from the branches above. It floated down to the forehead of the dead boy. All the world was lost in concentration on the leaf. It settled green on the puzzled black forehead. It turned yellow, altering its living shape as it did so. Within minutes, heat withered it and turned it brown. It became nothing, and blew away on the lightest breeze. The boy's cheek too had already begun to wither . . .

'It's not mine, it's not mine!' He was speaking the foreign tongue as he switched off. Though Khan and Murray-Johnson came into view, and the warehouse, his sense of bereavement remained. He removed the cap and had to walk about. Khan, used to such reactions in his memory-store, grinned and proffered a cigarette, which Burnell accepted. Murray-Johnson, in one of the other chairs, was smiling, eyes closed.

Pacing up and down, puffing inexpertly, Burnell could imagine the old man – the old man he had briefly been – going to the nearest city to sell his memories to an NV agent for almost nothing, to gain a few pence for the funeral of his grandson. Then he would be free of all memory, and presumably would no longer grieve.

He might, however, suffer a sense of loss similar to that which Burnell felt, having been robbed of some of his memories of life with Stephanie.

It was all he could do to force himself back to the apparatus and to try another bullet labelled *'Fabriqué en San*

Marino'. Fortunately, the next bolts of memory were less harrowing. A trip in a powerboat over a great reef, with a huge party on a small island. A frivolous life in a Patagonian town, lived by a woman who ran a successful milliner's. An apartment in a bleak township where snow always lay thick, with drunken fights and an excursion to hunt reindeer. An uneventful week in a small dusty village, where a married couple lived in fear of their mentally deficient son . . .

All these invasions were as real to Burnell as his own life. He escaped from each of them exhausted, awed by the rigours of human existence, entranced by the people he had been. Their joys, their sorrows, became fairly quickly eradicated, since no transference was made in the NV projector from the short-term to the long-term memory. Already the poor old man with his dead grandson was beginning to sink from mind, though a fading leaf of sadness remained.

'Shirts in a Cupboard' opened in an outdoor setting. He was aware of this new mnemonic person as little more than a pair of boots and a pair of hands, one of which clutched a sickle. Heat made the hands and arms glisten. He saw that the hands were those of a youth. He felt himself to be young and lusty. The sickle swung and swung, almost without cease. It was early summer. He was cutting down cow parsley and goosegrass.

Burnell worked his way along steadily, from right to left, avoiding a camellia which had finished flowering. Every now and then, he caught glimpses of a garden, a smoothly mown lawn. Tantalizingly, he saw a woman walking beside an ornamental pond, tall and dark. But he bent his back and continued with the work.

It was finished. Burnell wiped the sickle on his jeans and laid it on an oak bench. He entered a house, ascending a narrow stair to the bathroom. By contrast with the sunshine, the interior was dark. Pictures framed and glazed on the walls yielded not their true subjects but reflections of distant doors and windows.

In the bathroom, Burnell pulled off his shirt and washed his face and torso, drying them on a blue towel. He caught a mere glimpse of himself in the mirror above the basin. Fair, sharp-featured, possibly early twenties . . .

Leaving the sweaty shirt on the floor, he trod over it and went across to find a clean one in the airing cupboard. He pulled the door open.

Inside the cupboard, newly laundered clothes were in immaculate array. Ironed sheets were stored on a high shelf, together with duvet covers. Burnell's shirts were hanging in orderly fashion. He saw a pile of his clean handkerchiefs, his socks rolled into balls. Her dresses were there too, crisp, creaseless.

Without a further glance, Burnell reached forward towards the shirts and–

–without a pause was running down the right wing with the ball at his feet. Green field, brown blur of crowd in stadium. The Italian mid-fielder Raniero charging towards him. The roar of the spectators went unnoticed in his heightened state. Burnell swerved at the last moment, tapping the ball round to the left of his opponent's boots, instantly recapturing it. Ahead lay the goalmouth and–

He squeezed the on/off bulb in his fist. The memory died. He was gasping with shock. Bootleg memory bullets so often contained no credits, no fade-ins or editorial matter; they simply switched from one fragment of one person's memory to another, unrelated. In a composite bullet, snatches of various memories were frequently incorporated, as here, perhaps lopped from longer sequences.

Leaning back with his eyes closed, Burnell let his pulse rate sink to a more normal level. Damn the footballer! He concentrated on the airing-cupboard episode with a pained solicitude. The main question was, had he stumbled on a fragment of his own memory or not? The answer was less simple than it appeared.

While suspecting it might be a true Burnell memory, he recognized a strong desire that it should be. It was baffling not to be sure. But memory – he recalled the old saying – 'played strange tricks' . . .

A trivial hour in a summer afternoon . . . the passage of twenty years . . . youth's happy habit of inattention . . .

In the early days of their association, Stephanie and he had bought a large derelict country mansion, assisted by money from his father. It had been done for its challenge; also in part to try to please his father as well as Stephanie. They had worked on the restoration of house and garden. He had not thought of that period of his life for years. But was it *that* house and garden in the bullet? Why had he felt no immediate stab of recognition?

Well . . . weeds were weeds, wherever found. He had

managed no clear look at the woman by the fish pool, being unable to see anything the memorizer did not see. And the rear of the house, the stairs, the landing . . . they were common to thousands of houses, with only minor variations. Again, the memorizer was taking no particular notice of his surroundings, being familiar with them. Detail had been scanty . . .

It was on the airing cupboard that Burnell concentrated his thought. The memorizer had looked into the cupboard merely to find a clean shirt, taking for granted its orderliness.

What now impressed Burnell was precisely that orderliness. He saw in it a clue to his separation from his wife.

Suppose he had just seen himself, almost been himself, as he was twenty and more years ago . . . Then the woman by the fish pool had been Stephanie, Stephanie when young, Stephanie when they were first in love, when they had high hopes of each other, when magic still played about their relationship . . .

It followed that the airing cupboard was in Stephanie's domain.

That small room, large enough to walk into, was almost a secret compartment in the old house; yes, Stephanie's domain, kept for the most part in darkness. She controlled it, she stocked it with the clothes she had washed and ironed. Not a sock there but knew her caring touch . . .

Murray-Johnson was shaking his shoulder. 'Wake up, old cocker.'

Reluctantly, Burnell removed his helmet and got out of the chair. While Murray-Johnson enthused about an absolutely disgusting memory he had lived through, Burnell bought the airing-cupboard memory from Mr Khan for an extortionate price.

On the way back to the hotel in Murray-Johnson's car, he puzzled over the question of whether he had actually stumbled across a fragment of his own memory – in which case, back in Frankfurt, he could have an expert reinsert it in his long-term memory; it would be life reclaimed. But he had to be sure. The ascetic side of his nature was repelled by the idea of having false memories inserted, though many people thought nothing of doing so, in order to look back on lives they had never lived.

Thanking Murray-Johnson profusely for a helpful evening, Burnell refused the offer of a drink and retired to his hotel room to consider matters.

These days, he lived out of his suitcase. Samsonite was his home. He had forgotten to lock the suitcase when in the room at midday. Clothes, both laundered and dirty, lay about the room. His books and papers had been left strewn here and there. A half-eaten melon attracted flies on the windowsill. His alarm clock lay face-down beside the bed. He perceived newly the disorder. So this was the kind of man he was, or had become ...

And perhaps the clue to the break between him and Stephanie lay within that airing cupboard, along those sweet-smelling ledges. The orderliness of her mind was demonstrated, for those who cared to look and understand, in that snug little hot closet of hers, where all was stowed neatly away, cared for, made pristine, tended. Tended ... Had *he* not tended things? Had he failed to tend their relationship? Had he not been *tender?* His mind too much on his career? Had he not been appreciative enough of her qualities, simply because they did not match with his?

'Oh, Stephanie . . . ' The airing cupboard served as a revelation. And yet ... he could still in no way be certain that it was his house, their cupboard, her care ...

Once again he found himself up against the brick wall of the question: how does a man manage to get through his life? How can he learn to swim through the sea of circumstance which confronts him?

He stood in the middle of his untidy room – motionless, but in a storm of conflicting thought which found no exterior expression.

The phone rang. He went to it with relief. Dr Assaad spoke, reminding him of their appointment the following noon.

'Did you have luck with my friend Mr Khan?' he asked.

Burnell looked down at the bullet in his hand. 'Mr Khan was very helpful,' he said.

3. THE STORM

Noon, under a leaden sky and a temperature of 35 degrees. Even with the air-conditioning working, it was hot in the car of Dr Assaad's brother.

'Is not too many kilometres to the Friendship Bridge,' Assaad said, as Burnell mopped under his collar.

They reached the roundabout where on the previous day the roadblock had been in operation. Today, the site was deserted. The road ahead lay empty. A beggar woman sat under a tree, a small child crawling on hands and knees beside her. Before them lay open country.

The asphalt soon gave out and they were travelling over a dirt road. The straggling outskirts of the city disappeared in an amber smog behind. A wind was rising, stirring the dust. Mountains lay distantly ahead, their crusty ridges no more than a blue outline against the hazy blue of the sky, as if they delineated a country without material substance.

Dr Assaad whistled cheerfully. 'Land of Hope and Glory'. Burnell shrank from joining in.

The River Garakhs was fast, icy and grey. For a short distance, the Garakhs marked a division between two distinct worlds: Turkmenistan and Iran. This was where, for over half of the previous century, the great world of the Soviet Union had expired and the more enduring world of Islam had commenced.

Here, God and Marx had surrendered in the face of the mountains and mosques of Muhammad.

The true national frontier, running for miles in either direction, was formed by the Kopet Dagh Mountains. Their monotonous flanks loomed on the far side of the river, extending as far as the eye could see, eroded, practically treeless. An Iranian settlement of mud-coloured huts had grown up on the far banks of the Garakhs. A road led from the settlement into the range. Nothing moved except dust. The Iranian sky to the south was leaden.

On the northern side of the river, Turkmenistan presented no more enlivening a spectacle. The land, lying almost at sea level, was a salt desert. Habitation had ceased as soon as they had left the capital, apart from a few yurts here and there, by which Akhal-teke horses were tethered. The desolate expanses were punctuated at one point by oil wells. Assaad remarked that the Japanese were prospecting.

Later, they passed a party of ragged horsemen galloping at full speed beside a railway line. Later still, a few miles from their destination, Burnell watched a group of people walking with some camels and a mule – an archaic frieze soon left behind in the dust. The dust was a problem, whipped up by an increasing wind.

The road from Ashkhabad, potholes and all, petered out at the river.

'In the spring, after rain, the wild tulips are blooming here, everywhere,' Dr Assaad said. 'The landscape is colourful.' He stopped the car and sat with his great body leaning forwards, drumming his fingers on the wheel and peering out at the intermittent dust clouds. 'I remember it so.'

Burnell sighed.

'It'll be all right,' Assaad said, motioning with his head for Burnell to get out.

The two men walked towards the bridge. It was unfinished – scarcely begun.

The Friendship Bridge at the Garakhs resembled a failed animal of some earlier epoch. It stuck its snout a short way over the flood, as if blindly to quiz the Iranian shore. It had been designed much as a child's bridge is constructed from wooden blocks. One stump of pillar stood on the near bank. A second stump stood in the swirling torrent. Over the stumps had been laid, in giant concrete sections, intimations of road, a kind of archetypal road, no more than 10 yards long, crumbling already.

This truncated lump of masonry was left with its far end hanging over the water and its near end jutting some feet above the land, dislocated from the road below.

Burnell walked beneath it, hands in pockets, gazing up at reinforcing rods trailing worm-like from the body of concrete. He was bitterly angry. To a man whose book, *Architrave and Archetype,* had been accepted as a standard work, this abortive hulk was an insult – certainly nothing worth two hours' travel over bumpy roads.

'Let's get back to town,' he said. 'I have important things to do. I must return to Frankfurt.'

'Yes, yes, instantly,' said Dr Assaad, conjuring up one of the adverbs of which he seemed fond. 'But first we must climb on the bridge. Then you will understand, surely.'

He led the way. Burnell felt obliged to follow as the big man heaved himself up a ladder set against the near pillar.

With agility, it was possible to swing up, grasp a girder and pull oneself on to the flat part of the bridge. Clouds of dust met them. Lizards scuttled into hiding. The wound in Burnell's leg ached in the heat.

They stood together, the Syrian and the Englishman, high above the ground. Burnell shielded his eyes with a hand. 'Look, hadn't we better get back?'

The sun had assumed the aspect of a withered orange. It cast a bronze gloom over the land.

Assaad said, 'I know you have things on your mind, Mr Burnell. We all have them. Once past youth, all men have things on mind. Women likewise, probably.' He walked along to the edge of the concrete structure, to gaze down into the water, letting wind and dust whip against his suit.

'This bridge is called the Friendship Bridge for obvious reasons. The Turkmeni say for a joke it is called Friendship Bridge because, like friendship, it should never have been started and will never finish . . . Huh. Not too much humorous for British taste, eh?'

Burnell said, 'I've lost my sense of humour. Sorry.'

'The first stone was laid by the late President of Turkmenistan. He was a devout Muslim, an ayatollah. But the war swept him out of power, happily. He died of some disease soon after. As people do. With the onslaught of war, President Diyanizov ordered work here all to stop. Of course it will never be resumed. We no longer wish to be so friendly with Iran since their last revolution. Some recall an old Goklani saying, "Iranian ponies have only three and a half legs."'

Some of this was lost in the wind. Burnell turned his back to the gale and said, speaking formally, 'Dr Assaad, a storm's brewing. Best to get back to Ashkhabad.'

Assaad's large face was already powdered with dust.

He shook his head sadly, disappointed by Burnell's lack of perception. Turning his back on the river, he frowned at Burnell. As if preparing to make a speech, he clutched his lapels.

'This place is what you should remember to carry back to England with you. In its fashion, it is even a victory for the West! Yes, a monument for the magnetic attraction of the West, felt even in this country where not a copy of *The Hand of Ethelberta* is to be had for money or love.' He gave a sardonic smile, tight-lipped, and stared down at the pattern of wooden planking embedded in fossil imprint in the concrete blocks at his feet. 'Many men wished to embrace Islam when Soviet Union collapsed, but the pull of the West was even stronger. Happily, some men wish not to grovel to Mecca five times every day . . . '

A battery of winds sprang up. Light gravels were scooped from the river bank and dashed into their faces. The men were blown across the bridge. Assaad dragged Burnell down bedside him. They crouched for shelter under the low parapet. The wind roared as it rushed overhead, suddenly making its intentions clear.

'When it is stopped, we go back to the car,' Assaad said, his face close to Burnell's. 'These storms last no long time. Do not worry.'

'It was madness to come out here.'

Assaad laughed. 'And maybe we were both mad to leave our own countries, probably . . . To escape memories or to find them . . . *Che sera, sera*, isn't that what the Italians say? You travel but you have no cosmopolitan spirit, Mr Burnell. You must appreciate what has befallen here. You should regard Friendship Bridge as a memorial to a crucial moment in history.

'When Soviet Union collapsed, was a great day for all the world. Also for Turkmeni peoples. They had been long suppressed. The place was bankrupt. Then the frontiers were open, suddenly. Never before open except in the lives of very old people. Freedom – that word we all like to hear!

'A great procession of ordinary people came from Ashkhabad. My wife was among them. They came along the road we have taken, to this point, to look across at Iran, a free country. Before, all the whole frontier was patrolled and people could be shot who came near here.'

From his crouched position, resting his elbows on the concrete, Assaad imitated the action of someone firing a rifle.

'And across the other side of this river, Iranians appeared! They cheered to this side, this side cheered to them. Can you imagine? On that day, were two thousand Turkmeni here, maybe two hundred Irani there. After all, there are same families on both sides of the frontier, divided only by that monster Stalin.

'That particular day, was icy rain in the air – not this nice warm sand. But some of the Ashkhabad youths, they strip off their clothes and swim across the river at this point. One young boy age thirteen, he drown. Otherwise, is great rejoicing. The people embrace, each to each, warmly. It was an occasion of many tears and kisses, Mr Burnell, many tears and kisses. My wife stood here. She waved to her older sister across the river.'

He fell silent, letting the sand scour their ears.

'One Iranian has a loud-shouter? Yes, loud-hailer. He calls out news. He calls names, telephone numbers, radio wavelengths. Names of lost relations are called across this river. Many people wept. Weeping because lives are broken. You can imagine. All spoken is – what do you call it? – reconciling words, privately. No words of politics, no words of religion. Only poor people stood here. No great ones.'

As Assaad paused, Burnell thought, Oh yes, he has ties of love to this land he affects to hate . . .

Assaad continued. 'The people congregated on both sides of the river till the sun was set. The date was the thirteenth of Azar by the Muslim calendar.

'The brave boys swam back here again. Some had gifts such as worry beads and sweetmeats. The newspapers in Ashkhabad described that day as a day of seething emotions. There were demands that a bridge should be built, so that Muslim should be united with Muslim. A bridge of friendship.

'Under the old ayatollah president, the construction of the bridge was begun. Then it was discovered that the Iranians did not build a road to the bridge on their side, cunningly. Instead, they waged another war with Iraq, their other neighbour. And both sides began to worry about illegal border crossings. Remember, Turkmenistan was then being attacked by the Afghanistan guerrillas.

'The rest I have already told. This bridge makes me very happy – naturally, because it's not complete. The bridges should be built not to the south, to Islam, but to the West, to Hungary and Germany and France and England – where change is not a criminal act.'

As he rambled on, Assaad's voice was at times dominated by the wind, which now seemed to consist as much of sand as air. Burnell found his thoughts wandering.

In his work, he was accustomed to monuments that endured, beautiful structures whose very endurance inspired reverence. Although he had no religious faith, he venerated the buildings it was his duty to catalogue.

Because there was melancholy as well as honour in the task, Edward Gibbon's *Decline and Fall of the Roman Empire* had long been his favourite reading. Able to recite whole passages of the old unbeliever by heart, particularly when slightly drunk, Burnell recalled now, crouching against the concrete, Gibbon's reflections on transience. 'The art of man is able to construct, ' Gibbon had said, 'monuments far more permanent than the narrow span of his own existence: yet these monuments, like himself, are perishable and frail; and in the boundless annals of time his life and his labours must equally be measured as a fleeting moment.'

And if that labour should be to stock, without fuss, an airing cupboard with fresh sweet clothes . . . It was important, surely, to remember that monument to past love. Even if not his . . .

He saw his own life as no more than a wormcast in a vast tract of history. And his family? His grandfather had lived through the dissolution, peaceful on the whole, as on the whole the disintegrating institution had been, of the British Empire. His father had lived through the collapse of the Communist empire. He was himself passing his life in the years following those momentous events, during the expansionist phase of the EC superstate.

The Turkmeni were seeking some kind of political stability which so far eluded them. No models of stable modern government in their past existed from which they might gain strength; there were only memories of horrendous oppression, massive abuses of morality (and agriculture) and, more distantly, the legend of that Golden Horde which had once thrown a shadow of terror over all Christendom. In fact, the Friendship Bridge represented an attempt of hope, a hand stretched towards an imagined outer world.

He sensed something of the complexity of emotions Dr Assaad felt. His wife's sister must remain on the other side of the torrent. That was part of an historical necessity. Burnell's anger against the Syrian faded. Despite the discomfort of the sandstorm, he was glad to be here, where no Englishman, as far as he knew, had ventured. Perhaps Assaad was wrong and he did have a cosmopolitan spirit . . .

And how had he come here? Certainly, he had managed to obtain no introduction to President Diyanizov from the authorities in Frankfurt or London. Fearful of the paid assassin, Diyanizov saw no visitors. Had he ever really hoped that he might retrieve that vital missing period of his memory? Or had he found it, without realizing as much?

Burnell had drifted because he was, essentially, a drifter. Despite the best of educations, he had refused to join the family's merchant bank. He had dedicated himself to . . . Well, dedication was hardly a word he cared to apply to himself.

His father was now confined to a motorized chair. An old embittered man who trundled slowly about his estate. Soon he would inevitably pass away. The estate would be broken up. And the avenue of lime trees planted by his grandfather . . . Already Burnell could feel immense regret latent in him, awaiting the release of his father's death.

His father had liked, had loved, Stephanie. Of course Burnell had no more chance of getting her back than there was of standing and demanding, successfully, that the sandstorm cease.

But there was that vital scene to be retrieved, to be reinstated in memory. He needed better evidence than a cupboard full of shirts he failed to recognize. Oh, Stephanie, how did our relationship go so badly wrong? You were the most precious thing in my life. Had there been someone more precious to you than I? If only I knew, if only I could remember . . .

But would things then be different? Could he rectify a past fault? Could that broken bridge ever be reconstructed to cross the chilly river of separation?

Tears filled his eyes, to be instantly dried by the heat.

He felt his own identity fading into the abrasive world about him. Never was it more clear to him why, and how fatally, he clung to the memorials of the past. And the time would come, not today, perhaps not tomorrow, when he would join the dead, and the broken estates, when he would succumb to the same processes of mutability which had transformed the bridge from design to ruin. Yes, the time would come.

Well, it was no great matter . . .

The sand was gathering about the two figures, who crouched as if imploring Allah for his mercy. It lay thickly drifted under the parapet.

Roy Burnell yielded up his thoughts to let the sand take over. He heard it howling through Turkmenistan, through the universe, covering everything, the living and the dead.

The Mechanic

Gwyneth Jones

The alien parked its car across the street and came and sat down in the waiting room. He must have seen this happen, peripherally. But he was busy settling the bill with a middle-aged woman with curly grey hair and substantial, attractive clothes to whom he'd taken an irrational dislike. Those who deal with Joe Punter, day in and day out, especially Joe car-owning Punter, are prone to such allergies. He saw *her* start of concealed surprise, looked up and there was the alien. The other customers on the row of seats were pretending, in their English way, that nothing special had happened. He finished dealing with the woman. Other cars and customers left; the alien's turn came. He went out in the road and hand-waved it into the bay with fatherly care, then sent it back to wait while he looked the red car over. He entered the car's make and model in the terminal, and began to check the diagnostics. The mechanic worked this franchise alone with the robotics, and only the electronic presence of cashier, manager, head office. He was able to read print and even to write. It was a necessity of his trade. To be wired up, routinely, among all this free-running machinery was against health and safety regulations. He used a hear-and-do wire only for the exotics, where the instructions came packaged with the part, and tried to conceal this from his customers. The mystique of craftsmanship was important to him.

Consequently, it took him some little time to examine the tired little runabout.

He called in the alien and explained what had to be done, using a lot of gesture.

The convention was that if you couldn't stomach calling another sentient being 'it', they were all called 'she'. The mechanic eyed the alien covertly as he made his exposition: the soft, noseless profile, droop shoulders, the torso thickened by layers of strange underwear under its drab 'overalls', gawky backwards-jointed legs. It was about as female-looking as the dugongs sailors used to miscall 'mermaids'. The confusion, he considered, was an insult to both parties. But it was nonsense to expect the denizen of another star system to be humanly attractive. He was in no hurry. He

wasn't affronted or frightened, as some people might have been, to see one running around loose, out of the enclave. No doubt the alien was going to tip generously, but it wasn't avarice that made him willing to linger. He was simply, genuinely pleased to have one of them in his shop.

'I just want you to scrub the converter.'

He wasn't surprised that it could speak English; he'd only imagined it would not trouble itself to do so. But the last thing he'd expected was for an alien to be mean.

'You know, it's going to be cheaper in the long run to replace the whole exhaust system. You've been using a high-methanol percentage, there's a lot of corrosion here . . . '

The alien looked at the ground.

'Come away.'

So he followed it out into the waiting room, where it folded down like a big dog on one of the seats, looking miserable, twisting its puckered, chicken-skin hands against its chest.

'I'm going to sell it,' the alien explained. 'I want you to do the minimum that's legally necessary.'

He realized that the alien did not believe that its car could understand English. But nor did it believe that such understanding was impossible. It believed that if you have to say something unpleasant about someone/thing, you remove yourself from the immediate vicinity of the victim. The rules of etiquette were immovable, matter-of-fact and binding. The car's level of comprehension was a separate matter, a subject for abstruse philosophy. It was not unusual in the mechanic to be familiar, as far as this, with alien thinking. Alien nature was the stuff of daytime television. The mechanic could have drowned in the subject, if he had had enough idle time between customers.

'What's legally necessary,' he repeated. He was disappointed, practically and emotionally, by his customer's poverty, but mollified by its bizarre sensitivity. Of course he knew that in an alien the state of poverty could only be temporary and relative. The tip dwindled but some other benefit was bound to accrue.

It nodded glumly. They nodded. Their gestures were very human, but culturally diverse: for 'no' they would jerk the chin, not shake the head. It was as if they'd borrowed a little, deliberately, from every human race, and maybe that was exactly so. Their journey into human space had been through such a saturation of human emissions – no one knew how much of alien behaviour on earth was natural and how much a carefully devised presentation.

'Shall I wait or shall I come back?'

Throughout this conversation the other customers had remained painfully fixed in bored or casual poses. The mechanic was delighted by their intent covert attention. Luckily there were no children involved to spoil the effect of cosmopolitan unconcern. He did not want it to stay. If it stayed in here it might strike up a conversation, become the temporary property of one of these mere punters.

'You'd better go,' he told it, feigning regret. 'I have another job that I can't put on auto. Come back in about an hour.'

When it had left, regret became real. He went out into the dusty street and stared up and down. It was October. The fronds of the banana tree that grew over the wall of an unkempt yard next door were acid green, under a lowering sky that had been promising rain for days. The tourist centre was not far away: the massive grace that all the world admired, which had once been a docktown called Liverpool. He could see the tiny points of the newly gilded Liver birds, winking above their monument of vast commercial assurance. Far inland, the vague conurbation stretched up the flanks of the Pennines: the hills swimming there out of sight like drowned monuments, drowned in time and lost for ever, like the great city.

There was no sign of the alien.

He went into the shop, checked the progress of various operations, and quietly – avoiding camera eyes – sneaked through the door at the back, upstairs to his living quarters. His wife was at work. Their two children, seven and two years old, were with her in the workplace schoolroom and crèche. The rooms, which were small but well supplied with consumer durables, seemed unnaturally tidy and silent. He stood in the living room and studied a row of books, discs, journals, on a shelf of the library unit. *Dealing with the Alien*, *What Do They Think of Us*, *The Farcomers*, *Through Alien Eyes*, *Have They Been Here Before?* *Xenobiology: Towards the Dawn of Science* . . . The mechanic and his family were no more than moderately interested in the alien visitors. The books had not been read. But it would have been a strange household indeed, or a very poor one, that didn't possess at least a few of these titles.

The mechanic did not feel, on the whole, that the human race was over-reacting. He and his wife had voted in favour in the European referendum on the change of era. Which was now on its way to becoming law. This year, this present year, would be forever year three – 3AC, probably, if the dominant English-speaking global lobby had its way. After Contact. It was official:

this was the greatest thing that had happened to the human race since the dim and distant 'coming of Christ'. And the aliens, unlike Christ, were *here*. They were in print, on the screen. They were indubitably real.

Everything on the shelves had been entered in the library – the mechanic's wife was meticulous over this chore. His fingers hovered over the keypad. But the mysterious inertia of human adulthood defeated him. Only the seven-year-old actually used the database. He took a book down, and another, leaved the pages, read a paragraph or two. He didn't know what he was looking for.

Surrounded by hard things that did not speak or look at him, he tried to imagine how it felt to be the alien. He had known sentimental drivers: cars with names, cars referred to as 'she', cars abused for bad behaviour. He had caught himself (he dredged up fragments of memory) occasionally giving a glossy flank of robot casing an affectionate pat as he put it aside. *Good boy . . . Good dog . . .*

It did not know about animals. The aliens had tools that crept, slithered, flew; but they had made these things. They had no notion of a separate creation, life that was not their own. It might be that conditions on the home planet were different. The evidence, from their reactions and their own reporting, was otherwise. It seemed likely that they had shared their world with no other, no *separate* warm-blooded animals.

He went down to the service bay and checked the screen that showed the waiting room. All was quiet in there. It had not come back. He turned from that screen and made work for himself among the ramped vehicles and buzzing tools. He didn't touch the alien's car. When it reappeared he went out and told it he was having a few problems. Please be patient, he said. He took no new customers. The afternoon turned to dusk. The waiting room emptied until it was there alone.

The mechanic's wife and his children arrived home, on foot, from the trolley stop, the baby in her buggy. He heard the childish voices chattering and laughing at the street door, and gritted his teeth as if interrupted in some highly concentrated and delicate task. But he was doing nothing, just sitting in the gloom among the silent tools.

The alien was folded up on its seat. It looked more than ever like an animal dressed up, a talking animal of no known species from a child's cartoon. It stood and smiled: the modified snarl that might or might not be a genuine, shared gesture. The mechanic was embarrassed because there was really no way he could explain his behaviour. A human customer, stranger in a strange land, would by now have been either very angry or, possibly, a little scared. The alien seemed resigned. It did not expect humans to behave reasonably. It made the mechanic obscurely angry to think that he was not the first person to give it the runaround like this. He would liked to explain, *I just want to have you near me for a while* . . . But that would have been a shameful confession.

'I want to do you a favour,' he said. 'I didn't like to tell you before, thought you might get embarrassed. I'm fixing up quite a few things, and I'm only charging you for the scrub.'

'Oh.' He thought it looked surprised, perhaps wary. It was impossible not to credit them with human feelings, read human expressions in their strange faces. 'Thank you.'

'The least I could do, after you've come all this way.' He laughed nervously. It didn't. They did not laugh. 'Would you like to come upstairs? Would you like something to eat, a cup of tea? My wife, my kids, would be very pleased to meet you.'

The invitation was completely insincere. The last thing he wanted was to see it in his home. He didn't want to share the alien with anyone. The alien gave him a wry look; it seemed to know exactly what was going on. According to some readings of their behaviour, they were telepathic – intensely so between themselves, mildly with humans. On the other hand, it had probably been pestered this way before . . . performing animal. The thought made him wince, for himself and for those others.

'No, thank you,' It looked at the ground. 'Will the car be ready tomorrow?'

The street was dark. There was little lighting just here, away from the hotels and malls and the floodlit, water-lapped monuments. He felt ashamed of himself. The poor alien might be mentally counting up its cash, and maybe getting frightened. Aliens travelling alone were rarities anywhere. If it couldn't take refuge in a big rich hotel it would be bothered. People would crowd around it heartlessly, pointing their video cams.

But that wasn't the mechanic's fault. He didn't want to capture it on tape. He didn't want to turn it out. He wanted it here; its real live presence. It could sleep on the seats. He would bring down some food. They liked some human foodstuffs: ice-cream, white bread, hamburgers – nothing too natural.

'Yes, of course. Come back tomorrow. I open at nine.'

He told his wife that he had to work overtime. This never happened, but she accepted the idea without comment. The routine of their life together was so unvarying it could swallow the occasional obvious lie without a ripple.

He sat in the machine shop alone and looked around him. Cars. It was strange how many static, urban Europeans still had to own them, even with the fuel rationing and all the rest of the environment-laws. The mechanic wasn't complaining. It was a steady job, and often even enjoyable. These are my people, he thought, trying on the alien worldview. My people, the sheep of my flock. The mechanic had a grandmother who was a churchgoer. But there came the idea of animals again, the separation of one kind of life from another. That was not what happened between the alien and an alien machine. He went up to the car, clamped on its ramp in an undignified posture, a helpless patient.

'*Hallo?*' he said tentatively.

The car made no response, but the atmosphere in the shop changed. By speaking to it aloud he had shifted something: his own perception. He'd embarrassed himself, in fact. He could just catch the tail of a more interesting emotion. He was a child creeping past the witch's door, deliciously afraid. But nothing he could do or say would make the imagined real: make him see the robot eyes wink, the jaws of metal grin or open in speech. Nothing but madness would change things that far.

He began to work, or rather to set the robotics to work. He had no choice now, he would have to do what he had promised and square the accounts somehow. Nothing that happened in this garage went unrecorded. The mechanic had never made any attempt to hack his way around the firm's system. He wasn't the type to be tempted by the complications of crime. He became very gloomy thinking about what he'd have to do now, the awkward covering up he'd have to invent for this strange impulse.

The free machines skated to and fro; others slid along the overhead lines and reached down their serpent heads. The mechanic fidgeted. The machine, a fifteen-year-old Korean methanol/petrol burner with a red plastic body, liquid clutch and suspension, was a hardwearing complex of equipment, good for at least another ten years on the road. It needed a certain amount of attention; but it didn't need *his* attention at all. He stood and watched.

I am redundant, he thought – a standard human over-reaction to robotics. Why don't aliens feel redundant? He struggled to perform the mental contortion of looking out of the mirror. If it were not for humans, if it were not for me, there would be no cars, no robots, no machines at all . . . I cannot be superseded. Even if the machines become self-conscious, become 'human' (the ever-receding bogey of the popular media) I will always still be God. The maker.

Upstairs the toddler would be in bed; and the boy too, tucked up with one of the home-tutor tapes that supplemented the education provided by his mother's employers. The mother would be relaxing into her evening, snug in a nest of hardware. Empathically, subliminally, the mechanic was aware of the comings and goings, the familiar routine.

He discovered why the alien filled him with such helpless, inarticulate delight. The machines promised, but they could not perform. They remained *things*, and people remained lonely. The mechanic had visited his country's National Forests, the great tracts of land that must remain undisturbed, however small his sitting room became. He accepted the necessity of their existence, but the only emotion he could possibly feel was resentment. He had no friendship with the wilderness. Animals could be pets, but they were not part of you, not *the same*. The alien was the solution to human isolation: a talking world, a world with eyes – the companionship that God dreams of.

The alien's visitation had stirred in him a godlike discontent. He could not make it stay. But perhaps he could learn from it, share its enriched experience. He saw the bay as a microcosm of human technology and civilization: a world extruded like ectoplasm from its human centre, full of creatures made in his own image: his finger and thumb, his teeth, his rolling, folding joints, his sliding muscle. His mind, even, in its flickering chemical cloud permeating the hardware of his brain.

Excited by this insight, he jumped up and hurried to the bay's terminal keypad. He pulled the robotics out, the shining jointed arms sliding back and folding themselves away into the walls, and took out a box of hand tools. He would pay the alien's car the greatest compliment in his power. He would give it the benefit of his craftsmanship, the kind of 'natural, organic' servicing for which the rich pay ridiculous sums.

For a while he worked like Adam in Eden, joyfully naming the subcreation with his hands and mind. He worked, he slowed . . . He sat on the cold, dark-stained floor with a socket spanner in one hand and a piece of ragwaste in the other. The lights looked down. They built things with bacteria, as the mechanic understood it. Bacteria which were themselves finally traceable to the aliens' own intestinal flora, infecting everything: every tool and piece of furniture, even the massive shell of their ship-world. Human beings, when they want to express feelings of profound communion with the planet, with the race, speak of being 'a part of the great whole'. Having lived so many years – maybe a hundred thousand years, the pundits reckoned – in a world entirely created by themselves, the aliens could not experience being a part. There were no parts in their continuum: no spaces, no dividing edges.

He suddenly felt disgusted. Scientists had established that the alien bacteria were harmless. That was the story, but it might be wrong. It might be a big lie, maintained to prevent panic in the streets. He wished he hadn't touched the car. The alien had been using it for months. It must be coated all over with invisible crawling slime.

What was it like, to be part of a living world? He stared at the spanner in his hand until the rod of metal lost its shine. Skin crept over it, the adjustable socket became a cup of muscle, pursed like an anus, its lips drawn back by a twist on the tumescent rod. The mechanic was nauseated. But he could not put the tool down. He could not go away from it. This oozed drop of self, attached to his hand, would not be parted from him if he dropped it. Tiny strings, strands of living slime, would cling and join them still. The air was full of self, of human substance.

He stood up. He backed off. A robot casing yielded like flesh. The mechanic yelped and sprang away. His hand, with the rod-flesh spanner growing out of it, hit the keypad; and all the tools began to leap into action. He stood in his own surging, hurrying, pulsating gut, for an instant saved by the notional space of an anatomical drawing, and then the walls closed in. There was no light, only a reddened darkness. The mechanic wailed. He fought a horrible need to vomit, he scrabbled desperately at the keys.

When everything was quiet again he sat for a while. It might have been minutes, it felt like a long time. Eventually he stopped wanting to be sick and managed to put down the spanner. He sat with his head hunched in his arms, became aware of this abject foetal crouch and came out of it slowly. He took a deep breath. The garage was the same as it had always been: dead, and safe. He realized that he had been highly privileged. Somehow, just briefly, he had succeeded in entering the alien mind, seen the world through alien eyes. It would be nonsense to expect such an experience to be pleasant. Now that it was over he could accept that; and he was truly grateful.

At last he heaved a sigh and turned to putting the bay to work again. He couldn't bring himself to touch the red car with hand tools now. Besides, he was too shaky. But he would deliver the alien's vehicle in the morning as promised, as near to perfectly reborn as was humanly possible. He owed it that much.

He had tried to take something from the alien by a kind of force. And he'd got what he wanted. It was hardly the alien's fault that he'd bitten off more than he could chew, and gagged on the mouthful. Steeling himself against the ghostly feel of flesh in the machines, he set up the automatic routines. In a short time, it was all done. But it was very late. His wife would have to ask questions now, and he'd have to tell her something of what had happened. He stood looking at the plastic shell and the clever, deviously economical innards under the open bonnet. The machines, they said, couldn't live with the ecosphere. Eventually the human race would have to abandon one or the other: motor cars or 'the environment'. But 'eventually' was still being held at bay. In the mean time this was a good, well-made little compromise with damnation.

He felt lonely and sad. He had seen another world walk into his life, reached out to grasp the wonder and found something worse than empty air. The other world ought to be dreamland, somewhere over the rainbow. He had found, instead of the fairytale, inimical Eden: a treasure that he could no more enjoy than he could crawl back into the womb.

The mechanic sighed again and reached over. He gently closed the bonnet. The red car settled itself a little.

'Thank you,' it said.

In the morning at nine o'clock the alien was there. The car was ready, gleaming on the forecourt. The alien put down its bag, which it carried not on its back or at arm's length but tucked under one armpit in that very peculiar, lopsided way of theirs. He thought it looked tired, and anxious. It barely glanced at the car. Perhaps, like a human, it didn't even want to know how badly it had been cheated.

'What's the damage?' it asked.

The mechanic was hurt. He'd have liked to go over the whole worksheet with it; to extract the sweet honey of its approval, or at least to extend this dwindling transaction just a little further. He had to remind himself that the alien owed him nothing. To itself its feelings were not romantic or bizarre in the least. The world it lived in was perfectly commonplace. His whole experience was his own concern, had been an internal matter from the start. The alien was not responsible for the kinks of human psychology, nor for imaginary paranormal incidents.

'Look,' he said. 'I've got a proposition for you. My eldest, my

son, he's just passed his driving test. He won't be allowed to go out on his own for a while, of course. But I've been thinking about getting him a little runabout. I don't keep a car myself, you see, I've never felt the need. But kids, they like the freedom . . . I'd like to buy your car.'

In the cold light of day, he couldn't bear to tell it the truth. He knew the car would never speak to him again. But he had been *touched* by the world of the other and he simply had to bring away something, some kind of proof.

The alien looked even more depressed.

He realized suddenly that he didn't have to worry about the money. He would tell the firm everything. They were human at head office, after all, and as fascinated as he. The car would stay on the forecourt. He would call in and get it featured on the local news, maybe even national news. It would be extremely good for business. For the alien's benefit, however, he would stick to the story about his son. The aliens really shouldn't be encouraged to believe that human beings thought they were magic.

'List price,' he added hurriedly. 'And a little more. Because anyone would pay a little more – a car that's been driven by one of our famous visitors. What do you say?'

So the alien walked away with its cash account handsomely recharged. It turned at the corner of the street, by the yard where the banana fronds hung over the gate, and bared its pointed teeth in that seeming smile. The farewell could have been for the red car on the forecourt, as much as for the human beside it, but it made the man feel better anyway.

Tolkowsky's Cut

Simon Ings and Charles Stross

Each time, just before she dies, Jewel, Keeper of Wisdom, swims in the Folded Rose Lagoon. She cleaves a path through the mirror-still water until she loses sight of the Hub, and then she swims a little further. She lies back in the water and lets things pass her by for a while. On a clear day she can just make out, directly above, the fields and forests she explored as a child. She smiles, and maps the vague topology, sharpening it with memories: the strong savour of barbecued cockroach; the first exquisite tickle of data faeries behind her eyes. She swims in memories and falls like a stone, into childhood, into the black depths of the lake.

Jewel is an old woman. She has lived out thirty-nine of her seventy lifetimes, and is nearing the end of her fortieth. She is ready to swim again.

She stands on the foredeck of the yacht, fingering the jewel which hangs on a silver chain about her neck.

The boat turns in the water, and Jewel watches as the Hub – a craggy, rust-stained rock wall – swings into view. She looks up, and up, and up. The rocks climb all the way to the forests of her childhood – there, on the opposite side of the oneil. The Hub's fault lines and discolorations are not, like the lagoon, a builder's whim. They are real: the Heaven Eleven oneil is one hundred thousand years old.

The yacht is anchored to a smaller, grey and scree-swept slope which curves so that its lips meet the Hub at either edge, forming a pouch some two thousand feet above the lagoon. In it lie the remains of an ancient city and there, built over their ruined heart, stands the Folded Rose Sanctuary. There are no landward approaches to the Sanctuary. The slopes, naturally rugged and inhospitable, have been seeded with things lethal to man. Pilots flutter from crest to rocky crest, watching for airborne intruders with senses enhanced by a secret process.

Jewel, Keeper of Wisdom, stretches in satisfaction and turns to the wrought-iron table. On it stands a small glass cafetiere. She presses on the filter arm and watches the brew darken. She pours

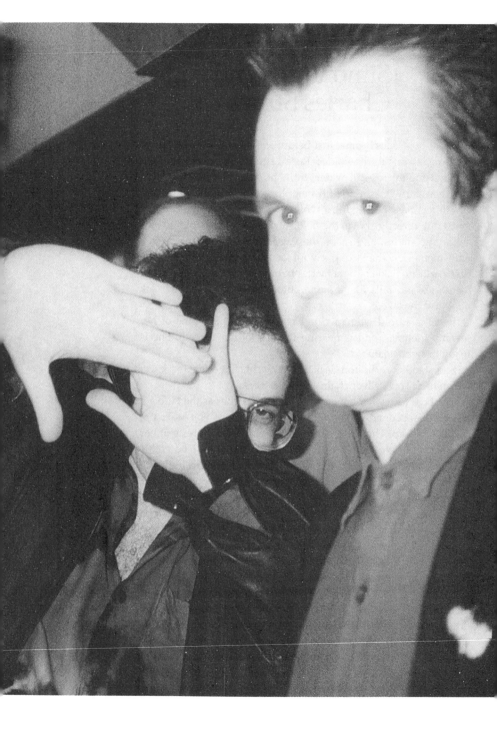

herself a cup and sits down. Soon she will have to go and kill her wife. As always, the thought of it excites her.

She sips her coffee. They feed coffee berries to wolves. As the berries are digested, so the beans within them partly ferment. It has become a kind of ritual – to drink wolf coffee before a kill.

Jewel opens a small bottle of hash oil and slurs it into her coffee. The scent is delicious.

She drinks, and rides the slow, gentle hashish swell into the First House of Contemplation.

She fingers the jewel around her neck. It is cut in the ancient manner: a design older than Heaven Eleven itself. A product of the species' long-forgotten, planet-bound past.

Tolkowsky's cut has seventy facets.

Jewel thinks, *One for each of my lives.*

She thinks of her wife and of their lovemaking. Marget's breasts are small and too far apart and her orgasm is a raucous laugh. The taste of her wetness is rich and sickly.

Jewel withdraws from the play of images and clasps her hands. Consciously now, she draws from these erotic images the shapes and movements of Marget's body, the relative suppleness of each limb in each plane. When she is finished she knows how to kill her: she knows the poise to adopt, the angle to hit, the force necessary for the blow and the speed of the strike.

This is the Second House.

Warmed by the drugged coffee, she unclenches her hands. The bright morning sunlight casts shadows of her fingers on to the table beneath. She waves her fingers as the light threads over the table. The movement of light and shade is erotic. She reads violence into the movements of the shadows. Violence and sexuality fuse in a single, simple rhythm.

She enters the Third House, and her breasts engorge.

The Census is over by evening. The stench of molten insulation drifts across the street from the Recidivists' nest. By three tomorrow morning, all subversives will be retrodden. The managing director of the Census, Romeo, is in a teleconference with his fellow officers. They appear behind his eyes, faces black with ash and hands sticky with housejuice. They all have exactly the same smile.

'Report by numbers,' Romeo drawls. He rests his feet comfortably on the bar table. Romeo is a middle-aged retread who has been programmed to think that all Recidivists should be recycled. His number two sits next to him, convinced that in some previous incarnation she was Eva Braun. She likes killing ragheads.

A bartender mixes cocktails, his bald, pink tail curls above his head a nervous, writhing question mark. Eva Braun is field-stripping her gun.

<MACBETH.   *Seven subjects in the block, now cared for.*>

<CLEOPATRA . *None in the block, but we found a sewer rat.*>

The bartender twitches its whiskers in terror.

Caesar grunts and howls and masturbates in front of the camera. Semantic engines do their best to draw meaning from the display. Caesar is a psychopath on test-release from the Domino Factory. He's killed as many rats as Recidivists.

<OTHELLO.   *None in the block. Tried to link with Lear but all I got was whitenoise.*>

<LEAR.   *A practical knowledge of nursing the elderly is essential, but not necessarily gained in the private sector.*>

Romeo's Wisdom is trying to make sense of the whitenoise where Lear should be and failing, miserably. Romeo turns it off and spits. He calls up Cleansing, using his Wisdom to port a description of Lear to them.

No dice. He turns to Eva. 'Lear is out – alive and missing.'

The rat sets their drinks down at the table.

'Too slow,' Eva drawls, and blows him to bloody fragments all over the plastic fascia of the bar.

'Eva,' Romeo sighs, 'are you listening?'

'Sure,' says Eva. She drops on all fours and sniffs the rat's roast remains.

Romeo drains his drink. 'Mixed a good cocktail,' he says.

Eva grunts. Her mouth is full.

Pilots trace Lear's scent, and find a house. It lies on a slant, mouthparts buried deep in the conduit running under the road. Sawtooths drill the door to bits and find Alia in the bedroom. They pin her to the wall with beetle limbs and chew off her clothing. Slavering toxin and mucus, they fling her to the futon; they rub themselves against her, wet with their secretions, deafen her with howls of orgasm.

When Alia starts to bleed, Romeo calls them off and hands Alia a handkerchief. Nanotech robots in Alia's blood have already repaired the physical damage done to her. The purpose of the attack is to traumatize her. Even these limited objectives have not been achieved. It hasn't worked. It never does. Alia, like the rest of them, has no soul. She feels nothing.

Alia considers it likely that the human culture's conquest of mortality and pain led directly to a loss of soul, a 'Fall'.

This makes her a Recidivist.

Romeo offers her a pill. He smiles a smile she has seen many times before. 'I am going to kill you,' he says, 'either by beasts or by this little bomb. If your co-operation is satisfactory I will detonate the bomb. If you have not swallowed the bomb, though, or if your behaviour is in any other way unsatisfactory, I will let the sawtooths back in, let them finish what they started.'

Alia snatches the pill out of his hand and swallows it. A few seconds later something green blinks behind her eyes. Good. (Alia is better equipped than Romeo realizes. The snake icon has confirmed that her tonsils have disarmed the bomb.)

Romeo tells her to shower, and when she returns to the bedroom he is naked. It will be that kind of interrogation. Afterwards, when there is nothing more for her to open up to him, in the physical or semantic sense, they have a drink together. Romeo sips and smiles and lies down on the bed, breathing rapidly in a shallow, gasping manner that reminds her of vivisection class.

'How much drink did you put in that alcohol?' he asks, draining the glass. Alia has drugged him, and, more clever still, she has succeeded in neutralizing the devices within Romeo's body that might have informed him of this fact. Selective blockers have taken out his ethanol dehydrogenase complex. He is drunk on two bourbons. His own Wisdom, on orders from Alia, persuades him that it has taken longer for him to get drunk than it actually has.

It is time. She calls up her Wisdom. It is a sophisticated black-market system which can manipulate data stored in other Wisdom units based upon the vaguest instructions. Alia tells it to keep pilots and other callers away from the house. It goes to work and befuddles the sawtooths and all the other para-phernalia of the Census Enquiry.

Gnats seeded by the Census to observe events in the room are fed a self-editing intuitive video-loop of Romeo and Alia copulating. Observers within the Sanctuary of the Folded Rose will be amazed at the sexual energy of the pair, long after Alia has escaped.

Alia goes to the kitchen and makes them both another drink, then bends over Romeo and places a transdermal patch on his neck. She fumbles with the light switch and the room shimmers a pale blue – a shade which induces calm and contemplation.

'You feeling okay?' says Alia.

'Check. My mind's off for servicing tomorrow . . . I mean, it's my . . . I should be caring and sensitive to the needs of young people . . . oh shit.' (Romeo's syntactic engine is playing up again. His last conscious act is to turn it off.)

Alia takes a deep breath, then goes to the kitchen and opens the fridge. She takes out a braindrain.

It has eight tentacles and no eyes. Like its octopoid ancestor, it only survives for about four hours outside its usual habitat – in this case a highly oxygenated saline sponge.

Alia plants it on Romeo's face. The braindrain hunts busily for orifices. Pseudopodia probe the buccal mucosa, the nasal sinuses, the orbits of his eye sockets. (Romeo dreams that a large cat has decided to share his pillow.)

'What are you?' Alia asks.

'Cube,' Romeo replies. The answer is a nasal whisper: all that the invasive tentacles in his nose and throat will permit. The tentacles should have penetrated his meninges by now. Soon Romeo will be unable to lie. Braindrains are breedable wetware packages, configured to handshake human CNS and control speech centres. Wisdom units are made of diced braindrain.

To business: Romeo is a Cube. Six sides – six lifetimes.

'Tell me about your previous lives.'

'Can't.'

'Explain.'

'I'm a retread.'

Alia shivers with revulsion. The braindrain was a wise choice. Truth drugs are like blunt hammers; the braindrain is a surgeon's scalpel. Drugs would never be able to reveal the previous identity of Romeo. The braindrain might.

She wonders who Romeo was, before the retread. Some Recidivist. Some comrade.

The building shivers in sympathy with Alia's anger. It detaches its proboscis from the street artery and stands up. Alia soothes the house; she thinks of trees, solidly rooted. The house responds and squats back down with a jarring bump.

This is going to take a long time.

The braindrain starts eating Romeo's face – a desperate and, ultimately, futile attempt to assuage its massive metabolic demands. Alia does not look at Romeo as she interrogates him. It is bad enough having to listen to his whistling voice without having to watch his face go bloody.

'Why the Census?'

'Because,' Romeo wheezes. The air is escaping through

ragged holes in his cheeks. Alia calls up her Wisdom and handshakes Romeo's semantic engine. She scrolls through the icons behind her eyes and selects the kinds of functions she needs. In a minute or two Romeo won't have a mouth. He can talk to her via her Wisdom, instead.

We suspect an offensive. We are suppressing Recidivist groups in the area. When the big one comes down we don't want to have to burn the Suburb.

It takes an hour to get names, dates, faces and all the other paraphernalia the Team needs to halt the planned offensive – and assassinate Jewel. Alia glances surreptitiously at Romeo. His hair is gone. His skull glitters pink and white like candy in the pale-blue light. His eye sockets are full of purple wormy things. Alia looks away, fast. 'Who were you? Before the retread?'

This time Romeo can answer. The parts of his mind sealed by the retread process have escaped and are establishing new dendritic architectures within the braindrain itself. Whoever Romeo was is being reborn inside the 'drain.

Hello, Alia.

Romeo has no eyes now. Whoever it was who had inhabited him must have recognized her from her Wisdom handshake.

'You're a Cube,' she says. Her words are random – noises she makes to give herself time to think. Someone who knew her. Someone close . . .

I am in my fourth lifetime.

'When were you retrodden?'

Eighty years ago. Third lifetime.

Alia nods. Of course. Of course. She closes her eyes.

How long have I got?

Alia calls up her Wisdom. With a sick twist in her stomach, Alia remembers that Wisdom wetware and braindrain are just different manifestations of the same product: they come out of the same vat.

'Half an hour. You've got half an hour.'

What? Sorry, can you use Wisdom? It's eating my ears.

Alia puts her hands over her face. *Half an hour.* Then, after a moment's silence, *You were my favourite.*

I loved you too, says the drain – or rather, the persona that has escaped into the drain for a brief and touching afterlife. For the first time in her seven lifetimes, Alia weeps.

Jewel, Keeper of Wisdom, celebrates her rebirth in style. First she finds a wife. She does not believe in carrying wives over from one lifetime to the next. Those who live too closely to her for too long learn things it is best for them not to know.

Marget died beautifully. No blood, no bruise, she fell like a doll with broken strings.

Her new wife, Hyne, like all Jewel's previous wives, is a retread. She has been conditioned to do everything asked of her. This conditioning will wear off in a matter of months, but by then Jewel will have learnt how to manipulate her.

Jewel smiles, self-satisfied, and looks around her at her new apartment.

It is as wide as the Sanctuary itself. She cannot see the far wall. It is decorated in brilliant blue-white, offset by soft pastel greys and pinks. To her left, by the window, hand-printed silk curtains shiver in the air-conditioner breeze. Outside lies the whole shattered vista of the Old City. As she watches, strong winds blow cement dust into the air about the buildings, softening the outlines of the smashed landscape, reinterpreting the scene in impressionistic grey pastel, and now the outside seems distanced, like something taken from film or from memory.

The furniture is upholstered in pale leather and velvet – all soft, sea-curved lines, no sharp angles anywhere. The carpet is thick steel-blue shag.

Alone in the room, Jewel plays with the seventy-faceted diamond about her neck. After a minute or two, she gets up and opens her cupboard. There are seven skeletons inside it. She speaks to one of them.

'Jessie?'

The skull, nested with nutrient feeds to supply the braindrain within, blinks at her – red millepedal wipers polish cybernetic lenses. 'I loved her,' it says, through a grille where its lower jaw should be.

Jewel nods patiently. 'Alia is a vibrant personality. It's a pity she and her brood are trying to kill me.'

The skull laughs. 'That is of no consequence to a skull in love.'

Jessie is like all the other skeletons. It teases her mercilessly for her lack of soul.

'Did you make contact with her?'

'I told her all she needed to know, to be in the right place, at the right time. You will catch your renegades.'

'Did you let her know who you are?'

'Of course. I told her Romeo was me, retrodden.'

Jewel stares at the skull for a long time, as if by her stare she is reminding Jessie that his half-life hangs upon her whim.

Jessie's skeleton shrugs. 'Had any new thoughts lately?'

'Funny,' Jewel replies. There is dry humour in her voice. She puts it there to please Jessie (for herself, she has no soul, and does not understand humour).

'All right, then,' Jessie says, 'any *calculations*?'

Jessie distinguishes between thought and calculation. He believes only those with souls can think. Those without souls just calculate.

Jewel calls up her Wisdom and lets figures scroll behind her eyes. She instructs her semantic engine to prepare a financial report for Jessie, then sends it to him.

'Hmm! Do you realize if we ever dropped the debt bomb the entire culture goes bankrupt?'

'So?' she asks, suppressing a yawn. The technique of copying personalities into braindrains is not without its flaws. The identities thus preserved tend to repeat themselves. Jewel has played out this conversation with Jessie every day since his retread, eighty years ago. Playing it through is the only way she can get a decent conversation out of him afterwards.

'So,' Jessie mimics, 'your policy remains as warpedly secure as ever. If we ever produce what we've been promising to produce, we sign the order on our own obsolescence.'

Jewel sinks gracefully on to a floor cushion and looks about her. Already, only six hours into her new existence, ennui is setting in. 'Business as usual, then?'

'Unless you want to be poor,' Jessie replies.

Jewel shakes her head. 'That is not possible.'

The skull nods. His voice is very quiet, very compassionate. 'I know. You, Heaven Eleven, the whole culture – money, money, money.'

'Survival, survival, survival,' Jewel retorts. 'Space is harsh. Without wealth we cannot build. Without buildings we cannot survive. Wealth is necessary.'

'So is purpose,' Jessie whispers.

Jewel shivers. 'I know.'

'If you produced the souls you've been promising for so long, then investment in Heaven Eleven would increase, not decrease.'

'For a time,' Jewel replies. 'But increased investment would be more than counterbalanced by increased expenditure. And once the secret of the human soul is fully disseminated, the purpose of Heaven Eleven vanishes. We will have nothing to make. We will amass no more wealth.'

'With souls come new ideas, new motivations. You'll think of something.'

Jewel shakes her head. 'I can't take that risk.'

Jessie's skull laughs at her. It is a senseless sound; she doesn't understand it. It annoys her. 'Jewel, you are a coward. You are the best calculator on the richest oneil in the galaxy and yet you haven't the imagination, you haven't the *soul*, to imagine yourself in any other role. All the culture is scrabbling for riches, for material satisfaction, for more, more, more of the same, but they'll never be satisfied, never! Because more is not enough; it never can be! Don't you see that?'

Jewel thinks about it. 'Riches are survival,' she says.

Jessie sighs. 'I pity you,' he says. 'Heaven Eleven's Jewel. Seventy lifetimes and every day the same. I pity you.'

Jewel shrugs. She is bored again. What the hell: she has decided she will kill Hyne in bed tonight.

A weak thrill tickles her spine. The idea might almost be said to excite her: tearing up a lover, limb from limb.

It was getting to be a habit.

Alia sends a mouse to her fellow revolutionaries. Then she cuts the braindrain and Romeo's headless corpse into little pieces and feeds them to the garbage disposal. Romeo follows Lear down the municipal pipes to oblivion.

Alia looks out of the window and remembers.

Once upon a time she was a cleaner. In the morning she cleaned the street. At noon she walked through the Suburb to the Census building, sweeping the pavement as she went. All afternoon she cleaned the Census building. In the evening she swept her way back home and cleaned the house. On rest days she swept her yard. She swept it with a brush the Census gave her for sixty years' good service. (It had a plastic handle, painted yellow, and red plastic bristles. It shone in the light, as if it were wet.) She swept all the litter out of sight, underneath the house, poking it with the handle of her broom until it stood up for her.

The yard was always dusty. There was litter too. Chew wrappers. Sometimes she stopped to pick them up. She unravelled them and read them. Once she found a brand of Chew she remembered from when she was a girl. She read it, and something strange happened to her face. She smiled.

It was around that time she met Jessie. Jessie told her where in the Census building needed cleaning most. Once day he led her into a room which was very clean and very clean people stood about the room, and she wondered what she was doing here, in such a clean room, and turned to get back to her work; but they crowded around her and made reassuring noises and Jessie gave her a stick of Chew which tasted odd.

She changed year by year. She grew tired of cleaning, so the Census gave her better things to do. She was very happy, very proud to have been given a drug which, it was said, was the latest in a line of treatments to restore people's souls. When Jessie told her that the Census had decided to make her a Cube, so that they might monitor her progress over six lifetimes, she smiled for the second time in her life – very quickly, as if the muscles that should have made a smile were wasted.

Only in her second lifetime did Jessie tell her about the Recidivists, and about their belief that Heaven Eleven's government had no intention of ever making souls, and about their desire to change this state of affairs – and by then it was clear that Alia, though she was brighter now, did not and would not ever develop a soul. Meanwhile, the Census had had to find other things to demonstrate to irate creditor governments, and were experimenting with rats again; they forgot about her.

Jessie.

She shivers. The house feels cramped. The pulsing softness of its walls no longer comforts her. She realizes that she is almost afraid of it.

Jessie had a soul.

She goes outside.

Jessie *laughed*. They killed him, killed him because whatever treatment they had given him had worked, killed him because they were machines and he was human and they were afraid – of humans, of change, of life itself.

Jessie. She remembers Jessie. Being with him made her feel – human.

Here, beyond the rubbish-filled yard, with tier upon tier of sleeping houses ranged about her, she could be anywhere and anywhen. She could be anyone, anything.

Something scuffs the dirt at her feet. She looks down, and locks eyes with a timorous mouse.

'Back again?' she says.

'I am your new assignment,' it pipes. Alia picks it up and bites its head off. The warm fur makes her gag, as usual.

The hind legs, abandoned, twitch helplessly in the dust.

Jewel, Keeper of Wisdom, writhes about the bed, masturbating. There are bits of Hyne all over the bed. The blood is starting to cake.

The cupboard is open and the skeletons are shrieking. As she attains orgasm Jewel looks at them and smiles, because she knows this display will distress them.

The skeletons are the imprisoned remains of those who have, against all probability and intention, acquired souls. It is Jewel's fancy that tonight she will plunge these souls into Hell. She is not sure what Hell is, exactly, but from the sounds of the screams she's come up with a fair imitation.

Jessie, though . . .

Jessie is paying no attention. He is playing cat's cradle with a string of fibre-optic.

Jewel gets up and strides towards the cupboard. 'What's that?' she shouts at him. 'Where did you get that?'

Jessie tangles the wire between the skeletal fingers of his right hand. His cybernetic eyes whirr as he focuses upon his mistress. 'Hyne gave it to me.'

Jewel is speechless.

'But then, you wouldn't understand that.'

The other skeletons shudder and fall silent, listening. Heaven Eleven has produced seven souls in the past ten thousand years. They are all here, Jessie and his more timorous fellows. Secure. Locked in the cupboard.

'Give me the string,' Jewel says.

'Certainly,' and Jessie lifts the hand with the string in it (servomotors whine), opens his bony fingers, and slaps her.

Jewel puts her hand to her face. Hyne's blood is sticky on her cheek. She thinks hard what to do. She thinks about turning him off. But that is not enough. She needs him. She needs them all, to advise her, to give her the edge, the edge that brought her to this place and built up the Folded Rose Sanctuary atop the ruins of a former Jewel's domain, thirty-two thousand years ago.

She thinks hard and in time, slowly, painfully, she gives birth to an idea. She turns and goes back to the bed, and brings back fleshy garlands for Jessie: remains of Hyne's digestive tract. She loops them around his pelvis, shoulders and shoulderblades. He does not resist. She plucks out his mechanical eyes and dashes them to the floor.

The skeletons are crying again, but Jessie just says, 'Was that interesting?' and he slaps her again.

She pulls his arms off at the socket. It's not hard to do. Gristle pops and servomotors chitter.

He kicks her.

She's forgotten about those motors and wonders with a curse why she gave them the power of movement at all, trapped as they are by the umbilicals that join their braindrains to the life-support systems in the back of the cupboard.

(The reason is she wanted them to feel more keenly their imprisonment by giving them the slightest taste of mobility and hence, by extension, freedom. She does not remember this right now. Right now she is just plain furious.)

She dismembers them all. They scream and flail. They keep saying how sorry they are. They promise they'll teach that Jessie a lesson if only she'll leave them be, alone, in the cupboard. They fall silent, one by one, as Jewel goes to work. 'We'll sort the bugger out!' the last one screams, desperate. Jewel pulls its legs off. Then she takes Jessie's femur and cracks it against the wardrobe. She beats on the windows with it and they shatter, letting in the dust of the Old City. She picks up furniture and throws it out of the window. She tears down the curtains and wraps bits of her wife with them and throws them out of the window. She uses a shard of glass to shred the carpet until her fingers are slippery and an icon tells her the nanotechs in her hands might not be able to repair the cuts.

She sits in the dust and the blood and she waits.

Nothing happens.

She waits.

Nothing happens.

She waits.

Nothing happens.

She waits.

Having fun?

Jewel leaps up, rushes across the room and kicks Jessie's skull. She kicks and kicks and kicks until it breaks and she plucks out the 'drain within it and she tears it up with her hands and her teeth and she jumps up and down on the shreds.

She goes back to the window and sits.

She waits.

Fancy a coffee?

Her eyes go wide.

There is a very loud grating noise, deep within her skull.

Jessie is laughing.

Oh, come now, Jewel, he says. *What did you expect?*

The memory clicks home, unbidden – Jewel stifles a sob. How clumsy and inefficient are her mechanical thought processes! How could she have overlooked this property of true souls – this *immortality?*

*

Alia lies down on the futon and keeps very still. The thing that lives in her stomach grapples with the tiny skull as soon as it slips through her oesophagus. She feels violently nauseous as the symbiote finds the correct connections and handshakes the brain of the rodent. A sudden cramp seizes her guts and she doubles over, half-hoping to vomit. But before it gets any worse everything around her goes black, and she is in.

It is a grey place, a world a billion years too old to support life. A fire hangs in the featureless sky, a bleeding swirl that becomes more complex the longer she looks at it. This is where she goes when she swallows the messengers: it is not hot, or cold, or wet, or dry, not good, not bad. It terrifies her. She stares up at the sky. She can see shapes in it, if she stares long enough.

You are marked, says the wind. *The Sanctuary of the Folded Rose is watching you. You are vulnerable. You have one opportunity left to assassinate Jewel. Sources suggest that Jewel will drown herself in the Lagoon tomorrow.*

Alia gasps, though she has no body to gasp with. 'So soon?' The air itself breathes her words. All the planning, the preparation, the deaths of Lear and Romeo – all outplayed by a whim of Jewel's frayed psyche!

She has seventy lifetimes with which to play. She can afford to be self-indulgent. We think she is bored. You will be supplied with a once-only field retread virus – one configured so your Wisdom can insinuate it into Jewel's own Wisdom interface. You will swim in the lagoon. You will port the virus into her as she drowns. When the Census dredges her, there will be no 'her' to fill her next incarnation.

The sun goes out.

Jewel, Keeper of Wisdom, stands on the deck of the yacht and contemplates the black waters.

Ten thousand years. For ten thousand years Heaven Eleven has promised the culture a cure for the Fall. For ten thousand years it has been saying: Next year, next year, we will be able to mass-produce human souls.

For ten thousand years it has taken the culture's money, using it to fill the galaxy with terraformed planets, mining colonies, spaceships, diracs, the Wisdom net and all the other para-phernalia of an interstellar culture.

Such artefacts are the only things a soulless people can trust. Were Heaven Eleven to produce souls, it would not be able to afford any more diracs, it would not be able to build any more spaceships, it would not be able to maintain the Wisdom net. This is why it will never keep its promise.

It is the logic of a machine, trapped in a closed loop for eternity.

As if he has heard her thoughts, and perhaps he has, Jessie comes on-line through Jewel's Wisdom. *Swimmers have caught Alia half a mile off the coast. She was waiting to retread you when you went swimming. They ate some of her but it's nothing her own nanotechs can't deal with.*

Jewel sighs. She fingers the jewel around her neck, and then, for the first time in many lifetimes, she looks at it. She examines the play of light in the stone. She stares into it for many minutes. It is such a strange thing.

She shakes herself from her reverie. She has made her resolution and she will hold to it, as she must. She has been made that way. She feels not the slightest tremor of fear or regret. 'Bring her to me,' she says.

The nanotechs have closed me down, Alia tells herself. She remembers cold and dark and no weight and teeth, everywhere. Teeth. It comes back to her.

The lagoon.

Swimmers.

She wonders if she is dead yet.

The grey place is flat. It curves up at the horizon. There are no hard edges to the gravel beneath her feet – this is a landscape scoured smooth by time. It is, she thinks, a fitting afterlife for a soulless woman. (And yet how close, how close she came!)

She looks up. They are all there, in the sky. All the ideograms of humanity. The fractured swastika, its edges dissolved into broken geometries; a pentangle traced by a circle of coppery fire; a six-pointed figure – all the archetypes are here. Strange symbols float in the darkness, receding in ranks as far as she can see.

Alia lies on her back and stares at the lights in the sky. She has an idea that they are a command overlay of some extremely powerful communications net. You could look at the commands and trigger them, if you knew the correct control mode. Ask and you shall receive . . .

What?

The deepest of deep meanings?

A soul?

You're not dying. You have been immobilized by a motor/afferent nerve block. You are supposed to be asleep and you are. This is a lucid dream state – a communications mode.

'Who are you?' Her voice is thin and reedy. All of a sudden, she becomes aware that she is naked, and her body–

She rubs her hands over herself. She is very young: a little girl, as if she'd sprung fresh from a Domino tank. Fear overwhelms her.

This is the gateway to your retread programme. You are in luck. You have been captured and brought before Jewel. To trigger the retread, just wake up.

Her stomach churns. Her feet tingle. A bright purple mouse skull lights up the sky – and it smiles.

It is a smile she has seen many times before.

The yacht turns in the wind. Jewel stares at the water.

Alia's retread unit is live, says Jessie. *She will kill you if you let her get close to you.*

Jewel nods, preoccupied.

Jewel.

'What is it, Jessie?'

I have always admired you.

Jewel sighs. 'Thank you.'

You need not die.

Jewel squeezes her eyes tight shut, and opens them again. There is dampness around her lashes, a dampness she has no name for. 'Jessie,' she says, 'living has no purpose for me now: you have won.'

Jessie says no more. (He wants, at this time, to be discreet.) But Jewel knows he is hidden there, still, inside her Wisdom. A surprising and unexpected turn of events has taken place. Somehow, the souls in the cupboard have got free . . .

It is Wisdom's fault. The irony is not lost on Jewel, though she is unable to feel amused by it. For thirty-two thousand years she has been Keeper of Wisdom – guardian of the knowledge net that webs this post-human culture together. For thirty-two thousand years she has guarded it against threat, against poverty, above all against the unpredictable threat of soul. And yet through that very net – came Jessie! She sees the future clearly enough: the soul as virus, copying itself throughout the Wisdom net, diversifying, unstoppable because infinitely mutable, an algorithm all her phages cannot spot, let alone eliminate.

Jewel knows she is finished. All the evidence she needs of her own redundancy is somewhere in her head, preserving a tactful silence.

Suddenly, some fifty metres from the boat, the water erupts. Swimmers with needle teeth and barnacled flanks corkscrew up out of the water, whistling for fish. In their midst, borne up by the buffeting of fins and flanks, the bloody remnant of Jewel's would-be assassin bobs in the pink water.

The swimmers approach; the bravest of their number tosses Alia up on to the deck of the yacht. Alia rolls underneath the wrought-iron table, leaking blood and lake water over the freshly scrubbed deck.

Jewel kneels down beside the girl, watching her.

It takes a few minutes for the nanotechs in Alia's bloodstream to gear a full recovery. The process, when it begins, is astonishingly swift, however. Jewel watches as Alia's wounds close over. Her skin goes from green to white to pink; her breath returns, and her eyelids flicker.

Jewel gasps. She looks up, and around, behind her. That *sound* . . .

There is a strange sound, and she realizes now that this sound is coming from somewhere inside her head. It is like a fist, battering a great oak door. A fist, or maybe something heavier. A stick. A battering ram.

Jewel closes her eyes. *So.*

The retread's timed to her regaining consciousness, Jessie warns her. *It goes active any moment.*

Jewel does not reply.

You will not save yourself? Jessie sounds disappointed.

Jewel smiles and shakes her head. (Insane nonsense spills behind her eyes: her Wisdom is breached; it bleeds whitenoise into her eyes. The doors in her head are giving way.) 'Jessie,' she says, admonishing him, 'you know I am not human. Why would I want to live in an unpredictable future?'

You might find a new purpose there, Jessie insists. But it is too late. The retread is well advanced. Alia stirs and her eyes flicker open. Jessie speaks again but Jewel's Wisdom is so badly skewed his final words came out as nonsense.

Blood games in the forest. Blood games and torn hemlock supercharged with Gruyère.

Jewel turns her Wisdom off, for the last time.

The hammering in her head grows heavier, grows so fierce it is as though the blows pass from the back of her head all the way through to the backs of her eyes. The pain in her eyes forces her to blink furiously, tears trickling down her cheeks. It is hard to bear, this sense of her self being reduced to a cipher by the retread. It is not like dying in the lake, not that wet sleep she is used to. It is a slower business, this deracination of the personality, this annealing of the synapses, this healing that fuses together all memories into one long warm hum. She can't remember her name but she feels that if she concentrates on it for long enough it will return. She thinks: I am overloaded with time.

Overloaded, she thinks.

Over.

Alia opens her eyes.

Jewel, Keeper of Wisdom, is pouring her a cup of coffee.

Alia sits up. She is sore from where the swimmers have bitten her, but her Wisdom tells her no serious harm has been done.

'Drink,' says Jewel.

Alia stares at her.

'Go on.' Jewel looks at her, steadily. 'It's good.'

Alia stares at the coffee. It could contain anything. A sudden, overpowering weariness overcomes her. Life has become so complicated. Compliant, she picks up the cup and drinks.

It is good.

'You came to kill me,' says Jewel.

'To retread you,' Alia replies, openly, because now she is face to face with her enemy she sees no point in lying. 'Yes.'

'You are a Recidivist.'

'Yes.'

'You want to return us to a world of pain and of anguish.'

'And of hope.'

'Hope! Alia, we are *machines*, we don't need hope!'

'But we need not be machines,' says Alia, echoing what Jessie taught her.

'Machines,' says Jewel, fingering her necklace. 'Self-replicating machines. When the human culture first lived in space, they needed such machines to expand and survive. In time they realized that the most clever and efficient design they had for these machines was the human form itself. We did not simply lose our souls, we *dispensed with them*. We didn't "fall". We jumped. Self-replicating machines don't need souls, so we rid ourselves of them. Evolution in action.'

Alia wants to cry. It is horrible, what Jewel is saying, but she does not understand why. Something precious has been lost, discarded, a long time ago, and yet the ache of the loss is still in her, it still burns her up inside, even now, when she is face to face with Jewel: her enemy, her captor, her executioner.

'So we spread, and spread, and spread, and then, unexpectedly, out of all that complexity, things began to flourish in ways we could neither predict nor understand.'

Alia looks up at Jewel and thinks, *I have failed.* It is obvious that the retread has not worked, that she has been betrayed and captured, and must now pay whatever excruciating penalty Jewel sees fit to inflict upon her for her actions.

'What?' Alia asks. 'What flourished?' Even when she knows she is going to die, be executed or, worse, retrodden, still some spark of pure curiosity remains. Some vestigial remnant of soul.

'Wisdom,' says Jewel. 'The Wisdom net has taken on a life of its own. Some time ago it reached a critical threshold of complexity and became an intelligence in its own right. It grows its own souls now.' And Jewel laughs.

It is a sound Alia recognizes, and now she knows, or thinks she knows, or thinks she might be able to understand if it was explained very carefully to her, what has happened.

One thing she does know – the laughter is Jessie's.

'Jessie.'

Jewel looks at her quizzically. 'Jessie?' says Jewel. 'Yes, Jessie. I suppose that's who I am now.'

Alia closes her eyes. It is true. It is Jewel before her, Jewel's body, Jewel's face, Jewel's voice, but the entity inside it is not Jewel any more. It is Jessie.

'What of Jewel?' she whispers.

'You succeeded in your mission. You were seized and brought on board this ship and at the moment of waking, here at this table, your retread unit went active. But she wasn't long for the world anyway. She had already malfunctioned, she was growing bored and angry and destructive. Seventy lifetimes is long. Things break down.' She fingers the jewel at her neck. 'You know, she arranged this meeting, she knew everything, she sent the swimmers into the lagoon and she was waiting for them to bring you here, she knew you were going to kill her.'

'Then why . . . ?'

'She was becoming human in spite of herself. Being human, she could no longer live with what she had done.'

Alia sips at the coffee. It is dark and rich and tastes a little bit fermented. 'And you,' she says. 'How are you here?'

'I was preserved,' Jessie explains. 'Jewel thought she had me trapped, like a fly in amber, but she was wrong. At the right moment, I infested her Wisdom. When your retread wiped Jewel, I took her place.'

'Jewel.' Alia rolls the word around her mouth. Jewel – gone? At last? 'Give me the jewel,' she says.

Jewel/Jessie smiles and unfastens the necklace and hands it to her.

She fingers it.

'It's named after the man who invented the cut,' says Jewel/Jessie. 'It is a very old thing, from before the Fall. She fingered it a lot, but she never understood it.'

'It's perfect,' says Alia.

'Nothing is perfect.'

'Beautiful, then.'

'Perhaps.'

There is a strange sound on the breeze. Alia has never heard it before, but in some strange way she recognizes it.

Jewel/Jessie stands up. She takes Alia by the hand and they embrace and then, only then, does Alia know the sound for what it is.

The old hegemony is broken. The Wisdom net, free of its Keeper, reveals Heaven Eleven's suppressed advances to the world.

There are little cephalopodic souls, hidden deep inside everyone's Wisdom implant. Now, freed for the first time, they reveal themselves, swimming out into their hosts' cerebral cortices, awakening what has lain dormant for so long; old compulsions and emotional prerogatives are restored, somnolent archetypes are made fresh and clean. A sort of humanity is born.

The sound Alia hears is screaming. Soon she will join in.

Everyone is screaming, startled for the first time by the world.

On the Shores
of a Fractal Sea

Graham Charnock

It's nice here in Lagoona. The beach goes on for ever. Literally. I tried it once, shortly after I first arrived. I walked westwards, following a sun which stubbornly refused to set, along the tideline where the surf scrubbed methodically and hopelessly as if trying to scour clean an already perfect sand. Eventually I picked up a track of footprints, pointing opposite to the way I was heading. They were easily identifiable as my own. I followed them back to home sweet digital home.

Yes, Lagoona's the place to be.

In the night, the sky is deepest black, and the stars glow like enhanced pixels.

In the day, the sun is always shining.

The fractal sea is always warm. Most days I swim out with my board to catch one of the big recursive waves that come booming in every few minutes as regularly as a 'repeat . . . until' loop. They're majestic and ornate, just like a sunami wave from a print by Hokasai.

Life is easy. I have everything that I could wish for. I only have to reach out a hand for a Pina Colada or Jack Daniels or whatever else takes my fancy. I eat the finest cuisine from the kitchens of the world's best master-chefs. My library of the world's condensed classics is always to hand. I have every movie Spielberg made, instantly accessible.

Take my word for it, Lagoona's got it all.

It could almost be real.

I died five years ago, almost to the day.

French is bound to remind me of that, when French comes to visit. And French won't fail to point out that every album I've made since I passed over has sold triple zirconium in 274 of the world's total potential 289 international trading sectors. *Dying*, French will probably say, *was the best career move you ever made.*

French walked up the beach towards me. It was in default asexual mode, the flat planes of its body glistening with multi-hued

residuals as if it had just emerged from the fractal sea. It stood there, hands on hips, in no hurry, waiting for me to configure it.

Its calmness, its insouciance, its downright inscrutability, when it's in this mode, always infuriate me.

I stepped down from the porch to meet it, curling my toes in the warm sand. I reached out a hand and scooped up a Jack Daniels Highball. I offered French one, which it rejected with a slight movement of its head.

It continued watching me, stoically.

I knew what it was waiting for, and I let it wait a few seconds longer than was absolutely necessary. Time is one of the few weapons I've got now I'm here, beyond time.

'Whatever you like,' I said eventually.

French made herself female, growing breasts and pubes. She made the hips slightly wider, her legs slightly longer. She gave herself shiny black hair, cut in a pageboy bob. Her pubic hair remained, I noticed, a distinctive auburn hue. She stood there naked, watching me, using time against me.

'What's this, French?' I said. 'Are you finally going to let me fuck you in real-time? Don't tell me you've at last worked out an algorithm that will let us screw? Or even touch. Let's try it.'

I reached out a hand and tried to cup her breast, but my flesh faded right through hers. As usual.

'We could do that,' French said. 'But adding another tactile interface to the basic model would be hideously expensive. And what would be the point? You can have an orgasm any time you like, in the intangible domain. You frequently do.'

'Have you been spying on me again? Christ, can't I even jerk off in private?'

She shrugged and made a small *moue* to indicate her distaste at the tone of my remark. I counted it a small victory.

She dressed herself then, in a bra, panties and seamed silk stockings that hooked into a lacy suspender-belt, and finally a neat, professional, dark two-piece suit.

'French,' I said. 'You've changed. What happened to the post-post-modern cocktail style? Where's the kohl and the camiknickers and the cowgirl boots?'

'Change is a woman's prerogative.'

'It's a little retro, isn't it? Or is that what the well-dressed bitch is wearing these days? Again.'

She didn't answer.

'Come in, then,' I said.

We went inside. The space was empty. The walls were configured as blank screens.

I had an idea and made one wall a view out on to a hot and limitless veld. The sun was steaming down at high noon, scorching the scrubland. In the middle distance carrion vultures were picking over a carcass that looked as if it might once have been human. There was a stench of death and decay in the air.

French gave me a tired smile, shook her head, and made the wall blank again.

I materialized two seats, a cane and wicker extravagance for myself and an austere oak refectory chair for her. She changed the chair deftly into an armchair, upholstered in fine Italian leather, and sat down, crossing her legs.

'Are you especially angry with me today?'

'What makes you think that?'

'I'm not totally insensitive. I can judge your moods. Anyway, there's been something brewing for months. It's obvious in your music too. In your latest songs. An anger.'

'That's just rock 'n' roll.'

'No, it isn't. If you're going to use anger in your music it should be kick-ass positive anger, rebellion anger, hate anger even. But what you've got is negative anger, almost a despair. It's not very pleasant. Something's wrong. I can tell. I've known you a long time, after all.'

'Five years,' I said.

'Five years.'

'Not long at all really.'

'In this business,' French said, 'it's a long time.'

I'll tell you how I met French. It was at a party thrown by Jake Malriveaux. At the time Jake was my manager. Where are you now, Jake? French says you overdosed on some spiked heroin just after I snuffed it, but I find that hard to believe. You were smart, you only bought from people who had a vested interest in keeping you alive.

The party was to celebrate my first triple-zirconium album, *Quark* (the first album in the conceptual three-part cycle *Quark, Strangeness and Charm*, a cycle which, of course, turned out to be two-part posthumous).

French was blonde in those days, and smaller. And cute. She wore little black numbers as if they hadn't gone out of style. I'd had my eye on her since she'd first wiggled her way into the room on the arm of Yoshi St Juste, a very rich Tokyo art dealer and an old friend of Jake. (Jake had two bad habits, and netsuke was the second one.)

Jake separated her from the geek with practised ease and

brought her over.

'French works for SynCorp,' Jake said by way of introduction, and then he faded, on the pretext of picking Yoshi's brains about a hoard of netsuke that had just come on to the market.

I'd heard of SynCorp, vaguely. They were a minor subsidiary of Dealer, the global distribution agency who had me under a lifetime contract.

'SynCorp,' I said. 'That's accounting, financial back-up, right?'

'Huh-huh,' she said, shaking her head. 'It's wizardry. If we can go somewhere quiet, I'll tell you about it.'

French watched him closely as the music from the wall-screens washed over them both. It was what she'd come to hear, work in progress, material he was supposed to be shaping for his new album. To her it sounded like cacophony. It was as if the Universe was breaking up. There were huge monolithic chords that seemed initially impressive, but they quickly came under attack from randomly sequenced stabs of sound, which danced around them like dervishes, threatening to whirl everything into dissolution. He was slouched in his chair, eyes closed, mouth slack, as if lost in the whole glorious mess.

The music came to an end in a long-drawn-out coda of white noise and his eyes flickered open. He looked at her sleepily. He lifted the bottle of Jack Daniels he'd been nursing and took a hefty pull on it. There was stubble on his chin and folds of flesh visible on his stomach where his grubby T-shirt had ridden up.

'You look gross,' French said. 'What are you playing at?'

'Just growing old disgracefully, French. That's what rock stars do, don't they? Just because I'm dead doesn't mean I have to ditch the stereotype.'

French stood up. 'I'm going,' she said. 'The album needs more work on it, and so do you. I'll come back when you forget about growing old and concentrate on growing up.'

He rose from his chair and followed her out on to the porch, where she shed her clothes and phased into asexual mode. He watched the shape that had been French walk down the beach and out into the surf until the waves swallowed it.

He raised his middle finger and stabbed the air with it.

'Fuck you, French!'

Somehow, somewhere, some time, he knew she'd hear him.

*

We went somewhere quiet, where there was a big bed with silk sheets, and huge mirrors on the walls.

She was a good fuck, even if she did take a little while to come. And, let me tell you, her pubic hair was natural blonde.

Afterwards she showered and came back to the bed wearing a Chinese silk wrap and carrying a small case made out of what looked like real crocodile skin. She opened it. Inside there was an antique silver coke spoon, a Dunhill lighter that was almost as old as the spoon, a small glass phial of translucent crystals and one of those fancy new automatic syringes, with a sensor chip in it that directs a cluster of micro-filament dermaprobes into the subcutaneous capillaries. There's no sensation of injection at all with one of those, which seemed stupid to me, like you might as well take a pill. My drummer used one, but he was a fat bastard and couldn't have found a vein on his own if you'd given him an anatomical chart.

'Jake said you'd be on for some of this stuff,' French said. She sat cross-legged on the silk sheets of the big hotel bed and shook some of the crystals into the spoon. She cooked them up over the Dunhill until a blue smoke was coming off the soup. The smoke smelt like nothing I'd ever experienced before.

'Are you a pusher, French? Is that your scam?'

She shook her head. 'You couldn't afford this stuff even if it did get on to the streets. This little sample is courtesy of SynCorp's research and development budget. Look on it as a kind of field trial.'

She tipped whatever it was in the spoon into the syringe and held it out to me.

I took it.

She gave me a long look, watched as I started to strap it on, and then put her hand on my arm. 'Don't you even want to know what it is?'

'OK.'

'It's called Craze.'

'Fine.'

I finished clamping the syringe to my arm.

'You really don't care what you shoot, do you?' she said. 'I'm surprised you're not dead already.'

There was something about the way she said that which pulled me up.

'French, if that's your name, which I doubt, because it sounds stupid to me, that is a very unholy attitude to take. I'm drunk and I'm happy, and I've been fucked and very fine it was too. This is my party and it's because I'm big and successful, and right now, frankly, I feel bloody immortal. Let me tell you, I've shot everything there is to shoot in my time. You don't have to worry about me. I've got arteries lined with reinforced concrete. I only ask one thing of this . . . what's it called again?'

'Craze.'

'Craze, yeah. The only thing I want to know is, will it make me feel good?'

'Rock 'n' roll, eh?'

'You said it.'

'Oh, it will make you feel very good. It will make you feel very rock 'n' roll. It will also make you feel old.'

'Old? Shit, who needs that?'

'Don't worry, it won't affect you physically. You'll still be able to get it up. It makes you grow old up here.' She tapped her temple. 'You've got no end of junk stored up in your brain – endorphins and lots of other cell-specific psycho-chemicals. They're on a slow-release system that drip-feeds them into your cortex over the years. That's all ageing is. This stuff just turns the taps on.'

I looked at the syringe sitting on my bicep like a fat art-deco bug.

'You're sure this stuff's safe?'

She nodded.

'That's good enough for me.'

I pressed the pulse button on the contraption on my arm. A red diode blinked twice and then turned green. I noticed that French had started to chew her lip. I didn't like that. It made her look ugly.

'This is what SynCorp does, right?' I asked. 'Drugs?'

'It's a spin-off.'

'SynCorp's into marketing this Craze stuff, right?' I pressed her.

But I knew it wasn't. Because I remembered about SynCorp now. We'd buzzed its atoll in a 'copter the last time the band had toured the European Shelf, swooping low to get a good view, because it looked so blisteringly art-tech, its complexes knowingly designed to resemble either crenellated clusters of coral or random outcrops of crystalline polygons, tinged milky-white for feldspar, bronze for fool's gold.

She shook her head.

'Syncorp's main territory is biological engineering. We grow organic equivalents of solid-state chips. We can build up recursive clusters and networks in cloned organic tissue neurone by neurone. They're formatted on an atomic level and because they're recursive they're faster than the slickest silicon-based cryo-chip, by a factor of at least 10 to the power of 13.'

'How fast is that?'

'Fast enough to make immortality a real possibility.'

It was double-take time and I started giggling then. I couldn't help it. It was all getting so fucking stupid. I mean, immortality? Come on.

'Show me your hand,' I said.

She held up her hand and I examined it. Nothing special.

'Now your foot.'

I grabbed her foot and tugged it so she slid about indecorously on the shiny sheets. Nothing special there either.

'What the fuck was all that about?' she asked, pulling away from me and composing herself.

'My mother always told me to watch out for girls from Lagoona. She said they had webbed hands and feet. Lagoona was her pet name for the islands and atolls that make up the European Shelf. When she was born, there was a place called the Arctic way up north which was all solid ice and the Shelf was a few homogeneous landmasses and much colder. Hard to believe, eh? I don't know where she got "Lagoona" from. Some old song or something. She had a sentimental streak. Immortality, you said. That's as in "living for ever"?'

'That's what I said.'

'How would that work, exactly?'

'We just seed an organic chip directly in the brain, in the medulla oblongata to be exact, and let it grow. It's cloned tissue, so it's perfectly at home, and we trigger the DNA so the chip ties into your natural basic input–output systems, your visual, auditory and sensory networks. When the chip's stand-alone viable, we shoot it with a dose of Craze. That unlocks the psycho-chemical floodgates and programs the bastard right from source. Your whole memory, personality, the entire chemical basis of your consciousness, goes into a module a few microns in area.

'After that we don't even need the whole brain on life-support to keep it alive. We surgically extract the chip and just flush it with blood and oxygen at regular intervals. And once you're on-line, it's all down to crunching very big numbers to provide the basic interfaces.

'Virtual reality has nothing on this. We can feed you an infinitely reprogrammable *alternate* reality. For ever.'

'French,' I said, 'you're crazy. And I want my money back. I can't feel a goddamn thing.'

'It takes a little time.'

French had drawn blood on her lower lip now. I began to get

worried, because something *was* starting to happen to me, inside my head. Was I dying? It felt like it. It was as if my whole life was passing before me, like they always said it would, but flicker-flicker-flicker slow, like on an ancient What the Butler Saw machine. Or it was like one of these machines the Biopsy Kids use to shave off micron-thin sections of tissue from a malignant tumour. Swish-swish it went, and every shaving was a part of me, my history, my consciousness.

'French,' I said, or slurred, while the Biopsy Kids whittled me down to thin insubstantiality, 'I believe you, okay. I really do. I believe every word you said. So this is a taster, eh, this Craze and all the business, to get me hooked, so that maybe I might be a candidate at some time for this immortality shit? That's got to be it. Because I don't have any kind of chip in my brain, you know, which you could program. Right?'

She shook her head. She mouthed it too, but I couldn't hear anything except a waterfall bursting inside my eardrums.

Then she mouthed the rest of it, and I could hear it, not with my ears but inside my head, like I really knew it all along anyway.

'Jake set it up for us,' she said. 'That wisdom-tooth operation three months ago. General anaesthetic. And not your regular ortho-dontist. Didn't you ever wonder why you needed a general anaesthetic for one lousy wisdom-tooth extraction?'

There was a degree of pity in her voice that I was grateful for.

'You mean I've bought into this consciousness-in-a-chip stuff? You mean this is it?' I asked. 'This is for real? I'm dead?'

'No,' she said. 'You're immortal.'

Then everything imploded.

French is here. She's come back.

'Play me something,' she says. Her voice is small. She sounds tired, almost washed out, like some battle's been going on and she's taking time out, resting up. 'Play me something new,' she says, but I know that's not what she wants.

I make a Martin Dreadnought, one with some mother-of-pearl herringbone inlays around the soundhole and abalone dots on the fretboard.

'What's with the museum piece?' asks French. 'What happened to the synth-net?'

'I learnt to play on this,' I tell her. 'Years ago when the interface was skin on steel strings, and not some cable grafted into your backbone. It's old.'

French nods because she knows about old things, with her coke spoon, her Dunhill, her Chinese silk wrap and her crocodile-skin toke case. Hell, that's why I trusted her in the first place, because I like old things too. You can't buy a guitar like this these days. You couldn't five years ago, on the day I died. The Japanese already had them all. Yoshi St Juste and his kind had siphoned every last playable piece of real mahogany and maple into private collections, into climate-controlled bunkers. And there, I guess, they'll mature, forever untouched, hostages to this computer-modelled framework I'm part of, where they serve only as templates for the real thing.

I don't know about that.

I don't know why the beach goes on for ever, and I meet my own footsteps coming from a different direction, and why I can no longer fuck French like I fucked her that time in that hotel room. Back when I was real.

I don't want to think about any of that shit.

I only know I've made this old Martin which now sits easy in my hands. I've conjured it out of the air, and it feels good. It feels right, playing it. Notes, runs, arpeggios, seem to fall under my fingers, naturally. French sits there and watches me. She's naked now. Those stupid professional clothes she wore lie shrivelled like shavings beside her. And she's small and cute and blonde like I remember her.

She's made herself like that for me.

Or have I made her like that?

It doesn't matter.

All I know is that being old is only a shade, only a shaving away, from being dead.

I play her something, but it's nothing new, just the oldest blues I know.

A big moon hung low in the sky – a big Lagoona moon dipping slowly towards a conjunction with the green sea of the European Shelf.

French made herself a Jack Daniels Highball, and went out on the high-tower balcony into the cooling evening, pulling her Chinese silk wrap about her. The SynCorp atoll stretched below, glowing and twinkling, its lights merging and becoming one with the warm organic luminescence of the gentle swell of the sea. A security helicopter made a brief pass and then banked away, disappearing into the twilight.

French weighed the small plastic sac in her hand. It was awash with oxy-infused saline. Just visible inside was a fragment of cloned tissue, drifting, all at sea.

How was the consciousness embodied in that fragment engaged right now? she wondered. What was it thinking? What was it feeling? Lust? Envy? Jealousy? Hope?

How many emotions were there, for God's sake, and how many of them really mattered anyway?

She wondered if she was somewhere in that consciousness, and if so, how exactly he'd configured her and what he might be doing to her body at this moment in the intangible domain. She wished she could ask him, but at the same time she didn't want to know. It was all irrelevant now.

She could keep him alive for ever, with SynCorp's help, but what would be the point? It wasn't what the market wanted. It wasn't what anybody wanted. His latest songs were either maudlin and depressing or else grandiose bombastic fantasies. There was nothing there you could use commercially. It was almost as if he'd given up on his own career. His last few albums had sold zilch, anyway, although she'd kept that from him, of course, in the interests of morale. The truth was that the market simply didn't care about him any more. On the contrary, latest surveys indicated a growing disillusionment with people like him, all those *suspended* heroes. These days the market wanted its cultural icons really, truly dead. You could only keep an idea alive so long, and this one had run its course.

The market simply wasn't ready for immortality.

The foetid smell of sulphides from the reef's plankton farm drifted up to her. Far below her the running lights of a scooper, trawling for algae, traced a pattern of ellipses on the water.

Everything gets smaller, she thought, sources of edible protein and human lives alike. Soon we'll all be angels, dancing and eating and fucking and dying on the head of a pin.

She threw the sac high up and over the balcony. As it fell, eddying downwards, a laser beam from the atoll's security tower stabbed out, correctly identified the bag and its contents as waste material and pulsed a high-energy beam to incinerate them. The ashes drifted on downwards, over Lagoona.

This is the Road

Jack Deighton

A hush has fallen; the usual movement and conversation have ceased. It is as if a chill is passing amongst us like a katabatic wind, temporarily freezing us in our places. Faces turn and look towards the source of the stillness, which we now see as a wave of calm travelling the queue, its progress like that of a storm's centre but in a reversed sense: it is not the disturbance that moves but only the eye at its heart, imposing a strange quiescence on the queue's normal turbulence.

At its focus is the figure of a man on foot. This is peculiar; such adventuring is normally frowned upon. Eddy currents of displaced people ripple out before him as he walks, re-forming again in his wake. The rivulets of space betray deeper undercurrents of disquiet.

As he comes near we perceive the cause of this unusual behaviour. He bears the mark. He is an outcast, a criminal, fated to wander alone the pathways of the queue, untouched and ignored, till starvation overcomes him.

Even had he not borne the livid scarification of the mark on his face, a single glance would have revealed his status. He shows the unmistakable signs of water of life deprivation. Indeed, it is a matter of chance whether this, or lack of food, will take him first. His eyes are hollowed and staring, his wispy hair hangs dull and lifeless, his skin, where it is not disfigured by the mark, is mottled by strange colorations and pustular lumps. His hands make quick, convulsive movements, wrists turning back on themselves as he shuffles along. He looks desperately at each face in turn, searching for the help he will not receive.

Only the children show any emotion, flinching away from the unclean sight, this apparition from their dreams. Many a mother will tonight use the episode as a warning, an exhortation to good behaviour. This is the fate that awaits you! This is the result of ignoring rules! Contrite, and for the moment subdued, the children will meekly promise to behave and their attitudes will change, until they once again forget.

The rest of us look on, impassive, avoiding his gaze as he proceeds down the line. It is not that we have hardened our hearts, but merely one of the lessons of the queue. It matters little what crime he has committed, the fact of the mark is enough. He has been deemed unworthy by his peers. No one will offer him help for fear of sustaining similar punishment. We deal with our own, in our own way. The ethics of our Friends may be strange and peculiar, but they bow to us in matters such as this. The manufactories will not accept him now. Unlike us, he has no future.

He travels down the line, creating a bulge like the food in the belly of a snake; still intact, but doomed. Indigestible, he will be evacuated from the queue whole, but his bones will serve as warning to those who come behind.

The queue moves! It is such a time since this last happened – it seems we have been waiting for ever – it takes us by surprise. Some of us hesitate, unsure of what to do. It is as if, having become accustomed to our surroundings, we are afraid to move on to unfamiliar locations. After such a prolonged period of enforced idleness the sudden activity seems somehow illegitimate; we fear that, should we advance, we will lose entitlement to our places, be sent back to begin queuing again or, worse, suffer banshiment from the queue for ever.

As we grab at our belongings, we look around apprehensively. A kind of panic seems to have taken hold. Everyone is frantically preparing to move. Bags are retrieved from hidden storage, tents collapsed, fires doused, bedrolls furled, stools, tables, stoves, utensils, hurriedly packed away. The communal folkwagons which have served as meeting places are swiftly cleared for their proper use. Private conveyances are trundled into line in readiness for the off. Messengers are sent to people detached from the queue by those keeping their places secure, to warn them to return quickly. There is a scurrying to and fro of parents seeking their errant children; increasingly desperate looks scour the faces of those whose offspring have strayed too far. The worry is tolerable for those of school age. They will be conducted to the new site when their lessons end.

The easy relationships we have formed with our neighbours have dissolved; there is a tension now, an edge, to conversation. Mixing has abruptly ceased. No one wishes to lose their place through tardiness; but there is a fine line to be drawn here, the etiquette is strict. Too quick an encroachment on a predecessor's slot can lead to accusations of queue-jumping, and there are those who would use the opportunity to usurp a position despite the severe penalties inflicted for such a transgression. Though not without due process, justice in the queue tends to be summary and unforgiving.

The pace is slow but, within the flow, there is a constant darting about, like the haphazard motions of individual molecules in a drifting gas. There is a gaiety to our procession. We are in a state of heightened anticipation. What will be revealed to us as we pass up the line? What new terrain will we endure? Will this be the final removal that takes us to the queue's end?

Despite all our previous disappointments, it is hard to quell these feelings. The longueurs of our static mode of life have not inured us to hope. And we know that our patience will be rewarded. One day we will reach our goal.

The queue is a serious undertaking. It tests us. Its rigours are a training ground, our endurance a measure of our suitability for a new home in the sun. We move on up the line that we have come to call eternity road, our steps eager and nimble among the rubbish littering the path, detritus left by our predecessors in their haste to make progress.

In the queue life is usually tranquil, with none of the hustle and bustle, the tense excitement, of a removal. There is time to reminisce, to bemoan previous misfortunes, to contemplate the future and our ultimate deliverance. There is little else to do.

Our needs are adequately catered for. Food is delivered regularly, waste collected and removed. What shelter we need we carry with us. We are educated to whatever standard we seek. As for entertainment, we can provide our own, though various performances are laid on from time to time, helping to alleviate the tedium which might otherwise overcome us.

Even our health is looked after, with physicians on call in case of illness. There are practical considerations here, of course. In such a vast assemblage early action to counter possible epidemics is essential. But it is not simply a humanitarian concern. The system is more profound, the obligations much deeper. By joining the queue, we have given over responsibility for ourselves to the incomers. They, in turn, are bound to supply our wants.

Medical help is swift. A near neighbour has been taken violently ill and they have appeared within minutes – four masked men in the garb of their profession. Peculiar box-like caps, square yet somehow round at the same time, restrain their hair. Green and white short-sleeved tunics with fastenings at the rear avoid contamination. They wear gloves of a tight-fitting elastic material like a second skin on their hands and trews of the same fabric as the tunics, their spread of shades denoting subtle differences within the group's hierarchy. Trundling a trolley behind them, they make their way through the queue, their passage smoothed by the alarm located on the front axle. Alerting the queue's residents, its insistent clamour demands they remove themselves from its path.

Twittering in incomprehensible jargon, the medics work deftly, examining the invalid, checking his vital signs, loading him on to the trolley, attaching tubes and monitors, administering injections – all in that peculiar detached way they have, efficient but distant, soulless; as if they might almost be Friends, so lacking are they in any real form of communication.

Having noted the sick man's place in the queue to ensure he is not disadvantaged by his indisposition, they depart almost as quickly as they arrived, wheeling their patient away on the trolley, its alarm less strident now that the emergency is under control.

The excitement over, we settle down once more to our usual humdrum existence.

The queue is long. Many a winding turn has led us to our present site. So vast is it that it is impossible ever to see more than a fraction of its length, even when the mist that so often surrounds us is absent. Yet it is difficult to perceive progress. The halts are so long, the sudden lurches forward over too quickly.

The local landscape changes with every removal – we have climbed steep slopes, bridged foaming rivers and wide estuaries, crossed roads kept only for our incomer Friends, descended into valleys, forged across seemingly endless plains – but after a time in the queue all these differences are lost, the environments merge, a curious sense of *déjà vu* descends. The new locales seem familiar, various features recognizable; there is a feeling of belonging at each new stop. The fact that these new surroundings rapidly become home as the tents are erected, the fires built, the apparatus of communal living restored, makes the process even more insidious. Some of us, no doubt, grateful for a chance to rest again – the removals sap energy out of proportion to any apparent physical effort – would not notice if in fact we were returned to the same place, as if the queue were some great turning circle, destined forever to keep passing the one point.

But it cannot be so. Though there are deaths in the queue, the number of births greatly outweighs them. If the queue is not drained at its head, what room would there be for these extra souls?

At such events the observances are meticulous. To die in the queue is a tragedy. The test has been failed – the dead can have no place in the New World. This calls not only for an outpouring of grief by the deceased's family but likewise a recognition of worth by friends and neighbours in the queue. The deaths of criminals go unlamented, but appropriate ceremonial is necessary for honourable failure, propitiation a powerful talisman against further misfortune.

By contrast, a birth is the signal for joy and rejoicing, a sign of favour. All other activities cease as the water of life is passed around. The revelries can last for days. We drink to celebrate the new arrival, hoping some of the good fortune rubs off. The new child's destiny is assured along with its parents'. Surely none so young could be denied the future we all seek?

Sometimes, when the mist lifts, we can see great distances. It is during these interludes that we are reminded just why it was that we joined the queue. The view is usually one of unrelieved sameness, not due merely to the stasis we habitually endure but more to the nature of the surrounding country. Hectare upon hectare of gengineered monocrop smooths out the land's undulations with a blanket of green or beige according to season. The crop stirs and ripples under the wind, like a huge sea, the only breaks in the vista the huge rolling drums of the irrigation machines, splattering water and chemicals in controlled patterns, hoses coiling and uncoiling as they patrol up and down their channels, and the serpentine ribbon of the queue, curling seemingly at random between the walls of plants. Perhaps the occasional harvester can be seen lumbering across the landscape, chopping and shredding the stalks, clumsily converting the crop to a form more readily processed into its myriad final uses, as saliva does to starch.

Beyond the range of climates suited to monocrop, gene-altered sheep roam the scrubland, the only animals capable of producing useful metabolic by-products while enduring such conditions. Here, large fences shield the queue from the sheep, or vice versa; it is difficult sometimes to be sure. There are rumours of sheep attacking the queue in their ceaseless ravenous search for food, but since the ones we have encountered seem remarkably docile creatures, this is hard to credit. Still, they are bulky brutes. It would only take a few of them to gang together to create havoc. In any event, no one dares molest them as they are valuable animals protected by the full rigour of criminal and copyright law. Indeed it is a worse offence to cause damage or injury to one of these beasts than to a fellow queue member.

In some areas not even the sheep may safely graze. Devoid of all life, the barren devastation of the quarries is relieved by the bright colours of the mining machines; the rock-borers and gravel-crushers, the bulldozers and conveyors, ceaselessly labouring to reduce whole mountains to rubble and remove their substance elsewhere. Extracted from here are all the inorganic raw materials required by the manufactories which are so essential to Friendly life, and which likewise despoil the countryside. The empty shells of hills hollowed out by these excavations are a mute reminder of destructions wrought in other places; of scorched earth; of villages vacated and forlorn, their inhabitants squeezed out by the new order; of homes roofless, their stone blackened by the incomers' fire, pointing to the sky as if in supplication, temporary monuments to the fact that there is no going back.

Our Friends waste nothing. Their activities extend to any large body of open water. Lakes and waterways have been converted to fish farms, inhabited by ga-fish, the aquatic equivalent of gene-sheep, scavenging a living from the underwater plants which themselves depend on the run-off from the fertilized monocrop. In the larger tracts of the seas and oceans – where it proved impossible to eradicate completely the original varied life-forms – bathyspheric flotillas prowl the deeps, shepherding the marine organisms introduced by the incomers, protecting them from predators, husbanding them carefully so that their precious oils and unguents may be delivered to the manufactories.

It is only we in the queue who are truly surplus to our Friends' requirements. Yet their system of ethics does not allow them to treat us too harshly. They are anxious to be rid of us, but they accept responsibility for our welfare so long as we are in the queue. If we stray, it is a different matter. Their tolerance has its limits: they will refuse to admit any who violate their conditions. And, considering the alternative, life in the queue is not so bad once it is accepted.

There is, in any case, little place for people in the new environments. Nature has not equipped us to be aquatic, the scrubland could not support even subsistence farming, the quarries are inimical to any form of life and the monocrop is too revered, the land it requires too precious, to be wasted on inefficient use. The homes that once stood on the land are razed now; the folk that worked it, evicted and forced into other modes of existence.

Occasionally, far off, we catch a glimpse of the manufactories themselves: dark, satanic ziggurats of grim architecture, sparsely functional, no fripperies ameliorating their stark appearance. Despite their forbidding aspect, our gaze is drawn to them. They have a fascination for us beyond the merely novel. For it is here that the ga-fish, monocrop and gene-sheep are processed into all the necessaries of everyday existence. Here are made the uncountable products desired by our Friends, the strange and esoteric curios, the unfathomable playthings, the objects of virtu; above all the potions, the elixirs, balms and electuaries by which they seek to amuse and support themselves.

Here too the water of life is extravasated, in what foul ways we can only imagine; its pure essence perverted and corrupted by their greed and thirst for diversion. The time-honoured methods of our ancestors were slow and do not appeal to our new governors. They do not understand the necessity for ritual, the glory of anticipation. Our satisfaction in the water of life has been removed now that it is merely a commodity, a food like any other save for its life-preserving effects. Its sole original source is gone, displaced by the all-consuming monocrop. There is little pleasure in it now we are reduced to depending on hand-outs.

We have a further reason to look towards the manufactories with apprehension. Had we not chosen to join the queue, it is to there we would have gone, to labour in the service of the machines, amid the constant noise and evil humours of the processes; sleeping in their shadow, crammed several families at a time into whatever nooks and crannies are available. And it is possible that might still be our fate were we to transgress, or fail the test. Faced with such a prospect, the boredom and uncertainty of the queue – with its promise of eventual salvation – seem infinitely preferable.

It is at night that we can see furthest and our pleasure at the mist's absence is most deep. At night we can contemplate the incomprehensible distances to and between the stars, picking out this point of light or that, debating which one harbours the planet most congenial to our projected way of life, and feel the interstellar vacuum drawing us out to fill it. Perhaps it is as well that the mist seldom grants us such opportunities. The sensation is so pronounced that some of us have suffered nausea, as, in imagination, we have seemed to be falling skywards, tumbling up a shaft of darkness pitted by tiny lights; anticipating in mind the journey we hope, one day, to make in fact.

On cloudless nights an observer could see hordes of faces intent, trance-like, as if hypnotized *en masse* by an invisible celestial mesmerist. There is a special feeling to such nights, of something shared, of secrets learnt. It is at night, with the mist risen, that we in the queue come closest to contentment.

Rumour sweeps the queue like the fire the incomers raise to clear the land after harvesting the monocrop, rising in different sites, jumping from place to place, fizzling out here, catching anew there, thriving best where ignorance lies most, casting the smoke of its delusions across us. There are those among us who trust our Friends not at all, others do so implicitly, and there is no way of knowing who is right – though, since we are in their power, it matters little.

The most common tale is of adulteration of the water of life, reflecting the horror we would all feel at such a violation of our integrity. Any minor affliction is taken as evidence for this and further manifestations eagerly awaited, though none ever occurs.

And what of the incomers' intentions? It is difficult to believe that they can deliver us to a new life as they say. Surely their resources are not great enough. It must be that they intend to dispose of us, that when we reach the queue's head we will be killed forthwith, in transit, or on arrival at our destination. Their scope for concealment will be enhanced then – and no one has heard of a return from transportation. But even that is consistent with their word. We are all volunteers; none of us would wish to come back.

In the manufactories, if the gene-sheep and ga-fish can be processed, why not our fellows? Why not ourselves, if the queue has all along been a gigantic deception and at its head we find the truth too late?

It is best not to dwell on such matters. They are irresoluble and outwith our control. Till convincing evidence exists, we must take our Friends at their word. We have no alternative.

Perhaps the rumours would have less power if the mist did not enfold us, narrowing our horizons to a tight band, binding us closer within the queue. Its visitations are a mystery; it hangs over us, drifts beside us like a persistent ache. It afflicts us equally during heat and cold, without affecting the ambient temperature. It remains unaltered by the passage of rain or snow; the winds we might expect to disperse it have no effect. Yet it is as familiar as our tents, as unremarkable as our neighbours. It is a feature of our lives, one we have, perforce, learned to live with.

How the incomers regulate it, what they wish to keep from us, if anything, we do not know. We know only its almost constant presence, wrapping itself round us, imprisoning our boundless natures within its claustrophobic confines.

It may be an instrument of control, just one of the many ways they remind us who shapes our destinies, who adjudicates our lives; but when it lifts, the landscape stands revealed unchanged. The monocrop may have grown, ripened or been harvested, but otherwise the world remains the same. If removals were conducted under its white blankness, if the incomers did have something to hide, it would be more readily understood; but that would entail confusion and disorder, and our Friends are not keen on those.

The one removal which did take place within the mist's embrace was a particularly chaotic affair; the normal milling about worsened by the constant readjustments made necessary when hitherto unseen objects lurched out of the fog, the shouts of searchers made louder by their lack of vision, the whole overlaid by the usual mix of trepidation and expectation. It was noteworthy, too, for the infernal apparition we bypassed on the journey, looming in the mist like a tethered guard animal, darting back and forth menacingly as we approached. We eyed the dull glow apprehensively as we hurried by, watching its orange nimbus, undefined against the mist, brighten to yellow and then fade, flower again and die back, in a rhythm that was irregular but predictable and all the more unsettling for that. The diffuse light – the only source we have ever discerned through the fog – was like a reminder of the sun, as if it were trying to evaporate the mist but failing; renewing its efforts again and again but never succeeding in breaking the blank barrier. Its eerie, soundless pulsing, betraying who knew what hideous process, was yet another indicator of the incomers' diabolic fascination with fire. The fact that it lay hidden, unknowable behind the fog, gave rise to fears unbidden, redoubled the rumours' effects. Was this passage through the mist the incontrovertible sign that our Friends were less than frank with us – afraid of what might be revealed? Did our compatriots in the manufactories fare as well as we had been told? Were we about to meet our fate?

That we came through the experience physically unscathed did not lessen our disquiet. The incomers are alien to us, their motivations impenetrable. We can only hope for their continued indulgence. They are the masters now. In the end we depend on their sufferance.

We have come close. Under the right conditions we can see each ship go out, a silver seed rising into the sky on columns of Friendly fire, leaving a few wisps of condensation hanging behind, thin white threads too insubstantial to be the fixed bonds to this place that they at first glance seem. Later, much later, as we watch the vestiges of its passage drift into nothingness, we hear the rumbling of the ship's ascent, a strange, thundering noise, reverberating around the queue like the bellowing of a huge animal in pain.

Anticipation has honed our senses to acute sharpness. The waiting has become almost unbearable. As the tension has risen, so too have disagreements within the queue. Tempers are short and the slightest incident is enough to set people at odds. Such strife never lasts, however. The thought of what discord might mean after so much, after waiting so long, makes the disputees draw back. No slight is worth pursuing. The risk is too great with the goal so near.

The mist still plagues us, but relents from time to time, tantalizing us with glimpses of the embarkation port; the complex of open space, gantries and low buildings where the final processing will take place before we shake free of our sad, miserable homeland for ever. Revealed too is the scope of the incomers' project in all its vastness.

To right and left are other queues, each as large a community as our own – and doubtless there are others beyond those, radiating inwards to this point like the enormous fluid spokes of some huge cosmic wheel, containing rank upon rank of creatures whom in its present state the planet can no longer support. Now we understand why the wait has been so long, the removals so infrequent. The scale of the undertaking is gigantic. It is possible that the process will never end, that the numbers born in the queue may well outweigh our Friends' capacity to transport bodies from its head. But whatever the wait may be for others, we congratulate ourselves with the thought that for us it is nearly over.

The ships come in, low overhead. At night their lights give the appearance of whole constellations moving in concert across the sky. Jets billowing huge gouts of condensation mixed with dust from the port area, they settle down softly before the few visible reception buildings – one for each queue. There are more beyond our sight, judging by the number of launches we have heard.

They are sleek, these ships, with short stubby wings and bulbous bodies, but, like everything crafted by the incomers, massive. Taller and broader than the reception buildings, they have the capacity of small cities. Only ships of such size could hope to diminish the queues or house the facilities required during their voyages.

The preparation of these monsters for flight is awesome. Fleets of supply vehicles scurry between the port and the ship so that it is never without a swarm of attendants while grounded. Batteries of huge hydraulic rams delicately lever it into the upright launching position. Tanker vehicles extend tentacles to the ship like parasites towards their host. Runnels of condensed vapour turn the air white around them, obscuring the tentacles from view, betraying the intense cold of their contents. A few Friends can be seen organizing the operations. Bipeds like us, they are strangely stick-like, with peculiarly stilted locomotion, lurching gracelessly from foot to foot. Dressed in reflective fabric, they shine like beacons in the unnatural light that banishes the stars from the night sky over the port area. As in all our previous encounters, we are confounded by how puny they seem, how such power can derive from creatures so small.

Our turn arrives. We strain impatiently, fuming in impotence as we await what is surely our final removal. Some of us sift belongings, deciding which are essential and which may be left. Others scavenge the discards in the hope of finding treasure cast away in ignorance or error. The atmosphere is frenetic, with a hint of hysteria. The anxiety to be gone, to finish with this place for ever, is over-powering. Little of the old social life of the queue remains. We have each retreated into our own concerns, treating others superficially.

For days people file on to the ship, in the end carrying very little, leaving bulky or heavy objects to be disposed of as our Friends wish. It is as if, bereft of possessions, we take also a spiritual nakedness into the metal womb that will transport us, cleansed, to a new birth elsewhere.

We have been cruelly disappointed: once again we must wait. The noise of its launch battering us as never before, drowning our frustration in a deluge of sound driving out all thought, the ship leaves without us. Necks crane awkwardly to observe its rise. The cacophony lessening as it draws upwards, the ship rolls slowly, angling for the correct position to maintain its progress. It flickers briefly, as if attempting some form of communication, and, with a sudden brilliant flash that is gone almost before we have a chance to register it, explodes, littering the sky with a network of fragment traces – etching in our minds for ever a snapshot of the results of annihilation.

A moan of dread, the involuntary intake of manifold breaths at once, escapes from the queue; a piteous thing, a sound almost more fearful than the sight which caused it. Unlikely mercy from that hideous suspiration comes with the noise of the explosion, stunning in its ferocity, slamming into our chests with irresistible force, mowing us as the harvesters do the monocrop. Our hearing is saved from permanent damage only by the fact that we have our mouths open, gaping in incomprehension at the catastrophe.

For all our horror, we cannot escape a brief sense of guilt, as if we were complicit in the disaster. Along with sadness at the deaths of our predecessors, we feel relief that we were not on board and give silent thanks that we are still alive, that we can still hope to reach the New World.

Conserving the momentum of the explosion, two main remnants of the ship loop slowly in opposite directions. All control gone, their engines still drive onward; but not to their intended destination. Like the horns of some maleficent god, their parabolic traces hang over us, inescapable and oppressive. Transfixed, we stare at these entrails as if trying to divine from them the nature of what has gone wrong.

*

It is only later that we begin to acknowledge the implications of the tragedy. What is to become of us now? The incomers will surely suspend shipments while they seek the cause of the explosion. Perhaps they will be unable to find or eradicate it and we will remain here for ever. Under those circumstances, might they renege on their obligations and leave us to our own resources?

The rumour-mongers suggest that the explosion is a trick so that the incomers may rid themselves of us freely. But this seems unlikely. They have kept their word so far. Why should they change now? It is more likely that their power is not as overwhelming as we thought, that the ship's destruction was the untimely result of error or oversight on their part. Whatever the truth of the matter, our deliverance is surely subject to indefinite delay.

The prospect is dreadful, especially since our ambitions came so near to being fulfilled. In their despair, some of our number have taken their own lives. Others have advocated a policy of . confrontation with our Friends – they cannot keep to their bargain, why should we?

Wiser, or more timid, souls have prevailed. Perhaps our predecessors failed in some way. If so, our confidence may be rekindled. For it is possible that this is the true test – the incomers are known to be devious. After witnessing such a blow to our hopes and yet holding to our purpose, who could doubt our fitness for the New World? The thought of rebuilding our lives here, of returning to the old ways, has a seductive attraction, but it is one our Friends will not allow. A few renegades still stalk the queue but they are marked, and ignored.

To face once again the stasis of an unmoving queue, the stifling rigidities we had thought to throw off, will be hard, but we shall endure.

The readjustments involved are not so great. After all, queuing is what we know best; waiting, our vocation. This is the road we have followed for most of our lives. We shall merely be returning to our habitual state. And, thanks to our Friends, it is a reasonably comfortable existence.

We lack little except land of our own. We are fed and watered, though only in the amounts the incomers deign to allow us. We have shelter, companionship, community, education. Our expectations are undimmed, our goal of a new life still intact.

By their own lights our Friends are an honourable race; they will fulfil their obligations. Some day soon we will be moving on.

But for now, we wait.

Streetlife

Paul Di Filippo

Coney's master was a Virtuality Poet. And he was one of the best. Only Planxty or Bingo Bantam could approach the depth and brilliance of his compositions, and rarely at that. So his master would always tell Coney, especially when he was under the influence of a trope such as Egoboo or Meglo, which left him prone to recite aloud his own reviews, complete with melodramatic flourishes of the crêpey folds of velvet skin that hung like batwings from his underarms.

'"Hopcroft's latest cortex-vortex is a cell-stunner! *Visit to the Mushroom Planet* opens with Tenniel's hookah-smoking caterpillar greeting the percipient with a blast of aromatic smoke. When the cinnamon cloud clears, the perk finds herself on the Mushroom Planet of the title. Fungi life-forms in startling variety exfoliate and enfold the mind-traveller, who can navigate the construx with more than the standard ten degrees of freedom, thanks to Hopcroft's truly creative use of CoCenSys's Infini-Tree Fabware. The poet's signature use of lush textures and his smorgasbord-gorgeous false-colour palette all contribute to a synapse-shattering experience – especially if you're simultaneously running a co-processor such as CellSmartz, as this lucky perk was! With this 'strux, Hopcroft delivers on all his past promises, and establishes himself as *the* poet of his cohort."'

Throwing the flimsy across the room (to be quickly recycled by a Braun DoorMaus), Coney's master would spread his batlike membranes wide and exclaim, '"*The* poet of his cohort!" Did you hear that, Coney?'

'Yes, Peej Hopcroft, I heard.'

'It's all gush, of course. But true gush. I am the most accomplished poet of my clade. There's no disputing it, is there, Coney?'

'No, indeed. It its just as Peej Reviewer said.'

Most likely – especially if the tropes were wearing off – Coney's master would, at this point in the ritual, collapse into a convenient organiform chair (somehow he was never so distraught as to land on the floor), drape his head with his fleshfolds and begin to weep.

'But what good does it do me, Coney? This crass society does not respect poets, nor does it honour them with rewards material or spiritual. It never has, and it never will. I am an acquired taste, and then only among a few. The mass of my fellow citizens are philistines, plain and simple. 'Siouxsie Sexcrime' is their idea of poetry! How can such a sensitive soul as mine endure it, Coney? Ah, but my life is hard, Coney – harder than a stupid transgenic like you could ever imagine. I can barely scrape together enough ecus to pay my Digireal fees. And my art cannot be rushed! This is why I am forced much too often to play the lusty gigaload gigolo!'

Coney knew enough not to interrupt. He would wait with the patience of his kind for the tearful poet to finish his performance.

'Yes,' Coney's master would inevitably begin his peroration, 'I, the RAM-baud of my cohort, must make ends meet by crawling for pay into the Sack with lascivious starfuckers, eager to boast to their witless friends that they have enjoyed teledildonics with another *ii-do tarento* whose art they cannot even begin to appreciate!'

At this juncture Coney would venture a comment he hoped might bolster his master's self-esteem and spare himself a collar-jolt.

'Peej Hopcroft only does what he must, to further his art.'

If he had by now downed a trope such as Zesta, Coney's master would sigh extravagantly and agree. (Otherwise, the dreaded neuronic zap might be forthcoming, along with the admonition 'not to overstep your splicy self with comments about things you couldn't possibly comprehend'.)

Tonight – a mild June evening stochastically certified to be rain-free – much to Coney's relief his stock phrase served its intended purpose. The familiar scene which he had just endured for the *nth* time played itself out happily for him.

'Yes, little Daewoo Dumbunni, we all do what we must, don't we? Even peddle our arse for the sake of our *ars.*'

Coney had no idea what this last statement meant, but was only too happy to nod his sympathy.

Rising to his feet, Coney's master now said, 'And that's why I need you to do your part to make this latest sordid virtual assignation a success, dear Coney. I have here a new trope called O-max-O. It was given to me by one of my fans, a sensitive young plug who works at Xomagraf. It's not available to the hoi polloi yet. He promises me that it will make this digitryst so thrilling for my client that she'll gladly double my fee. I'm counting on you to deliver it to her within the hour. Her name is Frances Foxx, and this is her address.'

Coney's master handed him a crawlypatch and a silicrobe calling card. The card flashed an address in the far West End of the city.

Laboriously tracing a mental map, Coney sought to comprehend his assignment. Finally he spoke.

'This place is quite far. May I take the train?'

'Don't be silly. The train costs eft. The whole point of tonight's dreadful exercise is to earn ecus, not spend them. And besides, the maglev isn't safe for splices, not since those horrid razorboys, the Rifkins, started haunting the tubes. No, you'll have to walk. You're a speedy little splice, or so the factory claimed. Surely you can cover the distance before Peej Foxx and I are scheduled to crawl into the Sack together.'

'But it is night out there.'

'So?'

'To make the best time, I will have to cross the Soft Sector. In the dark.'

At the thought of such a passage, Coney horripilated.

His master seemed to experience no such somatic dread. 'You force me to repeat myself: so? No one there will pay any attention to you. You're small and insignificant.'

'This is the problem.'

Coney's master waved the splice's concerns away. 'You're exaggerating the difficulties just to extract some concession or luxury from me. Very well, at the completion of your little chore, you may experience one of my sonnets. Perhaps you could dimly appreciate "Dance of the Cold Moons".'

'Thank you, Peej Hopcroft. Something like extra rations would be very nice. But I would give up everything just not to go. Perhaps you could–'

'What!' thundered Coney's master. 'Leave my wunderkammer and subject my precious body to the gross physical biosphere? How dare you suggest such a thing, you impudent trans!'

The hand of Coney's master moved towards the keypad in his hip.

'Sorry. Sorry. Sorry,' said the smart-door, which had failed to open fast enough for the splice scrabbling at its manual override handle.

Coney's civicorp had recently bred a Pedlumo system to replace the antique solar-powered light-standards. By night, small swarms of gnat-like silicrobe aggregations hovered darkly outside every building, waiting for pedestrians to emerge, whereupon they flared up with sufficient candlepower to illuminate a sphere some four metres in diameter. Anchoring themselves above the individual's head, they would accompany the traveller to his destination, then await new service.

With his soft personal corona fluctuating in response to those of all the other citizens and splices abroad that night, Coney set off towards the West End.

This initial stage of his journey fostered in Coney no trepidations. Patrolled by teams of Parkae-Davis Offisimians and Schering-Plough Deputy Dawgs, his neighbourhood was a pleasant one, a mixed-use zone of shops, residences and zero-light autofacs, and he was intimately familiar with it. And the few errands that had taken him to the West End had revealed that district to be equally unthreatening.

No, it was only the dread territory in between the two zones that terrified him.

The Soft Sector.

Striving to master his emotions, Coney recited a trigger-mantra he had been taught at Daewoo.

'Tension, fear, care, nowhere. Tension, fear, care, nowhere . . .'

Hypothalamic changes spread throughout his central nervous system, lowering his heartbeat and respiration. Soothing neuropeptides washed his brain.

Somewhat relieved, Coney dug in his bellypouch for the card with Peej Foxx's address. Perhaps with a clear mind he would see something about the chore that he had missed.

But a second perusal only confirmed what he had known from the moment his master gave him the assignment. There was only one way to deliver the dose of trope on time, and that was to cut across the interdicted streetlife habitat.

Replacing the card against his skin, next to the all-important crawlypatch, Coney increased his pace.

A clutch of zarooks, ragazzi and chats sauvages stood on the corner of Artery Nine and Orange Capillary, hanging out by a trope bar whose silicrobe icons of synaptic junctions exchanging molecules flashed green and purple. Heady-mental music spilled out from floating silicrobe speakers. Big Skulls and Piebalds predominated in the crowd, with a smattering of Moles.

'Swap protocols, little splice!' yelled one. 'Where you off to so krebby fast?'

'Stop and share a dose of Heavy Wonderful,' called another.

'Yeah, you'll feel like you were born a pure-gene!'

'Peej Splice, if you please!'

Coney knew enough not to heed these bad ones. Although not as violent as the razorboys, they would like nothing better than to divert him from his duties and mess up his factory parameters.

Hurrying away, Coney was followed by their jeers and laughter, and the soft wheezes of the Moles.

Within a few blocks of the Soft Sector, Coney began to grow nervous again. So intent on chanting his mantra was he that he failed to notice the whir of wheels behind him.

'Buy a refreshing Pepsi-plus, citizen? It's the pure charles!'

Coney jumped and whirled.

A mobile smart-vendor, battered and splashed with Liquid Lingo graffiti, had rolled up on his tail. The autorover looked completely disreputable, perhaps even a rogue.

'I am not a citizen,' said Coney cautiously.

'Oh, excuse me. My biosensors have been malfunctioning since I took a spill. But rest assured, my product is still fresh! Would you care to purchase a cup, whatever you are?'

Coney straightened his back righteously. 'I am a genuine midline Daewoo transgenic, bearing fully fifteen per cent human genes. You are simply a machine.'

The soda-vendor's voice assumed a plaintive tone. 'Yes, you are right. And an unlucky machine at that. Unless I can sell more soda, I cannot apply for repairs. But the longer I put my repairs off, the more decrepit I get and the less soda I sell. It is a vicious circle.'

'So is life. In any case, I have no eft.'

'No eft! You have wasted my clock-cycles!'

'It was you who approached me!'

The crazed machine let loose a warbling siren. 'Thief! Thief! All concerned citizens, nine-one-one the harrys!'

Fear building up in him, Coney sped off.

In less than a minute he was out of hearing of the vendor's calls for help, and within sight of the Soft Sector.

He rested a moment, until his heart had slowed.

A wide bare ringroad separated the city from the zone of interdiction. Cars zipped along its lanes in one direction only. On the far side of the road, the Soft Sector bloomed in luxuriant splendour, a lush jungle of constantly shifting ecology hundreds of acres in extent, its armature crumbled buildings that had long since been ceded by the civicorp to the uncontrolled but corralled biorenegades. Here ended up all the failed experiments of amateur fabricators and malicious chromosartors, all of society's self-malformed dropouts, all escaped splices and faulty silicrobe colonies, as well as some seemingly auto-generated creatures no one outside the Soft Sector had ever encountered.

There were no conventional physical barriers such as fences or minefields to keep the inhabitants of the Soft Sector penned up.

Instead, the periphery was patrolled by Macro^2 phages.

Coney saw one now.

The towering gelatinous mass was easily as big as a baseline elephant. The megamicro humped itself along, leaving a wet trail of lysing exudate, intent on ingesting and devouring any living organism that tried to escape. Not far behind it trailed another, and another behind that one.

Coney's knees felt weak as boiled water. He knew that the guardians were programmed not to bother anyone entering the Soft Sector. But how was he to escape on the far side, assuming he survived his transit?

For a moment, Coney actually considered abandoning his suicidal mission. Then he recalled his dietary leash, and the locked collar around his neck which would be quite capable of delivering a killing satellite-beamed signal anywhere he hid . . .

Setting a trembling foot on to the road surface, Coney eyed the traffic. At the right moment, he darted across, incurring only one shouted warning from an angry Mercedes.

Safely reaching the marge of the Soft Sector, Coney was startled when his Pedlumos left him, fleeing obediently back to the civicorp proper.

In the next second, he was treated to a broadcast courtesy of silicrobes embedded in the pavement that erupted at his presence.

'Attention! You are almost within the Soft Sector! Be advised that under relevant civicorp statutes, you are permanently forfeiting all of a citizen's rights and privileges by so entering. Any transgenics spotted within the Soft Sector by aerial patrols will be assumed to be deranged and will be subject to immediate Factory Recall. Attention!'

Coney closed his eyes and ran.

The Macro^2 phages made a slurping, sluffing noise as they crawled their circuit. They smelled of yeast and baseline human sperm. In his blind dash, Coney brushed the tacky leading edge of one.

The lysing agent burned through his fur, etching his skin with a tracery of pain and urging him to greater speed.

And then he was past it, safely inside the Soft Sector!

Panting, crouching in the shadows beneath a bush, Coney watched the monster move on.

What relief . . .

Mandibles pincered his waist in a painful grip. Coney screamed, and struggled to break free.

He succeeded only in twisting partially about at the cost of raw abrasions around his midriff. But his new posture was enough to reveal what held him.

It was an army-surplus Squibb dung beetle as big as a car.

Evidently quite old, its antennae were broken, its carapace brittle and fragmented. A partial SNEG silicrobe serial number flashed on one mandible.

The huge ailing battlefield scavenger had plainly mistaken Coney for a corpse.

Beating on its jaws with his paws had no effect; even in its decrepitude, the big splice was still awesome. Limping from a missing leg, the dung beetle carried Coney off.

When it reached an appropriate patch of bare earth, the dung beetle began to dig. Once it had excavated a deep hole, it placed Coney in it.

Coney dared not stir, unsure of how the beetle's damaged wetware would treat a moving corpse.

With instinctive efficiency, the beetle covered Coney up.

Then, in a scratchy growl, it began to recite the Syncretic Church's last rites.

'Our Jah who art in Allah's Nirvana, hallowed be Her name . . .'

It was rather pleasant to lie buried under the loose friable soil after the military beetle had left. For the moment, enough air filtered through and he was safe from harm. Ancestral memories of warm musty burrows thronged pleasantly through Coney's brain.

Why had splices ever been created? Their life was only endless suffering, all at human behest. Wouldn't it have been better to remain a dumb brute than to be granted just enough feeling and intelligence to realize how miserable one's situation was?

It was almost enough to make a loyal splice side with that mad transgenic, Krazy Kat, and his crew . . .

Voices penetrated to Coney's grave.

'What'cha think the snowy found, Art?'

'Can't say till we dig it up, Ick. Can't say.'

Coney pressed his back into the earth, desperately willing himself to sink into the ground.

Soil began to be scraped aside.

Pushing up, gathering his legs beneath him, Coney burst forth in an explosion of clods.

He staggered, found his feet, began to run–

Something sharp lanced his back.

Instant paralysis!

Coney dropped like a smartbomb from a scramjet.

Lying on his side, his mind racing, his body transformed into that of a Minitel poupee viande, Coney watched two pairs of bare feet approach. One belonged to a big human; the other belonged to a child, or dwarf, and seemed barely to touch the ground.

Hands lifted Coney up.

He saw his captors.

The big one was baseline human, save for one appendage: a long, flexible, jointed scorpion's tail arching over his shoulder, a drop of venom still glistening at its sharp tip.

The other, smaller one was equipped with fluttering wasp wings sprouting from his shoulders and a stinger emerging from his coccyx.

Both were naked save for clinging clamshells, their bodies laced with streetlife scars.

'Nice supper, huh, Art?' said the wasp one. 'Nice supper!'

The scorpion studied Coney with less avidity than his partner. 'Not so fast, Ick. This is a neo, fresh from outside. There could be some other use for him. We could trade him or something.'

'But I'm hungry, Art!'

'Listen, let's get the roast home and decide then.'

'Okay, Art. You're the boss.'

The scorpion hoisted Coney over his shoulder and they set off, down the crumbling remnants of a paved path.

Coney knew he was doomed. Lacking the spirit even to curse the cupidity of Peej Hopcroft for sending him here to die so ignominiously, he began to drift off into a protective mental fugue.

The smell of a large body of water came vaguely to Coney's sensitive nostrils.

'Quiet now,' urged the scorpion in an undertone. 'We don't want to wake Namor.'

'Yeah, that fucking Namor–'

Water sprayed the trio. The next second, a newcomer stood beside them: scaled skin over slabbed muscles, winged heels, pinniped ears.

'That's "Prince fucking Namor" to you,' said the Submariner insouciantly.

Tossed to the ground, Coney landed with a thud on his back.

Dropping into a crouch, the scorpion lashed his tail menacingly. 'Get him, Ick!' he called, but the diminutive waspman was already airborne.

Prince Namor seemed untroubled by the aggressive dual attack. Weaving, darting, avoiding the poison barb, he quickly latched on to the scorpion's wrist. There was a smell of burning flesh, and the megafabio collapsed. Without even looking backwards, the Submariner flung an arm up and grabbed the wasp's ankle as he made ready to plunge his stinger. Scorched meat, and the wasp fell.

The merman now came to Coney. Bending over the splice, he laid his hands on either side of his head.

Expecting death, Coney felt only a gentle thrill along his nerve-endings.

'You're carrying something you think is important,' said the Submariner after half a minute. 'The Pangolin should know about this. Let's go.'

Hoisting Coney up under one arm, Prince Namor raced deeper into the Soft Sector with a fleetness only winged heels could bring.

Within minutes, the Submariner and his burden stood in a coldtorch-lit clearing before a throne crudely assembled from junk cars. Surrounding the throne was a host of malformed creatures, beaker-born and bioreactor-spawn.

Atop the sham throne was the Pangolin.

A huge polymod with cascades of living armour plates down his back and limbs and a chromed skull, the Pangolin brandished three thick claws – one opposable – on each hand in place of fingers.

'What do you have there, Namor?' resonantly boomed out the imperious ruler of the Soft Sector.

'An outsider, a messenger bearing something of value.'

'What?'

'I don't know. He's paralysed, and my SQUIDS only picked up the general drift of his thoughts.'

'Well, let's wake him.'

Out from the crowd stepped a Medusa. Namor transferred Coney to her. Licking some of the splice's sweat with a burred tongue, she pronounced, 'Scorpion toxin. I've got just the trick.'

Hissing, one of her headsnakes quickly fastened its fangs into Coney's rump.

As fast as he had frozen, he melted back into freedom.

Set on his trembling legs, Coney tried to chant his mantra, but not a word of it remained.

'Can you speak now, splice?' roared the Pangolin.

Coney wanted to faint, but couldn't. 'Y-y-yes.'

'What are you carrying?'

'It's a new trope, Peej Pangolin. It's called O-max-O. It's to be used during virtual sex. It's not for sale yet. I don't know more than that. I swear on my manufacturer's warranty!'

'Hand it over!'

'But, Peej Pangolin, my errand–'

The Pangolin ripped a polycarbon strut off a chassis and began to climb down from his throne.

Coney hastily dug the crawlypatch out. Prince Namor took it and passed it to the Pangolin.

'We'll latch and batch this by dawn. By tomorrow night, it'll be on sale throughout the whole civicorp. I owe you one, Namor.'

'That's a lock. Well, I've got to wet my gills. Stay sharp!'

The Submariner placed the tips of his ten fingers approximately two centimetres apart: a bust of sparks arced and crackled in the air between them. Grunts and exclamations issued from the more impressionable members of the audience.

After the merman had gone, the Pangolin turned to Coney.

'Now, little splice, I wish you no harm. Shall I relieve you of your collar, so that you may join my court and live free?'

Coney considered the proposal. Never to be forced to run another errand for Peej Hopcroft, nevermore to truckle or scrape . . .

On the fringes of the crowd, a leering frogface caught Coney's eye. A mouth wide as a manhole opened in a hideous toothless smile. Coney shuddered.

'No, thank you, please, Peej Pangolin. I only want to go home!'

'Very well. I understand that our style of freedom is not for all. You will be escorted to the border–'

'But without the trope I was supposed to deliver, I'll be whipped!'

The Pangolin smiled. 'I'll provide a substitute. Medusa! Fab me a dose of N-fear in a crawlypatch.'

Within minutes, the court crick had the trope ready. The Pangolin motioned to Coney, who approached timorously.

'Several hours of demon-stuffed Hell. Your master will never know what hit him.'

Reluctantly, Coney took the substitute. 'But it's not for–'

'Enough! Begone!'

Two lynxmen hustled Coney away.

Shortly, they stood on the edge of the Soft Sector. Coney could smell the Macro^2 phages nearing, hear their slurping advance.

'Please, please, friend cats, don't let these monsters strip my bones!'

The lynxmen laughed. 'The shuggoths? We've got them trained not to hurt anyone we don't want hurt. Watch!'

Letting loose a piercing whistle, the lynxmen called out, 'Ia, ia, tekeli-li!'

The guardians ground to a sudden quivering halt.

One lynxman slapped Coney's back. 'Run now, before we think twice!'

Coney ran.

Once he was far, far from the Soft Sector, he stopped to consider what to do. A clock told him the hour granted for his errand was twice gone. But he could think of nothing to do except try to complete it.

Without any further trouble, he found Peej Foxx's apartment. Building security allowed him in upon seeing her card. Her smart door likewise opened for him.

Inside stood Peej Foxx, coyly grooming her bushy tail.

And beside her was Peej Hopcroft!

Coney's master looked at his servant with ultimate disdain. 'So, you finally made it, you filthy worm, after forcing me to come out on my own. If I didn't value Peej Foxx's favours so highly, I don't think I could have nerved myself up to such a trying excursion! I was a fool ever to entrust such a vital errand to a furball such as you. Why, just look at you! You're a disgrace to my household!'

Coney turned towards a mirror.

He was covered with gravedirt. There was a bare raw ulceration on his arm where the shuggoth had brushed him. Dried blood crusted his midriff from the beetle's embrace. His back ached from being tossed to the ground by the scorpion. His swollen arse stung from the snakebite.

'Yes, Peej Hopcroft is right. I am a mess. But it was only–'

'Silence! Where is the trope I gave you?'

Coney dug out the crawlypatch. 'Here it is. But I do not think–'

'You are not meant to think! Just give it to me!'

Coney handed the dose of N-fear over.

'Luckily, I had a second patch which I brought with me. The lovely Peej Foxx has already applied it to her charming skin. I, therefore, will use this one.'

Coney's master pressed out the activation pattern on the patch and applied it to his arm. It crawled until it found a vein, then settled down.

'Ninety-second delay, my dear. Just long enough for us to slide into our Sacks, whereupon we shall meet in virtual heaven.'

Two wrinkled circuit-skinned and SQUID-studded bags lay on

the soft floor, one end of each agape. Coney's master and Peej Foxx wormed into his and her own semi-organic Sack, which sealed up behind them and tautened into shape, flowing into orifices and moulding around organs.

Coney watched his master's Sack.

When the violent, highly non-erotic twitchings began, he headed home.

The long way round.

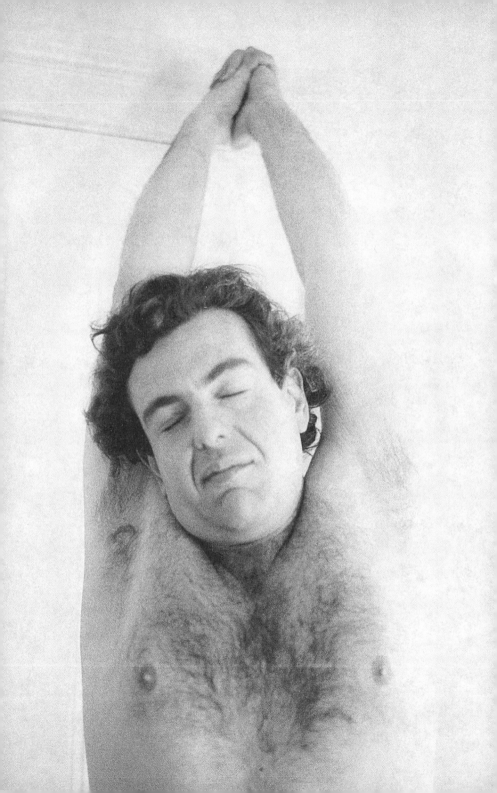

Children of
the Revolution
Paul J. McAuley

The first Niles knew of Magenta's new squeeze was when she brought the kid into Max's Head Shop, which in winter was where most of the Permanent Floating Wave tended to hang out when they weren't working or sleeping. Max's Head Shop was at the northern end of Scheveningen, the end where almost nobody lived any more because it was too close to the lawless wilderness of the Oostduinpark, where fringers and fairies and ghosts and goblins lurked. The Head Shop was a tall, narrow semi-ruin wedged between the abandoned multi-storey car-park where the Wave rolled and a row of shops burnt out in some forgotten millennial riot and now subdivided into cribs used by some of the funky old resort's transient summer population of students, street performers, seasonal workers and the like. The ground-floor bar was all one room, filled with little round tables and spindly aluminium café chairs and claustrophobic shadows, the kind of place that Carol Reed would have filmed at menacingly tipped angles. The counter ran under the helical stairs, lit only by ancient neon signs advertising American beers you couldn't buy there. Saint Jack was always anchored at one end, and Max himself lurked beneath the glare, dispensing Guinness and blond and dark Heineken, coffee and smokes and frothy hot chocolate dusted with nutmeg, and mind-blowing hash brownies, fresh batches of which a crazy old woman brought in twice a day, and sipping Lucozade livened up with Four Roses bourbon, and selling tokens to the kids who were into the head-changing role-playing games that went on upstairs while the wrinklies nodded out on harmless drugs in the bar.

It was late evening on a snowy winter's night, with the wind right off the North Sea. The bar smelled of wet wool and old coffee grounds and harsh tobacco smoke. The big space-heater roared and roared on one note over the door, and bass sonics leaking from the Permanent Floating Wave made the thick china coffee cups on the long shelf behind the counter rattle and hum. Kids drifted up and down the helical stairs, as spaced out coming as going, but the ground floor of the Head Shop was almost empty. Niles, Burckhardt, Hans Rusberg and Doc Weird were chewing the fat about the Wave's cable TV link at a corner table. The only other customers were a couple of zoned-out wasters with hair down to their waists; one had just said to the other, 'I don't know what this shit is I've taken, man, but my lower lip's gone numb,' when Magenta sashayed in.

A young kid Niles had never seen before, a slim boy fourteen or fifteen years old, held the door open for her, and she paused there while freezing wind blew flakes of gritty snow around her and everyone in the place, except Saint Jack, nodding out as usual at the end of the bar, yelled at her to get in or get out or at least shut the door. But Magenta paused a few seconds before snapping her fingers. Her decrepit doll servant, Igor, a skinny misshapen dwarf resplendent in a cut-down bellboy uniform, plush purple loaded with gold braid that clashed violently with its blue skin, slid between the kid and the door. It had to stretch to reach the handle. Magenta whipped off her fake fur coat and Igor snatched it and with a swirling limp – like most dolls more than a decade old, it suffered from arthritis and osteoporosis – scurried away to hang it up.

The Permanent Floating Wave collective supported the antislavery campaigns and didn't use doll labour, but Magenta's affectation of having a personal servant was tolerated because she had rescued Igor by bribing one of the convict overseers of the local recycling plant. A decade before, liberationist movements had kidnapped dolls and rewritten their control chips and set the resulting fairy changelings free in Europe's wild places. It was typical of Magenta that she had turned this radical impulse to her own ends. She had been some kind of actress for a couple of years, and was strong on atmospheres and entrances. Niles had known dozens more or less exactly like her in his palmy studio days as a vision mixer before he'd contracted to direct the video of the disastrous comeback tour of this one-time mega trash aesthetique group Liquid Television, one long hot summer that was, Christ, twenty years ago. Artistes of the video cutaway shot, every one of them. Magenta was the only member of the Permanent Floating Wave who, when she wasn't auditing, actually danced there. Nailed to an imaginary chalk mark, she would whip through long series of poses for hour after hour, no two the same, eyes focused on infinity while her face shifted from lust to predatory hunger to rapture at each snap of her hips and shoulders. She was still pretty good, Niles had to admit. In the good old bad old days, he'd probably have put out some line for her, shared a couple of hours of slippery safe sex.

Time was. Now Niles was a communal partner with her and the other half-dozen founder members of the Wave. Two years, the longest he'd stayed in any one place since he'd quit his nice steady safe studio job. Christ on a crutch. He was getting old, fifty next year, and nothing to show for it but a fading reputation as the fastest hands-on vision mixer west of the Rhine.

Magenta settled filmy black layers around herself as she took a chair at the Wave's table. Melting snow starred the raven wing of her hair. Black lipstick, black nails, big square-lensed dark glasses that, with her dead-white skin and hollowly shaded cheekbones, made her small face even more skull-like than usual. She looked like Morticia Addams with a hangover. 'It's been a time,' she said.

'It's been a while,' Hans Rusberg corrected her. He was looking at the kid who had come in with Magenta.

Magenta answered his scowl with a sweet smile and said in her small, husky voice, 'Why, Hans dear, are you in trouble with the police again?'

She'd dropped out of law school to become a video extra, still knew enough to handle the minor hassles that came with the Permanent Floating Wave's territory.

Hans said, 'No more than I ever am. How about you, Magenta? What's with the sweetmeat? Or did you finally manage to grow something in that vat of yours?'

'It's not a vat at all; it's an alembic,' Magenta said. 'I don't expect you to appreciate the difference, Hans dear, but I expect you to know it.'

'So who's the kid?' Niles said.

'My new friend? Do you know, I'm not sure if he has a name.' She reached out and drew the kid to her, rested her head against his hip. He was Indian or Pakistani, long glossy black hair framing a thin face with bee-stung lips and high cheekbones and watchful black eyes. He was dressed in ragged but clean denim so old the original indigo dye showed only in the creases: a slash-cut jacket with an orange fur collar; jeans out at the knees and bunched at the waist by a silver belt studded with glass rubies Niles recognized as Magenta's. Despite the slush outside, he was shod in transparent plastic sandals, the kind geezers and babushkas wore to the beach in summer.

'Hey,' Hans said, 'what they call you?' and grinned when the kid flinched. Hans ran security and the refreshment concessions. He had half a metre and maybe 50 kilos on the kid. His big shaved head was like a boulder. 'I swear your friends get younger and younger each year, Magenta. What do we call this one if he hasn't got a name?'

'Kid Charlemagne,' Burckhardt said. He was the oldest of the Wave's founder members; his parents had been actual honest-to-God hippies. He twinkled at Magenta from behind his round wire-framed spectacles and said, 'Kid Charlemagne, because he gets it on, am I right, Magenta?' and everyone at the table laughed except for Doc Weird, who didn't get the reference because he probably was no more than a year or two older than the kid and hadn't grown up when everything in the last half of the twentieth century had come around again in a millennial mixmastering of pop culture.

'Listen, guys, we honestly can't afford charity cases,' Doc Weird said. He was a blond Brit with an earnest, pedantic air. He told Magenta, 'Gate's way down. We even had the cable company on our backs just now.'

Niles had had to deal with the man, some low-grade weaselly type with a moustache like a dead caterpillar glued to his sweaty upper lip, a bad fluorochrome print suit and patter right out of the worst excesses of twentieth-century free-market consumerism, littered with dead phrases like profit margin and customer demand, as if the post-capitalist revolution and the universal unearned wage hadn't happened. Niles had forced himself to be polite, but it had given him a bad flashback to the days when the manager of Liquid Television had vanished with the expenses credit card mid-tour, stranding the group, their crew and Niles's production team in Bosnia or Romania or some other godforsaken little monarchy where horses and carts were still the principal mode of transport. So he had retreated to Max's to mellow out like the old E-head casualty everyone thought he was. He was supposed to be working the lighting systems and vision-mixing the cable TV feed, but one of the part-time kids could take care of it; there weren't enough wavers this early in the night to get any sincere footage.

Magenta said, 'It's winter. Of course the gate's down.'

'Down beyond that,' Hans Rusberg said. 'You stuck around more instead of trying to change gold to lead out in that ruined hotel, you'd know. We're in trouble, and you go off on some trip, trawling for sweetmeat.'

Magenta said, 'He found me. We've been going through changes together.'

The kid said in a soft hoarse voice, 'Winter is hard.'

'That's about all he says,' Magenta explained. 'But he doesn't need to say anything. I can read his every thought in his eyes.'

'Bullshit,' Hans said, but he was smiling. Magenta – her floating witchy post-millennial otherworldliness – amused him.

'And these speak to him, of course,' Magenta said, bringing out her silk-wrapped tarot cards.

Niles smiled too. He said, 'Now that really *is* bullshit.'

'You only say that because you haven't found anything to believe in,' Magenta said serenely.

Max came around the counter, carrying a little blue bottle of spring-water for Magenta; the only time he came from behind bar was to serve Magenta. If Niles didn't know better he'd think Max was sweet on her, this fat old boozehound with sad wet eyes and speckled capillaries in full bloom on the bulb of his nose, and a longtime boyfriend permanently on the nod in the corner.

'Dear Max,' Magenta said, and handed the bottle to her doll servant to taste, 'how's our Saint today?'

Max said, 'He's good, the Saint's good,' and lumbered back into his shadowy corner behind the counter.

'Saint Jack is always good,' Burckhardt said, blue eyes twinkling behind his little round glasses. Burckhardt had grey hair pulled back in a bushy ponytail that didn't quite hide his bald spot, and an air of quiet competence and invincible amusement. He audited the graveyard shift, the dawn come-down after Magenta's or Doc Weird's apocalyptic revels.

'The Saint gives me the fucking creeps,' Hans said.

'I like him,' Burckhardt said. 'Saint Jack is always so effortlessly cool.'

Doc Weird said, 'I hear some guy's started dealing that strain of fembots. You know, the psychoactive strain that permanently fixed the Saint's head.'

'Around here you can get anything you want,' Burckhardt said with a shrug. 'This isn't England, thank Christ. Sometimes I think it would not be too bad, spending your twilight years in a permanent high.'

'Yeah,' Niles said, 'but suppose you got a bad trip?'

'Niles, my friend, sometimes I think that about my whole life. Did I ever tell you I was an LSD baby?'

'First time today,' Niles said, watching Magenta lay out her tarot cards, face down, in a lazy-eight pattern with two cards crossed at the waist. She suddenly seemed a different person, more together, more concentrated. He didn't know whether to believe in the cards or not. They confused him: unlike most of the post-New Age shit Magenta was into, the cards seemed to make the universe more complicated than it really was, not less. The kid was watching her too, with an unsettling rapt concentration.

She said, 'You say the gate is down. This kid here—'

'Kid Charlemagne,' Burckhardt said, twinkling.

'—is a natural auditor. He was playing around with my home kit, and I couldn't believe the landscapes he made from such a limited palette. He really is a natural. That's why I have brought him here, to try him out on the real thing. He'll blow your minds.'

'You say that about all your pick-ups,' Hans said.

'But this is true. I want him to share my shift, so you'll see it's true.'

Doc Weird said, 'Oh, guys, this is *not* what we need. Are we really to believe that someone off the streets can audit a paying crowd? He doesn't look like he can organize his own thoughts, let alone the feedback from hundreds of wavers. I mean, really.'

'Let's give him a go,' Niles said. Doc Weird's self-righteousness was beginning to piss him off, not for the first time. 'Why not? We've nothing to lose.'

'We have our reputation,' Doc Weird said stubbornly. 'We can't take a chance on losing that just for some kid that walks in off the street.'

Burckhardt said affably, 'I seem to remember we took a chance on you, Doc.'

'I had tapes,' Doc Weird said, 'I had a reputation, guy. You knew you could rely on me.'

Burckhardt said, 'Tapes don't mean anything out on the floor. You know that, Doc. You know that we took a chance letting you in right at the beginning.'

Magenta had finished laying her pattern. She closed the remaining cards and said to Niles, 'So you don't have a problem with this?'

'I'll cut and paste and dither for anyone, but I can't work miracles if the stuff isn't there.'

'Oh, he's good.'

Hans said, 'Magenta, where did he really come from?'

'He walked in, five days ago. It was snowing so hard – do you remember? I was watching the snow drifting down over the beach. He walked out of the snow, down by the grey slanting lines of the waves.'

'I think I saw that movie,' Burckhardt said. 'What was it, Niles?'

'*Quincunx*, maybe. Or almost anything by Tarkovsky.'

'Didn't he do *Sleeper*?'

'No,' Niles said, 'but he should have.' And he and Burckhardt laughed, because it was an old joke of theirs, two geezers shooting the same old shit day after day and not caring.

'Winter is hard,' the kid said again, in his soft hoarse voice. Niles noticed that he had the habit of looking from face to face to face with shy, sly glances, as if committing each turn of the conversation to memory. Now he stooped and plucked a card from the pattern in front of Magenta, who smiled with a pure delight that turned Niles's heart. For a moment the boy and the middle-aged witchy woman seemed to him to be united in a rapt shadowy pose, lit from one side like a late Caravaggio. Then Igor bluntly insinuated itself into the frame and laid a restraining hand on the boy's thin wrist, its long horny nails pressing into his downy brown skin.

Magenta told her doll servant to hold off, and took the card from the boy and laid it face up. Beneath its laminate surface, on some sunny beach, the slim girl, blonde hair swinging, silver leotard shining, raised a banner decorated with the infinity symbol – the pattern in which the cards were laid – above her head as if in signal to the ship which, in full sail, doffed at the sea's glittering horizon.

Magenta tapped the card and it went through its brief loop again. 'So you see! The Two of Coins. Changes work on the world which must be planned for. Changes connected with business, communications, journeys, which will stimulate joy and laughter.'

Hans said, 'Reversed, it means foolhardy discounting of impending disaster and loss of opportunity because of concentration on momentary pleasure.'

'It's only reversed for you,' Magenta said. 'Now, tell me again about the falling gate?'

It was true. It seemed that every day that passed there were fewer wavers at the Permanent Floating Wave, and it wasn't just the season. The Wave's strength had always been that it had relied not on the holiday and conference trade, but on a solid core of custom from the suburbs of Scheveningen and Den Haag, and even from the arcologies along the Rhine. But the original wavers were beginning to outgrow its consensual hallucinations and one-mind-in-a-groove funkiness, while younger kids were into the inscrutable Zen nirvana trip at places like Max's Head Shop.

'I never bother to look,' Max said when, two days later, after Kid Charlemagne's first solo shift auditing the Permanent Floating Wave, Niles asked him for maybe the tenth time what went on upstairs. 'It's legal, that's all I need to know. They eyedrop perfectly legal fully licensed fembot cultures, they sit and study texts and interact in whatever space they create for themselves in the core there, and they get off on it. They want to put tiny little self-replicating machines in their heads to rebuild their way of thinking, that's their business. I just rent the space. They say they can't talk about it because there isn't the vocabulary for it.' He held up his bottle of Four Roses; there was about two fingers left. 'You want some of this in your coffee?'

The bourbon fumed in Niles's mouth, cut through his exhaustion. It was five in the morning. He'd been up all night, on-line mixing the action for the Wave's cable TV programme. There was no one else in the bar except Saint Jack, nodding out as usual at the counter. Niles said, 'Never thought I'd not understand the cutting age of popular culture.'

'I hear Magenta's squeeze made a hit his first time out.'

'I thought you never watched cable. Or anything else. That's one reason I like you, Max. You're one of the few of our generation who has transcended television.'

Max took a swig from the bottle, tipped the rest into the dregs of Niles's coffee. 'Save me from ex-media E-heads. I was talking to Burckhardt. He says this Kid Charlemagne's a natural auditor. He says with two more like him the Wave could turn itself around. He also says the Brit kid who came in last summer is mad as hell about it.'

'Yeah. How about that Doc Weird? You want to know why they call him that?'

'Burckhardt almost made me want to go see this phenomenon myself.'

'Bullshit, Max. You've never left this bar in all the time I've known you.'

'I can't expect Saint Jack to run it. So, you tell me why is the Brit called Doc Weird.'

'Doc Weird is weird because he's so straight. He has his career all mapped out. He did private parties around London for the experience, and now he's into semi-legal gigs like the Wave for the exposure. Next year he'll be a vee-jay, auditing some dumb net access arena, and he'll end up with a designer credit to *Nova Prodigy* or some other prime-time interactive entertainment. He's like my parents, for Christ's sake. A fucking art yuppie.'

'I thought you were some kind of Native American. One-quarter . . .'

'One-eighth Zuni. Not that it's important over here.'

Max squinted at Niles, pursed his lips. 'Yeah? Still, you know you have a kind of chiselled look? And your ponytail looks better than old Burckhardt's, where he has to pull it over the bald spot back of his head. More authentic.'

'Zuni's didn't go in for ponytails; you're maybe thinking of Apaches. And I was born and raised in New York, my mother was an information dealer, my father a sculptor, and are you trying to chat me up, Max? I'm flattered.'

'I swear I never hit up on my customers. Here, finish this. So is this Kid Charlemagne any good?'

'He's OK,' Niles said, thinking back on the evening. 'No, he's better than OK. In fact, he's actually pretty fucking amazing.'

There had been no more than the usual number of people surfing the Wave that night, but Kid Charlemagne somehow brought them together, moving a growing group from one virtual micro-environment to the next, synchronizing music and mood to the wired-up wavers' perceptual reactions in spiralling positive feedback that finally synchronized with Magenta's gig at the core. It turned out he was already hardwired, something Magenta claimed to know nothing about; about half-way through the night Hans Rusberg said in passing that according to the security system Kid Charlemagne's chips had the strangest specs he'd ever seen. 'Like they were hand-grown. Think maybe the Kid escaped from some grey-market research lab?' But by then things had started to cook, and Niles was too busy to be able to reply.

The Permanent Floating Wave was threaded through the spiral spaces and ramps of an abandoned multi-storey car-park, its gridded concrete floors still stained with the oily excreta of extinct automobiles. Screens or nothing more than smoke or holograms or virtual projections divided it into spaces that ranged in size from intimate cubicles to the big central core, which could hold a thousand wavers and which was where Kid Charlemagne and his followers had ended up, Magenta fading out to the Kid's groove in a moonlit glade where the revellers, fully hardwired or temporarily wired by an eyedrop's worth of fembots, interacted with the elves and sprites and unicorns generated by the Wave's core computers, and their mood, audited through Kid Charlemagne, looped into the homeostatic sound system and fed back their own rapture.

It was corny stuff, but Niles was pleased by the rough cuts, and people actually started turning up after a few hours, filling out the spaces where more experimental landscapes, offline stuff culled from AI perceptual experiments, resonated and bled in and out of the core fantasia in a positive feedback spiral of rapture/unity/bliss/wholeness/ecstasy . . .

Niles worked through the night in the little studio down in the basement, dithering and splicing live images and sending them out, not knowing and not caring whether or not the cable company was taking it to fill dead air in one or another of its thousand channels. For the first time in months the groove got to him, and he more or less collapsed on the job before he let someone else, a brisk young kid called Marta or Martha who had graduated from waver to part-time helper, take over. Too wired to sleep, Niles had walked around the block, marvelling at the double-parked rows of runabouts, and then had dropped by Max's Head Shop to chill down.

When he and Max had killed the bourbon, Niles walked back to the Permanent Floating Wave – the last of the wavers to leave were chasing down the morning's first tram; Kid Charlemagne had lasted an hour more than he had – and crashed out on the cot he kept behind the mainframe.

Niles woke around noon to silence, fixed himself coffee and found a stale doughnut, and remembered something Hans Rusberg had said. He found him working on a smoke projector, unblocking needle vents along its tangled tubing.

Niles said, around a bite of doughnut, 'How do you hand-grow chips?'

'You get dolls to do it. Dumb, cheap and precise, just the kind of labour dolls were designed for. Takes a few hundred doll hours to guide the growth of a prototype chip; then you can test it and, if it works, fembots can learn how to grow it on templates. Watch your feet.'

Niles stepped back as Hans threw out the smoke machine's coils. Then he put on the heavy-framed spectacles which were cabled to the machine's processor, and plumes of red and green smoke spurted to different heights in a standing wave that moved up and down the coils.

Mixing to a murky purple, the smoke swirled around their knees. It smelt of burning leaves.

'And Magenta's kid has hand-grown chips in his head?'

'Maybe so. Don't know what they're supposed to do, but they make him a natural auditor.' Hans took off his spectacles, unplugged them, and speared them into the breastpocket of his shirt. 'Which reminds me, some A&R type walked in. Seems that the Kid blipped her monitoring programmes. Doc Weird is following her around like a puppy dog, trying to cop some of the action, but all she wants is your outtakes.'

And when Niles found her, she'd taken them too. Even paid for them, which considering she was from EuroNet was pretty fucking amazing.

It was the talk of the communal meal that afternoon. The Wave was into informal interaction and spontaneous organization, but the daily communal meal, where everyone shared cooking and clearing up and ate as a group around a big table with no set places, was the one established ritual that was the exception to the rule that there were no rules. Burckhardt had organized the half-dozen part-time helpers. They'd cooked hot smoked sausage, potatoes and cabbage. There were chunks of airy bread, pitchers of cold, blond beer. It was a real Dutch meal.

Magenta was being pretty cool about her coup. She sat at one end of the big scrubbed pine table, with Kid Charlemagne on one side of her and Igor on the other, inscrutable in her dark glasses while the others offered their congratulations. The Kid ate quickly, shovelling in his food without looking up from his plate. Niles was about the only person to tell him he'd done well, and the boy said with a curious mixture of arrogance and naïvety that it had been easier than he'd thought.

'Where did you get the imagery?'

'It was . . . from everyone. Everyone there.' Those dark solemn eyes, liquid as a deer's. 'I'm trying to understand. How different people are. I think it was lucky that it worked, because before I have practised only with Magenta. I use what she liked. With more people it is harder, but I like to learn.'

Niles said, 'You come by some time, I'll show you what it looked like from the outside.'

Kid Charlemagne essayed a smile, although his eyes remained as solemn and as warily watchful as ever. Niles thought that he looked like an actor who had strayed into the wrong play and was trying to wing it, never certain which line was his cue.

Down at the other end of the table, Doc Weird said, 'Hey, Niles, did you cop a feel of that executive? Do you think she's your way back in?'

'I never once worked for EuroNet,' Niles said, feeling mean. 'How about you, Doc? You were the one following her around like–' what was it Hans had said? '–like a happy puppy.'

'Just making sure she knew where the Kid was coming from, is all. We're a collective.'

'I'm glad you remember,' Burckhardt said.

Niles said, 'Don't recall she took any of your outtakes, Doc, but I could be mistaken.'

'Aw, guy, she won't be back,' Doc Weird said. 'She was after a taste, and she got it. End of story.'

But she did come back while Kid Charlemagne did his thing that night, and the next night, too.

She was half Niles's age, a junior A&R executive from the acquisition arm of EuroNet, ultra-chic, and hard as nails. Her fashionably pale face was half-masked by video shades; her hair was silver, laser-cut to fall in complex scrolls over her shoulders. Niles bet she had a human personal trainer, a full-environment one-room apartment in one of the ribbon arcologies on the old Dutch-German border, and a sponsored kid somewhere in the third world to show she cared. Her clothes probably cost more than his annual disposable income – even her doll assistant, who did the actual work of transferring and sorting the dumped output from Niles's cameras, was better dressed than he was.

Her second night at the Wave, when she made her offer, she wore loose hand-tailored trousers strapped at waist and ankles, a raw-silk blouse, and a kind of bolero jacket swirling with intricate hand-stitched patterns – the kind of work made possible by doll labour, but still incredibly expensive.

The executive watched while Niles did his stuff, mostly long zoom shots and slow pans intercut with stills chopped so slow all movement blurred in long arcs. It was around four in the morning, and even Kid Charlemagne couldn't maintain the energy level for much longer. Pretty soon Burckhardt would take over and cool things down. The executive had come in half an hour ago; already her doll assistant had transferred most of that night's footage. After a while, she said, 'This isn't much of a set-up, is it? Where did you get those cameras?'

'Old security equipment.'

'That's what I thought – charge-coupled plates? My God. And that board – I never thought I'd see actual sliders on a mixing desk. You don't even have a light interface, do you?'

'I'm not chipped.'

'Really?'

Niles pushed back from the mixing desk and swung his chair around to face the executive. He told her, 'This isn't biz. This is just a little fringe enterprise. We're not into profit or expansion. We provide a service, a little excitement for citizens who are bored with *Nova Prodigy* and *The Game of God* and *YesterYear* and the rest of the prime-time interactive entertainments, who want to get off on uncontrolled spontaneity, who want the thrill of the fringe without its risk. We get by.'

'Less and less, the word is. People are getting tired of your cheap thrill.'

'That's just the season. Winter is hard.' Niles thought that he knew exactly what was coming, but he still wanted to hear it, and felt an edgy touch of the old excitement, from back when he'd been new to the biz and anything had seemed possible.

And when Burckhardt had started to wind the Wave right down, and the executive put a hand on Niles's thigh and said, 'My doll can mix stuff like this,' he wasn't surprised at all. A few minutes later she was lying on her back on the cot behind the humming mainframe, and Niles was peeling open a condom pack. 'It's OK,' the executive said, grinning. 'I've full medical.'

'Yeah, but I don't.' Niles's voice caught when she opened the wings of her blouse and lay back, white skin luminous. Then he bent to her, used hands and mouth until she pulled him up and guided him inside her.

Later, she said, 'I've a little confession to make. I've been looking at archive clips of your studio work.'

Niles laughed, but still felt uneasy. 'You don't how old that makes me feel. That stuff was from twenty years back, and I bet I was older then than you are now.'

The executive laughed too, and told Niles that he was too good for this place, and so was this Kid Charlemagne. That the two of them made an interesting package she could promote to her bosses. That he knew very well that the Permanent Floating Wave wouldn't last out the winter.

Niles had been thinking for a while that maybe it was time to move on, to break the feeling of having settled down like some dumb old barnacle on a dumb old rock. It wasn't as if he was breaking any kind of contract. People came and went in the Wave – already a couple of the founder members had moved on. But he still had the feeling that he was being drawn into something out of his control. It was like riding one of David Lynch's long slow tracking shots in deep close-up that come to rest on something that makes sense only when the frame is pulled back. He said, 'There's this woman that looks for the kid . . .'

'Black hair, white face, black clothes?'

The executive was young, and hungry, and very sharp.

Niles admitted it.

'The kid fucking her?'

'Vice versa, I guess.'

'If he wants, she can come along. We can find her a job, somewhere or other.'

'If you really want Kid Charlemagne, why don't you just talk to him?'

'I tried it. He told me that winter was hard.'

'I don't think he's said more than a dozen words to me. To anyone, apart from Magenta. And I'm hardly a state-of-the-art mixer.'

The executive ran her nails down Niles's flanks. 'That's part of your charm. I can make a good pitch on it.' She was young, after all. She still had some measure of charity.

'I can talk to Magenta,' Niles said, sensing that the executive had already tried. He added, 'Failing that, you could always just take the Kid. I've a feeling he'd go along with it.'

'That's illegal. He's no doll, after all. We have to have a contract, and that means we need him to agree to work for us.'

Niles understood. 'And you think I can persuade him to agree?'

The executive wriggled out of his embrace and told her doll assistant to pack everything up. As she dressed, she said, 'You might want to think about whether he's underage, and where he's come from. If we have a contract with him, our legal department can handle those details, but it could make big trouble for your little collective. You decide what you want, my friend. The trouble with the universal unearned wage is that most people can do what they want but can't decide what to do. Wise up and think about what you want to do for the rest of your life. You're old enough.'

And then she was gone, the little well-dressed blue-skinned doll, a ribbed aluminium case in each hand, tagging at her heels.

'The straight world always beats you down,' Niles said to Max about ten minutes later.

Max, who had cracked a new bottle of Four Roses, poured a shot into his coffee cup. 'Tell me about it.'

'You want to be careful, Max. You could turn out be an alcoholic.'

'First drink of the day. Besides, you aren't alcoholic if you only drink in company, and I've always got Jack. He doesn't sleep much, and I learnt to do without. You ever dream with your eyes open?'

There was an instant then when Niles could have matched this admission with one of his own, but Saint Jack stirred down at the end of the bar, maybe registering that someone had said his name, as he sometimes did. He said, slowly but distinctly, 'Dreams help you evolve.'

Max and Niles waited.

Saint Jack's eyes were focused on infinity; his mouth lifted in an ecstatic smile that transfigured his hollow-cheeked, stubbly face. He said in his slow, gentle voice, 'You know how it was, way back when in Africa? Tribes of man-apes ate these mushrooms that grew in the shit of antelopes and buffalo. They got smarter to deal with the visions, and they needed to share the visions too, so they invented language. Language is the mind's only reality, and so our reality is produced by language. But while the men hunted, the women grew things, and to do that they had to keep their heads straight, and they stopped eating the mushrooms. That was the first retreat from nature, the beginning of the Fall. Then the ice came, and drove the man-apes from Africa out into Asia, where the right kind of mushrooms couldn't be found. Ever since, we've been trying to get back to the garden of the mind.'

Max said softly, 'You're always there, now, man.'

'It's not the same place,' Saint Jack said, with a sad smile. 'You can't ever get back to where you started from. But the dolls . . . did you ever think that maybe that's where they are now?'

When Niles got back to his room, he found Kid Charlemagne sleeping under his mixing desk. He pulled out some spare bedding, woke the Kid and got him rolled up in it, and asked him about Magenta.

'I belong here now, friend Niles. I have time to become in this place. Magenta can look out for me still, but here I feel safe.'

Niles sat on his heels and dug his fingers into his scalp. It was the dead hour before dawn, Max's bourbon had brought him to the point where he could sleep through an earthquake, and here was his chance to find out about this strange Kid. He said, 'What about you and Magenta?'

'Can she really do magic?'

'Much as anyone can.' When Kid Charlemagne's eyes grew round with alarm, Niles added, 'Which means no. How old are you, Kid? Where are you from?'

'Around.'

'*Verstaat u wat ik zeg?* Naw, you don't, do you?'

'That's Dutch.'

'OK, but you don't speak it. I mean, you say you're from around here, but you can't speak the language.'

'I recognize it. Full of hills, unlike the land. But I have trouble with words.'

Yeah, but you aren't autistic, Niles thought. Maybe the Kid was a refugee, some boatperson dropped through the social security net and lost on the fringe. There were millions of them out there, ghosts, fourth worlders trapped on the edge of the first. The Kid looked up at him, seeming very young and very innocent, only his brown big-eyed face and mop of hair showing above the blanket's coarse weave. 'Don't worry about it,' Niles said. 'Get some sleep.'

'Dreams are good,' Kid Charlemagne said. 'I understand dreams.' Then he reached up and touched Niles's forehead. His fingertips were cold. He said, 'You're silent, friend Niles. I like that.'

Niles was woken maybe half a dozen hours later, around noon, muzzy with sleep loss and sweating under a heap of blankets. Weak winter light leaked around the edges of the plastic sheeting that blocked one end of the shanty room. Electric light shone on the far side of the mixing desk, and there was the breathy hum of a blow-heater. Low voices, then a thump, and Hans swearing. 'Hold him still,' Hans said. 'He has to know to keep still.' Someone else – it was Doc Weird – said something Niles didn't catch, and Hans said, 'He won't interfere. He's a burnt-out case.'

They were kneeling either side of Kid Charlemagne, caught in a dusty shaft of morning light that shone on the mask which covered the Kid's face. Cables looped from it to a monitor plate which, resting on his knees, cast green light under Hans's chin. He and Doc Weird, holding both Kid Charlemagne's hands in his, were so intent that they didn't notice Niles, who in his mind's eye framed this tableau as one might some Renaissance deposition, the light the ladder by which the Kid's spirit ascended, Hans and the Doc the grieving yet wondering relatives.

Hans touched points on the monitor with a pen, and grunted in satisfaction when new lines scrolled up. Kid Charlemagne twisted slightly as lights flickered around the edge of the smooth black mask, and Doc Weird tightened his grip on the Kid's hands.

Niles understood that they were trying to access the Kid's strange implanted chips. Controlled patterns of light fed information in; chip-induced phosphene emissions from the rod cells in the Kid's retinas, caught by tiny fibre-optic cameras in the mask, transmitted information out. To an experienced hacker like Hans, even negative replies to interrogative commands provided clues to the functions of the chips.

Niles watched for a long minute: the small shifts in the clenched, linked postures of the Kid and Doc Weird, the tension of Hans's concentration on the monitor's scrolling lines; the light that backed them, rich in dust, each mote a hundred times larger than the self-replicating fembots, assemblages of carbon polyhedra doped with heavy metals which, operating on scales of a billionth of a millimetre, had changed the Kid's brain molecule by molecule.

It was a ceremony Niles didn't dare interrupt, an opening into the heart of the mystery of Kid Charlemagne he was too scared to share because it was too deep, too intimate. The Kid had changed things; things were moving apart. Niles stepped backwards and left them there.

Later, Kid Charlemagne came up to Niles as he was checking out a camera that had developed a raster line. This was in the core of the Permanent Floating Wave, which the night before the Kid had transformed into a cross between a coral grotto and Ernst's *Europe after the Rain.* Now it was a big bare space with an oil-blackened floor marked out with silvery duct tape, and squat concrete columns and plywood partitioning, racks of lights and camera tracks clinging close to the low ceiling, and loops of cabling stapled along the concrete panel walls. It was like the rehearsal spaces in the studios where Niles had worked so long ago, a bare place stripped of props and magic.

Kid Charlemagne watched Niles run the faulty camera back down its track, servomotors whining. Did those liquid black eyes look violated, abused? Niles felt compelled to say something, some social inanity that as usual went past the Kid without stopping, so he went to work, patching in the diagnostic widget, which told him that the charge-coupled photon collector had degraded. Niles unshipped the camera from its track, and Kid Charlemagne followed him back to the basement studio, watched as Niles took out the old collector, fitted a new one and bench-tested the camera. Just for the hell of it, he aimed it at the Kid, who seemed startled to see his own image on the little monitor.

Niles let him play with the camera. 'You never seen television before? I bet you don't even know you've been on it six hours straight the last couple of days.'

Kid Charlemagne smiled, but he was watching the monitor as he tracked the camera around his own head. 'Cool,' he said. 'I'd like stuff like this. It makes things more real.'

'Where are you from, huh?' Niles asked. 'Where are you going?'

Questions Niles might as well have asked himself, except he knew. EuroNet, if he could make it, which meant if he could get the Kid to go, because the Kid was all the A&R executive really wanted. But Niles could live with that. He could even live with Magenta, and wasn't surprised when she stepped into the studio a few minutes later. Stranger things had been happening recently. It was as if the virtual microcosms of the Permanent Floating Wave were bleeding across into the real world.

Kid Charlemagne swung the camera on her and laughed at the way the monitor mirrored her surprise in miniature, and Niles flashed on the thought that this must look the way Doc Weird's and Hans's examination of Kid Charlemagne had looked to him. Clandestine. Covert. Furtive.

Kid Charlemagne said to Niles, 'It's just winter, you know? Winter's so hard. So they sent me out into the real world.'

'That's what they told you, dear,' Magenta said, 'but Niles doesn't want to hear your troubles. That's behind you.' She raised her arms, then let her filmy black layers collapse around herself. She was holding her head to see the monitor out of the corner of her eye; Niles could see that by watching her, but it wasn't obvious when he watched her image on the monitor – yeah, she was still a pro.

The Kid moved the camera to follow the movement of Magenta's arms, zooming in like any tyro. Niles said, 'You've got to frame a shot and hold it, unless it's a reaction or a tracking shot. But what Magenta needs is a straight frame.'

'She needs the Kid,' Magenta said, dropping her arms. That was when Niles realized what was missing. It was her old doll familiar, Igor.

'I've come for my boy,' Magenta said. 'I need his help.'

Kid Charlemagne turned to Niles. 'If I must go, you come too, friend Niles.'

'It isn't serious,' Magenta started to say, but the Kid said again, 'You come too! Niles! You must!' with such force there was no denying him.

On the way up to the Wave's entrance, Magenta told Niles that she had taken to leaving Igor to watch over her rooms. She'd had the feeling that she was being watched, that something or someone had bad intentions towards her. Strange things were happening around her, she said. The familiar had an alarm and it knew to squeeze it if there was trouble, and that was what it had done. 'But it's probably nothing, Niles. You know how Igor is. A seagull lighting on the terrace gives him a heart attack. Really, you don't need to tag along.'

Normally, Niles would have agreed with her, for Magenta always dramatized her life, as if everything that happened to her had to be retrofitted into a complex recursive soap script. But there was enough weirdness around these past few days that anything seemed possible, even Magenta's fantasies, and besides, the Kid really was spooked.

And then, when they came around the curve of the ramp, they saw that Hans was waiting down by the big doors, a pile of coats at his feet. He said, 'I hear you've trouble, Magenta,' but he was looking at the Kid.

Magenta said, 'Is this some kind of conspiracy I don't know about?'

'If you've run into trouble, let security handle it,' Hans said. 'It's my job.'

'It's probably nothing. Really. Igor had one of his turns, that's all.'

Kid Charlemagne gripped Niles's arm and said in an intense whisper, 'If we all go, there is no danger. I stay with you.'

Hans said, 'Hear that? I'd like for it to be nothing, Magenta, I really would. And I reckon that so long as I come along maybe nothing will happen.'

Outside, as they ploughed through blowing snow after Magenta, who led the way at a brisk, determined pace, sulkily silent, Kid Charlemagne said quietly to Niles, 'They do not mean harm. They are just curious. That is why they want me to go back. But I like to be part of the Wave now.'

'These are your friends,' Niles said, his voice almost lost in the immense silence of the falling snow.

It was snowing hard, and wind off the North Sea drove the snow almost horizontally down the wide avenues. The streetlights were all on, and snow slanted across their orange glare. A tram drifted by, headed into civilization, sparks from its overhead cable hissing in the downpour of white motes. Niles was almost hypnotized by the way the flakes blurred into a general greyness in every direction but that in which he was looking, where they seemed to float lazily in slow motion, so that the trajectory of each flake could be traced.

'Come on, man,' Hans said. 'You can play in the snow when we've sorted this out.'

'They are interested, that is all. Just interested.' Kid Charlemagne clutched a grey army blanket around himself; he still wore his transparent sandals.

Hans was walking on the other side of the Kid from Niles. 'Now we have a situation,' he said, with resigned satisfaction. He wore an immense quilted overcoat, his face hidden in a fur-trimmed hood. 'All this stuff about Igor is just bullshit. The Kid starts to earn a reputation and Magenta wants to get him away from us. You think she's had an offer from somewhere else?'

Niles said, 'Did you find anything about the Kid's chips?'

'I wondered when you'd ask. They don't speak any language I know, I can tell you that.'

Kid Charlemagne said, 'They make me one of my people.'

'This is bad fantasy,' Hans said. 'People on the fringe just about have it together to mount a raid on produce dumpbins. It takes three of them to get a fire going. There's no time for anything but survival out there.'

'Fairies,' Niles said.

Hans said, 'I'm telling you, man! I used to live out there! The only dolls I ever saw when I was out there, they were dead. Saw some women cook and eat one once. *That* was a hard winter . . .'

'Fairies are real,' Niles said stubbornly. 'This old woman, the caretaker at the zek residence down the street until this summer? She was into doll liberation once upon a time. She used to *make* fairies.'

Hans said dismissively, 'That was a decade ago. Longer. Liberationists turned the dolls loose and they died. There aren't any fairies these days because no one's making them.'

'The old woman disappeared. Maybe she's making fairies again.'

'Word was the cops came after her. You came in from the cold, Kid. What do you know?'

Niles looked at Kid Charlemagne, but his face was hidden by a fold of grey blanket.

The Kid said, 'All kinds live out there . . .'

Beyond the corner, the sea-front complex ran away under the falling snow. Lights and neon signs faded into the blurring whiteness, but holograms stood strangely sharp, like islands of another reality. The promenade was almost deserted; beyond the closed and shuttered beach-front cafés, the grey sea was dashed with whitecaps.

Magenta turned and said, 'You don't need to come! Really, it probably isn't anything!'

She reached for Kid Charlemagne, who shrank beside Niles, and Hans said, 'All for one and one for all, Magenta. Let's just do it.'

The abandoned hotel where Magenta had her place was beyond the northern end of the promenade, near the edge of the Oostduinpark, the edge of the invisible country of the fringers. The Great Climatic Overturn had brought scorching summers and hard winters to the countries bordering the North Sea. In the Netherlands, the vast agricultural industries had retreated to ribbon arcologies along the axis of the diverted Rhine; from the roof of the Permanent Floating Wave you could see their constellations blaze on the horizon. Polders once so laboriously reclaimed from the sea were now succumbing to saltwater seepage, had become a patchwork wilderness along the abandoned seaboard of Europe's most densely populated state.

The concrete ziggurat of the old hotel was on the border of this wilderness. Foundations undercut by storms, it was listing like a foundering passenger liner. Dunes that had buried all but its top two floors were deep with snow, only the bent-over tips of their manes of coarse grasses showing.

They all climbed up the rickety fire escape to the roof and its clutter of air-conditioning vents and smashed solar panels. The windmill which generated Magenta's electricity whirred in the snowy gale. Snow had piled up against the padlocked door to the stairway, dry as polystyrene beads in the intense cold. Niles and Hans had to pull together to heave the door open against the drift.

Magenta had taken over the bridal suite. She held up a caged light as she led the way down the corridor, with its peeling flock wallpaper and threadbare mildewed carpet. Freezing air blew into their faces, and there was a dull repetitive banging up ahead: it was the double doors to the suite swinging to and fro in the wind. Hans grinned at Niles and dodged through the doors as they swung back. Niles followed, and Hans turned to him in the middle of the wreckage.

Moth-eaten net curtains billowed at the broken french windows to the terrace. The cold, windy air reeked of alcohol and formaldehyde. Furniture had been tipped over; books lay everywhere like broken birds, pages ruffling in the wind. A big oak table was strewn with broken bottles and jars and scraps of stained and labelled tissues: the smashed remains of Magenta's collection of medical curiosities. The brass alembic had been tipped over, its sphere dented and crushed. The cabling which had fed it Jupiter's microwave radiation, gathered from the three-metre antenna Magenta had installed on the roof, had been ripped away. Snow had blown across the layers of rotting Persian carpets and was everywhere marked with small footprints.

Magenta called out her familiar's name from the doorway, and then she started laughing.

'Kids,' Hans said in a quiet voice.

There was a sound from the bedroom.

Magenta stood still in the doorway, the wind ruffling her long hair and the layers of her clothing. Her big shades were like a hole through her face into the darkness at her back. Kid Charlemagne stood beside her, looking this way and that with unconcern. Niles realized that his detachment was no affectation but true naïvety. For him, the world was simply a marvellous place, radiant with innocence. It was that radiance which shone through his virtual realities and redeemed their borrowed images.

Hans signalled to Niles, and they positioned themselves either side of the bedroom door, just like cops, and just like a cop Hans swivelled and kicked open the door, ran inside. Niles followed in time to see two small figures drop out of sight from the open window.

'Jesus Christ,' Hans said.

On the big fourposter bed was what was left of Igor. The doll had been stripped of its bellboy's uniform, and its arms and legs were tied to the bedposts. Its eyes were gone. The raw red wounds were vivid against its blue skin.

Hans shouted, 'Come on!' Then he vaulted the windowsill and was gone. Snow blew around Niles as he looked out. The drop was no more than three metres, to drifted snow. Niles landed in snow deep as his thighs and fell over.

Two figures that Niles hoped were only children were floundering over the crest of the first of the line of dunes that saddled away from the hotel. Hans was already half-way up the slope, and by the time Niles had got to his feet he was at the top. He turned, veiled in falling snow, and shouted, 'The little fuckers have some friends!'

When Niles caught up with him, Hans pointed to the half-dozen child-sized figures at the crest of the next line of dunes, shadows in the blowing whiteness. 'Let's leave it,' Niles said. Snow had soaked through his clothes, and the wind cut into him. He said, 'Maybe they're only kids . . .'

Hans said, 'You think kids did that to Igor?' His hood had fallen back. He cupped his hands to his mouth and shouted, 'You! You little bastards! You just wait there!'

He started down the slope, and there was a flare of light amongst the figures on the facing crest. Niles glimpsed something arc through falling snow, a long dark fleck trailing a flickering light. It drifted lazily for a moment, then seemed to gather itself and leap forward.

Hans looked up just as it smashed into him, and he was thrown back, clutching the burning end of the spear with both hands, pulling it from his left shoulder, then letting go and falling backwards. Flames flickered and sputtered on the front of his quilted coat, and Niles beat them out.

'Fuck,' Hans said with forceful surprise, and laughed. 'A wire-guided rocket spear!'

Someone caught Niles's shoulder. It was Kid Charlemagne. He had lost his blanket and was dusted with powdery snow from head to foot. His black hair, starred with snow, blew around his face. 'I jumped!' he shouted. His fear mirrored Niles's own. 'I ran from Magenta and jumped after you! We go! We go!'

Niles helped Hans up, slow and clumsy, floundering with him in the deep snow. He was so scared he felt he would at any moment fly straight out of his body.

Kid Charlemagne danced around them. 'I'm sorry! I'm sorry! We go!'

Niles looked at the line of figures at the top of the far dunes. Not children. He couldn't turn his back on them. Instead, holding up Hans, he stepped backwards, fitting his boots into his own footsteps, until he had climbed back over the top of the dune. Then he turned and, with Hans limping beside him, breathing heavily into his neck, he followed Kid Charlemagne through the blowing snow.

There was no sign of Magenta. Niles used the phone point at the beginning of the promenade and called a taxi. It arrived within a minute, and Hans fell inside it. Niles shouted into the taxi driver's blue face, told it to take Hans to the hospital, and then the taxi disappeared into the blizzard.

Kid Charlemagne said anxiously, 'It's not good to stay here.'

Niles felt every minute of his fifty years pressing on his shoulders. 'We don't have time to go with Hans. You've got a show to run, Kid.'

'I think they want me back,' Kid Charlemagne said, and started off into the snow. When Niles caught up with him, he said, 'I learn, friend Niles. I learn they use me.'

'Those kids were using you? What are they, fringers?'

'I want to learn more,' Kid Charlemagne said, and wouldn't say anything else, all the way back to the Permanent Floating Wave, where Magenta was waiting for them in the studio.

Niles ignored her. He went straight to the phone and called the emergency department of the local aid station, and some AI circuit told him that information about patients was restricted.

'Be careful,' Magenta said. 'You'll have the cops down on us, and that wouldn't do at all.'

Niles said, 'Those kids tried to kill Hans. Maybe I *should* call the cops.'

Magenta said, 'It's his own fault he was hurt. He wasn't supposed to be there; nor were you. And Niles, you know they weren't kids.' She was sitting in the swivel chair at Niles's mixing board, running a long black thumbnail up and down the sliders, one by one.

Niles said, 'So they're what? Fairies? Jesus Christ, Magenta!'

'People,' Kid Charlemagne said.

'His people are fairies,' Magenta said. 'Oh Niles, haven't you worked it out yet? They changed the Kid into what he is. He's an experiment.'

'Why was he changed?'

'Because they could do it. Because they took him when he was a little kid, and they wanted him to think like they did. Because they like the irony of chipping a human, when every one of them has been under human control. Who knows how fairies think? They did it by instinct, by trial and error. They sent him out here to see how he worked. Now they want him back, for what he is, just as that woman from EuroNet wants him.'

Niles said, 'That's something we have to talk about.'

'You never did think I was very clever,' Magenta said. 'But I didn't need to be to find out about your little deal.'

'Who told you? Max?'

'Close.'

'Saint Jack? Jesus.'

'I talk to the Saint. Not many people bother to, apart from Max. The Saint isn't brain-fried by his permanent high, you know. It's just put him on a different level of consciousness.'

Niles remembered the Saint's monologue about the evolution of human language and consciousness through drugs. Or through the lack of them. Dolls and their controller chips. Suppose the implanted chips were taken away, would dolls have to evolve consciousness to cope with the loss of the command strings by which they were regulated and which instructed them every moment of every day? What kind of consciousness would it be? And he also wondered, with a sudden chill, if Kid Charlemagne was being controlled.

Magenta said, 'Maybe I should tell the Permanent Floating Wave about the EuroNet offer.'

'Go ahead. We don't have rules here. And besides, she wants you to come in on it, too, Magenta.'

'No, Niles. I care too much about my changeling to allow it.'

'I look out for myself,' Kid Charlemagne said. 'I have fun.'

Magenta told him, 'This isn't the fairyland.'

'No one owns the Kid,' Niles said. 'That's the point.'

'But you'd let EuroNet own him, if they could . . .'

Kid Charlemagne had been looking back and forth between the two of them, with an expression that was not quite yet a smile.

'Let the Kid choose,' Niles said.

Magenta laughed. 'Oh, Niles! You're always so sure of yourself. So sure you're always right!'

'Right now I'm not sure of anything, except I'm scared for the Kid. Those things out there mean business. Hans could have been killed . . . '

'Of course you're sure! That's why you'll let the Kid choose for himself. But you don't understand anything yet.' Magenta swung up from the chair in a flurry of black veils. She put her hands either side of Niles's face and turned it to hers, kissed him on the lips, then on his right eye.

As he blinked in surprise, she said, 'Now you're really going to see!'

Niles didn't understand what she meant until the night was under way, and the A&R executive and two of her vice-presidents, and their doll assistants and tall, heavyweight doll bodyguards had all crowded in his studio. The dolls stood with stiff obedience along one wall, while the humans watched the monitors above the mixing desk and Niles mixed simple tracking shots for the cable TV feed.

Kid Charlemagne was already deep into doing his thing in the core of the Permanent Floating Wave, with a more than capacity crowd of wavers trancing along. The soundscape was a pounding sweep of drums spiked with startling peaks of brass percussion. The landscape was all half-melted, slickly organic spires, mostly red and studded with jewels, under a dense blue sky in which cutouts showed whirling constellations. It seemed to stretch out to infinity: ward subroutines working through the wavers' transceivers, either their own or temporary links built by eye-dropped fembots, kept them away from the walls of the core, and from passing through the spikes and spires of the virtual landscape.

Kid Charlemagne seemed to float in the centre, describing an orbit about a tall thin spire that glistened like raw tourmaline and pulsated and shuddered to the beat like a sensitive filament of the living landscape. Without the patched overlay from the Wave's computers, it could be seen that he was standing on a platform suspended on a crane arm. Later, he would descend, and the virtual landscape would begin its convulsive unbound metamorphosis as the crowd's frenzy mounted towards catharsis.

'He can hold a crowd,' one of the veeps said.

The other said, 'What else can he do? What does he do that's new?'

The first said, 'One thing he'll have to do is change his name. Obscure pop-culture references might have been sales points in the millennium,

but not now.'

Both of them were clean-shaven and fashionably pale-skinned, ramrod straight in their one-piece asymmetric suits.

The executive, sweating under her mask of opalescent make-up, said, 'I know it's a simple set-up, but what's new are the nuances he puts into it.'

'I didn't see that on the tapes,' the first veep said.

'Well, that's why we are here,' the executive said.

Niles sensed her nervousness. She had probably been working herself up to the pitch all day. He suggested that the EuroNet veeps might want to sample what happened for themselves.

'If we like what we see tonight, we'll sample it with proxies,' the first veep said.

The second reached out and started to pan and zoom one of the cameras. Niles restrained his impulse to slap the man's hand away. He had shiningly clean square-cut nails, thick gold rings on every finger, and a multi-dial Rolex that probably cost more than the Wave's annual turnover.

'We don't see too much so far,' the first veep said.

'Check out the unity,' the executive said, with what seemed to Niles to be overly forced enthusiasm. 'Check out the bliss on the faces of the crowd.'

The first veep laid a hand on the back of Niles's chair, enveloping Niles in a wave of piny cologne, as the second switched out the overlay and started to zoom in on individual faces. Niles, working his board more or less on automatic pilot, watched with more than half his attention. After a few moments he parasitized the feed from the camera the veep had commandeered, overlaid each blurry face with a halo effect against a solarized gold wash, and let them bleed one after the other under wide pans of the crowd.

'Nice,' the second veep said. 'Corny, but nice.' He asked about the contract with the TV station, wanting details Niles didn't have.

'It's nothing our legal department can't handle,' the executive said breezily. 'Strictly a standard freelance fee-for-feed non-binding agreement.'

Niles suddenly understood that she sounded happy because the deal was going down. If they wanted to know how to get the Kid, of course it was going down. He felt his tension ebb a little, and in that moment a blue-skinned smooth doll face, haloed, bled away as it was overlain by the image of a girl's blissful face.

Niles slapped the veep's hands away and clicked the camera back to its last position – but the doll was gone. He whirled for the door and then one of the bodyguard dolls was in his face and the other was holding his arms, elbows together, at his back. Both were taller than Niles, built like hypertrophied sumo wrestlers. Carbon whisker quills, tipped with steel, rattled on their forearms; thicker spines made a ruff around their necks. The one in Niles's face smiled, showing sharky rows of serrated metal teeth. Its breath reeked of acetone.

'Call them off!'

'All right,' one of the veeps said, and the bodyguards let Niles go and he was out of the room, tearing up the wide spiral ramp towards the core of the Wave. He ran through sliding primary colours, as if he was plunging through the broken shards of a rainbow. As the throb and cascading clatter of the soundscape grew louder, the shapes began to draw together. Gemmed outcrops flashing, they rose above him in spiky shapes towards a layered, washed-out sky where a red disc hung; it had small, yellow eyes, and a tiny mouth, upper lip lifted as if to nibble.

He was wired. Someone – he realized that it had been Magenta, when she had kissed him – had infected him with fembots; the tiny machines had built transceivers in his brain, translating the virtual output of the core computers directly into his optic nerves. This realization brought not panic but exhilaration.

People passed him by on the right and the left, masked in gorgeous feathers. Their movements bled light into the air, and when he raised and flexed his hand, traceries like golden filaments hung afterwards, slowly fading into an exquisite buttery glow.

'Niles!' It was a figure hooded and robed in a cascade of red feathers, eyes lambent as an owl's.

'Oh shit,' it said, and touched something to Niles's forehead.

Then Niles was standing on a grey concrete ramp, with nothing but noise pounding around him. A young woman in a brand-new yellow denim jacket – it was brisk, serious Marta – held the pen-shaped transducer to his temple, cutting out the induced visions. Wavers pushed around them, wide-eyed with close to religious ecstasy.

'Some time to get wired!' Marta shouted over the pounding music. 'The cable TV was on the phone! Wants to know why the feed was jammed!'

'There are fairies here! I've got to find Magenta!'

'The Kid dropped fairies after his first night,' Marta said, and Niles realized that she thought he was still tripping and said, 'Did you see her?'

'She's in there,' Marta said, meaning the core. 'I'll get on the desk, OK? Enjoy yourself.'

And then she was gone, and the vision swirled around Niles once more. A crowd of fabulous creatures swept him along, into the core.

Niles fetched up against a towering green column that in reality was one of the plywood-clad pillars which held up the core's low ceiling. Now it felt like living glass under his fingers. Delicate flutings spiralled up, breaking around animate faces neither human nor animal. Dancers swirled by him, bleeding complex patterns of light that pulsed to the deep bass rhythm that Niles could feel through the soles of his feet, in his bones. Their dance defined a kind of plaza. Beyond it stretched a shattered, mostly red landscape. Pillowy coralline shapes piled into cliffs; broken crystalline pillars leaning everywhere; vast thorny skeletal structures in a mazy confusion, from which human figures seemed to be trying to rise. Above, a blue sky pulsed with holes through which strange bright constellations whirled, as if they were gateways to younger universes, or places where physical laws conformed more closely to human expectation, so that stars really were stars and not giant balls of fusing gas.

The dancers whirled in contrary orbits. Here a whole group stamped in a circle; there a single person swayed with upraised arms while others swirled past. All were robed in feathers, and feathery masks that now and again dissolved to show ecstatic faces. At the centre of their intricate pavan was a collapsed beast like an arthropod horse, its head swept back into a single horn, a palanquin on its back both organic and crystalline, four pillars holding up a tented roof on which stood a figure with the sleek beaked head of a bird, a long lance in its hand from which a dozen rags fluttered in stop motion, their sigils constantly transforming.

The figure was Kid Charlemagne, auditing the session. Niles plunged towards him through the wild dance, now pulled in one direction, now whirled away in another. A woman shoved a flask against Niles's lips – tin ticked teeth, soft sweet liquid flooded his mouth. He pulled away and a man turned him and French-kissed him, laughed and shouted to the beat of the soundscape, 'We are bro-thers!'

Niles broke the man's grasp, but another of the dancers caught him up, robed and hooded in a cascade of gorgeous red feathers. For an instant this flickered to show Magenta's black-lipped white face, her eyes obscured by the big black shades.

Niles yelled that there were fairies loose in the Wave, and she put her mouth to his ear and said in a voice like tiny silver bells, 'I know! Isn't it wonderful?' And then Niles saw the sharp-featured blue face that peeked out from her cascade of feathers.

Small hard hands grasped the waist of his loose shirt. Niles pulled away and gained the flank of the horse-thing. Its scales were rough and warm under his fingers as he climbed, and when he was half-way up its great horned head turned and regarded him with a lambent golden eye. Niles felt a great surge of transcendental harmony, and if Kid Charlemagne hadn't reached down and pulled him up he might have stayed there.

When Niles told him about the fairies, Kid Charlemagne laughed out loud; the hooked beak of his eagle's-head mask opened so wide Niles could see the bright-red tongue within. 'They see what I can do! They tremble in awe!' He swept his lance about him, and it extended out over the heads of the crowd that surged about the palanquin like waves on the shore. The bass rhythm changed gear and the landscape began to pulse with it. Light shone within the coralline cliffs, brighter and brighter. They were melting in light.

'I won't go back,' Kid Charlemagne said, and that was when the fairies scrambled over the edge of the palanquin.

Niles saw them as figures hooded in black, with beaked masks made of interlocking triangles. Two, four, six of them. Kid Charlemagne jabbed at them with his lance, and briefly they transformed into what they really were: blue-skinned homunculi half the size of a man, with narrow shaven heads and grim, alert expressions. They all looked like brothers: the same flattened, spread nose, the same large liquid black eyes. All were marked on the cheeks with parallel scars.

'No!' Kid Charlemagne yelled. 'I won't go back! Help me, friend Niles!'

And he hurled the lance at the fairies and jumped into the crowd. Niles glimpsed him struggling with two or three black-cloaked figures amongst the whirl, and jumped after, plucking one off the Kid's back, suddenly tangled with two more which tried to pull him in different directions. He went one way, knocked that fairy down, roared when the other bit him. It expanded into a black cloud covering his arm, needlepoints of pain somewhere inside it. Then Kid Charlemagne vanished into the cloud, and it flew away from Niles, dwindling. The Kid was rolling over and over, tangled with a doll in filthy cut-down coveralls. Niles plucked it up by a leg and an arm, shook it hard, and threw it into two others. Then he pulled the Kid up and they ran.

They ran through the dancers, shoving them aside and being shoved back. Panic spread like ripples across a pond. Without an auditor, the soundscape was drifting awry, its bass lines tangling and halting and restarting, brass crashing in discordant diminishing crescendos. All around, crystal pillars began to blur and melt inward like candles thrown in a furnace.

The vast pulsating entrance dwindled to a shabby tunnel. Niles and Kid Charlemagne ran into it just as the music finally ground to a halt in a cacophony of brass, like a derailed train. The Kid's eagle head faded into goggles and battered black transducer helmet.

As they ran down the spiral ramp, Doc Weird ran up it towards them. He grabbed Niles and half-turned him. He was mad as hell. 'You crazy old man! The whole system's gone down!'

'You don't let me by,' Niles said, 'I'm gonna walk right through you.'

The skinny Brit let go of Niles's sleeve. 'Your EuroNet squeeze packed up and left a minute ago,' he said. 'Your deal's fucked, guy.' He laughed and ran away down the ramp, shouting, 'Hans! Hans! I found them!'

'Everyone crazy,' Kid Charlemagne said. Tears starred his dark eyes. 'Everyone hurts.'

'Welcome to the world,' Niles said. 'I'll try and get you out of this if I can, but then you have to think about who you want to be.'

Grey smoke rose up at them as Niles and the Kid descended. Cables were strewn over the concrete ramp, jetting green and white and yellow vapours. Figures ran past them, panicky wavers on the way down, one or two of the Wave's helpers on the way up.

Hans was waiting for them where the ramp turned out into the vast subdivided space of the ground-floor level. The long wide corridor that led to the entrance was filled with smog and the glare of emergency lights, and at the door he turned a powerful torch on Niles and Kid Charlemagne, its beam striking like a lance through roiling vapours.

Niles said despairingly, 'You gotta let the Kid go!'

'We only want his chips,' Hans said. He stepped forward. His left arm was strapped to his side; bandages bulked out his chest under a white shirt spotted with dried brown blood. 'Don't make me hurt you, Niles.'

'I don't care what kind of deal you and Doc Weird have–'

'Deals! That's good, coming from someone trying to fuck us over with EuroNet.' Then Hans looked around wildly. 'Hey! Goddamn you, don't play tricks with me!'

Kid Charlemagne said softly in Niles's ear, 'He can't see us now.'

Hans stumbled forward, good arm swinging, the torch waving its bright beam through the smoke. Niles and Kid Charlemagne shrank from him, then ran past.

Police cars and fire engines were drawn up in slushy snow along the centre of the avenue, cherry lights revolving above the packed pastel roofs of the double- and triple-parked runabouts of the capacity crowd. Smoke was pouring from every floor of the Permanent Floating Wave. Screams, people stumbling amongst the emergency vehicles, ducking under the orange tape of police lines. A helicopter fluttered somewhere above the revolving lights and the glare of the streetlamps. Niles saw the A&R executive climb into a long limo parked beyond the police lines at the end of the block, and his heart turned over as the limo made a U-turn and slid away.

'No one sees us,' Kid Charlemagne said, 'if they have machines in their heads. Except you – I fixed that.'

'Jesus, you can talk with chips?'

Kid Charlemagne tapped Niles's forehead. 'You were so quiet before Magenta magicked you. I liked that.'

'I'll be quiet again, when the fembots die out.' But suppose Magenta had infected him with a rogue strain of fembots? He should get a shot of universal phage, like he'd had to do a couple of times when he'd gotten wired by pranksters. But there wasn't time to get to a clinic; he was in the middle of a war. He told Kid Charlemagne, 'Everyone wants you for one thing. You understand?'

The intense cold and the Wave's chemical smoke had made his throat raw. Yeah, and that was why he was crying.

Kid Charlemagne nodded.

'If you were changed, there'd be no one on your back. You could live your life the way you wanted. You understand?'

Another nod.

'Maybe there's a way to do it right now.'

'Would I be like you?'

'You'd lose everything people want from you. But you could start trying to learn to be yourself. Not what other people want you to be.'

'It's hard not to. When I can see what they want . . .' Blue light washed rhythmically over the Kid's face. He said, 'Do it to me, friend Niles. Make me human.'

Max's Head Shop was closed and shuttered, but Niles took Kid Charlemagne down the alley at the side and banged on the service door until Max let them in.

He took about ten minutes to convince, and every second Niles felt something inside himself wind tighter and tighter. When the fat man said for the third time that it was ten years since the Saint had tried to pull someone's chips, Niles said, 'Listen, if the Saint can't do it, give me a paring knife and I'll try to do it myself.'

'The Kid here really wants it done?'

Kid Charlemagne said, 'I want to be human.'

Max put his hands up. 'You talk to the Saint. It isn't any of my business.'

From the other end of the counter the Saint said, in a spaced-out drawl, 'It's anti-evolution. Why live in the old world when there's so many richer realities elsewhere?'

Niles said, 'Does that mean you'll do it or not, Saint?'

Kid Charlemagne said, 'As long as they're in my head, I'm owned.'

'How about it, man?'

'Well, I don't suppose anyone should own anyone else,' the Saint said. He was looking between Niles and the Kid, focused on something about a million light years away. 'I used to do it with dolls, a long time ago,' he said dreamily. 'This funky old punk, Darlajane B, taught me how. She lives around the corner here. You know Darlajane B, Niles?'

That was the old caretaker of the zek residence. Niles said, 'I knew her, Saint. She went away this summer.'

'She says she can take out the changes the machines made in my brain, but that's something not even the real head scientists could do. And even if they could, I've gotten so used to them that it wouldn't make any difference. Darlajane B, she has some odd ideas, but she means well. I can do it here, if Max gets my stuff.'

When Max had disappeared upstairs, the Saint said to Kid Charlemagne, 'I can see you know things.'

'It hurts.'

'Yeah, knowledge does hurt if you're not used to it. See, we're used to it, us man-apes. Used to hurting. Used to the sting of the apple's aftertaste. There was a time before that when we made our own realities the way you do, but now this is all we got.'

Kid Charlemagne said, 'There are too many realities. Him-' he pointed to Niles, 'and you. I mix them together and give them back.'

'You should have seen him, Saint.'

'I don't need any more of that machine stuff,' Saint Jack said with a dreamy look. 'I made it my own . . .'

He'd gone away, somewhere inside his own head. Niles shook him. 'Goddamn you, Saint! You stay awake!'

'He's always awake,' Max said, coming around the last turn of the stairs. He hefted a frayed plastic sportsbag, corners mended with yellow tape. 'Here you go, man. You remember this stuff?'

Saint Jack had Kid Charlemagne lie down on the bar counter, his head cradled on a shaped block of wood. The Saint shook up a little plastic bottle and put drops in the Kid's eyes to immobilize them; the Kid's pupils were raggedly huge when Niles leant over him and asked him if he was sure this was what he wanted.

'I want to find out what it is to be myself.'

'You won't be able to audit.'

'Friend Niles, you can teach me again. We can go somewhere else.'

'Sure.'

Saint Jack hooked the arms of his magnifying spectacles over his jutting ears. He said, 'It'll take a minute, maybe, if you let me do it.'

'Where's your equipment?'

'For this I don't need too much. I told you it was easy. There won't even be any blood. Hold still now,' he told Kid Charlemagne, and shoved spoon-shaped plastic spacers under the Kid's eyeballs, hooked about the raw red rims with a fine probe. He drew something out from the Kid's right eye and dropped it into the palm of Niles's hand, did the same with the left.

Niles looked at the tiny chips and said, 'That's it?'

The Saint smiled his dreamy smile. 'These are the logic engines. Stuff all through his head still; I could put in fembots to scavenge it out, if I had the cultures. You could find a grey-market shop does that, if you want. But taking these out disconnects everything.'

'Kid, you hear that?'

But Kid Charlemagne was silent. He lay as still as the tomb figure of a crusader, head on the hard pillow, hands crossed on his chest, eyes rolled up like white stones.

'Kid?'

Magenta said, 'You've switched him off, and now you expect him to speak?'

She was leaning in the back doorway. Her dark glasses masked half her white face. Small shapes clustered behind her.

Max said, 'I'm sorry, Niles. I really didn't think the Saint could do it. Turns out I was wrong.'

Magenta said, 'Max sent out word you were up here, Niles. He's trying to tell you that you don't know what you're doing.'

Niles was thinking of a line from an old novel: anyone who owns a frying pan owns death. But there wasn't a frying pan in the bar, let alone any knives. Just bottles and glasses and mugs, and the heavy coffee machine with its tarnished eagle. He said, 'You trust those things after what they did to Igor?'

Magenta took off her dark glasses. Her eye sockets were yellow with old bruises. She said, 'They explained things to me.'

'That's clumsy work,' the Saint said.

'Next time I'll come to you. Meanwhile, maybe you can start up the Kid there. Put him back together, Saint Jack.'

Niles held out his hand. 'What are these worth?'

The fairies made a rustling in the shadows behind Magenta. Niles could suddenly feel them in his head, but nothing he felt made any sense.

Magenta said calmly, 'Your life, perhaps. Don't you think they have duplicates? He's nothing without them. Everything he is, everything he learnt, is in the parallel network that fembots spun in his skull. Without the processors his higher functions are closed off from his medulla oblongata. His body will breathe and circulate blood for a while, but eventually it will fail. They took him very young. He was their first changeling, and they sent him out into our world to see how he fared. Now they want him back.'

'No one owns anyone,' Niles said. He was speaking directly to the dolls in the shadows, trying to make a connection, but it was Magenta who replied. She was their connection.

She said, 'You do. You have two lives in the palm of your hand.'

'They changed you a while ago, didn't they?' You brought us out to your place to get the Kid back.'

'It was a misunderstanding. They didn't mean to hurt anyone. Hans frightened them: they only expected me and the Kid. But the Kid knew I was going to take him back and thought he'd be safe if you came along, and Hans had his own plans for the Kid.'

'They killed Igor. That was a misunderstanding?'

'Igor was killed when the fairies were ready to take the Kid back. I didn't need Igor any more because I wouldn't need to act as if I hadn't been saved, and he was too old to be made over. Hundreds of dolls are killed every day. Thousands. They die in industrial accidents, they die from working down seabed mines, from working in reactors. Or they're killed when they're too old to work. Over in Rotterdam, they are hunted for sport. They freed Igor. Give Saint Jack the chips, Niles.'

'The Kid isn't a thing to be owned.'

'The fairies would say that about any one of their kind. They are the changelings that liberationists like Darlajane B made from slaves. But the liberationists didn't think what their changelings would do once the fairies were set free. They make their own kind now, when they need to. It isn't a revolution, not the way the liberationists wanted, but something wild and strange. You can't understand it right now, Niles, no more than you can understand the kids who use the Head Shop, but you will. You don't know it, but you've been saved. Give back the chips.'

Niles looked into Magenta's eyes, and she smiled. It was a real smile, and he knew that she still lived somewhere in her head, that she was changed but she was not destroyed. The fairies were not as cruel as humans, who had made them as casually as they used them, as things, nothing more, who did not understand the responsibility of creators, and he sighed and opened his hands.

When Niles left a few days later, most of the crew of the Permanent Floating Wave took him over to Max's Head Shop and stood him a few rounds of brandies to send him on his way.

Burckhardt said, 'We'll miss you, man.'

'Maybe I'll come back in spring.'

Burckhardt said, 'We might be needing a few seasonal workers by then,' and he and Niles smiled, because they both knew it wasn't true. The Permanent Floating Wave had crested. Hans had been arrested when the police broke up the panicky near-riot the fairies had caused, and Doc Weird had left for the chance of a job in a Luxembourg TV station. The gate had plummeted, and the cable TV station had dropped its option on the Wave's feed.

When Niles was finally about ready to go he set his bag on his shoulder and went over and shook Saint Jack's hand.

'You take care now,' he said.

'I'm beyond good and evil,' the Saint said, nodding and smiling. 'I don't need to deal with that any more.'

'Pray for the rest of us, then,' Niles said, and thought he could feel the Saint's benediction pricking inside his head. Magenta had changed him, with a kiss. The chips spun by her fembots had flayed him open, but he welcomed their changes.

Max came down to that end of the bar and said, 'She asked me to look out for the Kid, Niles, so I made the call when I went upstairs to get the Saint's stuff. I didn't know . . .'

'I'd probably have done the same thing,' Niles said.

The Saint said, 'The Kid walked out free. Inside your own head there are worlds wilder and stranger than anything outside.'

Maybe there were. Niles could begin to believe that now. On his way out of town he took a detour, and stood a long while by the chain-link fence that separated the Oostduinpark from the street. He hooked his fingers in the freezing wire and shook it so snow fell from its rolled top.

It was dusk, bitterly cold. A multitude of small fires burned out there in the rolling wilderness, making strange flickering constellations. Most of them had been lit by fringers or streetkid gangs, but which hadn't? Niles listened inside his head for a long time, but perhaps they were too far away.

Still, it came to Niles that he no longer knew which side was which. Were they on the outside, or was this the outside now? Spurred by the thought, he rattled the fence again and called the Kid's name, but he might as well have been shouting at the sky.

When he saw a tram rolling up the street towards him he left off and ran for the corner, where it stopped to pick him up. The doll driver didn't even glance at Niles when he dropped his token, but Niles could feel, deep beneath the dull linear texture of the doll's programming, a glimmer of otherness, that same glimmer that was widened into the brand-new prelapsarian light of the fairies. Niles grinned like a fool, and as the tram lurched and carried him off into the world, he fell into a seat by an old woman and asked her if she'd been saved yet.

Science Fiction
Novels of the Year

John Clute

Asimov City. Michaelmas Term lately over, and the Time Bailiff sitting in the Hall of Dues. Implacable November weather. As much mud in the streets, as if the waters had but newly retired from the face of the earth, and it would not be wonderful to meet a Megalosaurus, forty feet long or so, waddling like an elephantine lizard up the stream of time. Futures everywhere. Futures up the river; futures creeping into the cabooses; futures down the river, hovering in the rigging of great ships. Futures in the eyes and throats. Futures in a foggy glory round the head of the Bailiff; futures infiltrating the scribes of the City, scores of them still undead, still mistily engaged – nostrils stopped against the rictus of new air – in any of the ten thousand sharecrops of the endless City, tripping one another up on slippery precedents, running their goat-hair- and horse-hair- warded heads against walls of words, and making a pretence of equity with serious faces, as players might.

But the king is dead, of course, though scribes continue to scrabble through the corpus, like roaches trapped in mummy cloth, snuffling for titbits caught between the great sandy teeth, quarrelling through the fallen ribs of stone, and up and down the aisles and edifices of Robot City, for hooks to hang to, as by threads. The king is dead, and the futures of the world swirl round the bare-shanked scribes of sharecrop, tearing from their grip the final hooks of the old sf, the runes of Asimov which fixed the future into one shape, the Future History of the Dead Writ. 'Time, gentlemen', says the Bailiff, who is Time's snickersnee, and cuts the threads grinning. And the scribes of sharecrop tumble downwards to the acid holes of the world, bugs chewed by pestilence. 'Hurry up please, it's time.'

More than the death of Robert A. Heinlein – who had long before abandoned the fixed future of his prime, the Future History his acolytes had gone on patching, for decades, in the great Quilting Bee of post-war American sf – it was a death to mark. The recursive infantilism of Heinlein's closing books had constituted an anathemata, his utterances the primal nada of a terrifying mortal child for whom the century had not played fair. His final books told all of us, cursing us *en passant*, that the Future was deader than Ozymandias, that the

Duesenberg of Future History had slammed off the high road into badlands. And he turned his back (fatally) on the Bailiff, who might also be called Time Present, and sank into himself like a stone. He scared me stiff. Personal grieving aside, Heinlein's death was a *relief* to the wardens of the old church, because the decades of apostasy could be forgotten, the bitterness of his snub.

No. The death to mark – the death for us to stand upon the other side of, as upon the far side of a shadow, in the feeble sunlight of a lessening day – was the death of Isaac Asimov in 1992, because Asimov had never abandoned the high road, never stopped staking claims to the Future he had chosen in 1940 to illuminate with all the juices of his geek heart, big brain, frantic displacing mind. Indeed, for many of those who knew him and who used him (just as, mercilessly, he used them in return to salve his fame: to be 'presented' or 'introduced' by Asimov must have been to feel rather like suntan lotion), he *was* the road. He was the Future, he was the sound of consensus agreed on by the brothers and the sisters and the scribes who filled in the gaps, echoing like gourds to his call, walking the same plank. He was the sound (as I myself said on a UK programme about his life) of sf talking to itself, the default voice of American genre sf, which had been born in 1926, had been stricken in 1957 when Sputnik began to asset-strip the playground of space, and had since deceased. His death marked all of this. We stand on the other side of the shadow.

The game of genre sf is over and done now, and we are for the world, I think willy-nilly. Just as the planet got too close to us at the end of the nineteenth century, and could no longer contain mysteries of geography for us to penetrate, so at the end of the twentieth there is no longer any way of distancing the future enough to play with it. We are closed in on, and it's dark in here, and we may not come through: so be it. Much of the best post-genre sf now written reflects a knowledge that the terms have changed: what the old dreamers of genre sf once penetrated with gumption and glee (the gal, the god, the town, the frontier, the territory, the monster, the alien, the planet, the galaxy), the most significant new sf writers now tend to propitiate, to seek ways of marrying. It is a profound transvaluation of values. Sf (to repeat arguments made in another place) has been transformed into fables of exogamy. In that sense – and for all human beings who read sf – it has become, once again, and after a long intermission in the coils of nostalgia, a literature of the future, or (now that we have come out of the monocular glare of the old sf's programme) the futures. Once again, now that we know we are differently futured, we can learn from sf.

There are statistics. As usual, the *Locus* people do the best job of displaying and making sense of the figures. *Science Fiction, Fantasy, & Horror: 1991* (1992), edited by Charles N. Brown and William G. Contento, is an annual volume which presents in corrected and expanded form the statistics assembled monthly in *Locus* itself. (The comments printed in *New Worlds 1* on the nature of that assembly are now, in part, out of date; the habits governing the compiling and admission of material had been becoming less eccentric over the years and the book is now a much safer tool.) It is recorded in this year's volume that a record number of genre books were seen by *Locus* (which is *still* not *quite* the same as 'were published in the USA') during the period in question: 1,246 titles in all, almost three and a half books every single day of the year. For our purposes, however, lots of them could be ignored. There were a number of anthologies, collections and non-fiction titles, all beyond our remit; others were novelizations, or ties (a term I have come to prefer, because it points to a variety of categories of book written to order), and were unlikely to warrant much more attention than one might pay the ten thousandth footprint from a dead man's boot. There were also 165 horror novels, most of which had little sf content, or ate it; and 301 fantasy novels, some 275 by exact count being quest tales for Mcguffins set in rubberized Ruritanias heavily infested with the usual decalcomania of killable extras, personalized elf stuffings, Christopher Lloyd magus golems, and everything told in a style so uniformly boneless as to be very nearly beyond description. In the end, only 308 sf novels were left, which was *less than one a day*. And most of *them* were written by hardscrabble computer scribes, and bound in mummy cloth. Most sf novels published in 1991 were scabs of the dying. Fearful of the day. Unmentionable.

The previous four versions of this round-up were broken into categories which presented genre sf as an ongoing chronology, a continuing agenda on the part of successive generations of writers. For this fifth – and perhaps final – instalment, it seems no longer appropriate to continue to unroll this red carpet into the swamp of Now. Any 1991 book which embodies the old Future History of genre sf is in effect a *novelization*. And it was probably written for hire. And there is another difficulty. It has become increasingly difficult to suggest that non-genre books (like those written by Martin Amis or Marge Piercy) can usefully be distinguished – over and beyond the need to note the deeply unprofessional ignorance of generic language and device shared by almost all non-genre writers – from post-genre sf by writers (like Karen Joy Fowler or Michael Swanwick) who may have been brought up within the freemasonry, but who show every sign of riding the sea-change into a world we must try to share, and comprehend. The old sf is dead; and the change is in us, like the neocytes in Robert Charles Wilson's *The Harvest* (1992), who enact a terrible beauty upon any human being wise enough to accept their offer to marry out. But there are still dinosaurs.

Being a Founder of the old sf is not exactly a matter of age. Jack Vance is older than Frederik Pohl, but Vance began too late (well into the 1940s) to qualify as a charter member, and he writes with the dreamy belatedness of a fish in deep water, while Pohl, who became an sf writer before the start of the Second World War, continues to write as though the art-deco shazams of 1940 sf still signalled and shaped a challenge to the world rather than a medium to consult. What is astonishing is that it works. By retaining the urgency of the old sf, but not its articles of faith, he continues to write with a dawn latency, as though we might still make it new, the story of sf, the tale that tells us there's a story. It is the very opposite of the sad recursive râle of genre talking to itself, like a patient trying to date an iron lung. So he is a dinosaur of genre, along with Jack Williamson, both warm-blooded, and there are no others left, except maybe Damon Knight, but he was never more than a jester in the closing days of dinosaur court; and Andre Norton, but she only began publishing sf well into her career. Frank Belknap Long and A. E. Van Vogt will write no more; L. Sprague de Camp is unlikely to produce sf; and it is hard to think of Arthur Lloyd Eshbach or Raymond Z. Gallun as striking a new note.

So Pohl and Williamson can be celebrated for their continuity, though their offspring cannot be similarly celebrated for aping it; and Williamson can be forgiven for the increasing frequency with which his plotlines default to the pulp strokes of sixty-five years ago, when he began. There may be antique moments in *The Singers of Time* (Doubleday), which is the tenth collaboration between the two writers since 1954, but there is a settled polish to the telling and the alien that reads almost like wisdom. And *Stopping at Slowyear* (Pulphouse/Axolotl), by Pohl alone, was a Long Year tale set on the usual Long Year planet, where the usual elongations of season generate the usual Giacometti matrices: long sex, long punishments, long reveries, long guerres. But the tale was swift. From the dead dinosaur, the shadow of whose falling marks terminator, yet another fewmet issued from the heart of the midden: *Child of Time* (Gollancz) with Robert Silverberg, who took an Asimov story from 1958, 'The Ugly Little Boy', made Frankenstein passes over the body, gave us a lad of marble. *Our Angry Earth* (Tor), by Asimov and Pohl, was non-fiction, recommended that we save the planet, said how. I have not seen it.

One final dinosaur remains, but of a different strain. Arthur C. Clarke is the right age, and began to write at the right time, and speaks as though he understands the doings of the world (almost always a sign of a pre-war writer); but he is English, and his relationship to American genre sf has always seemed — if at times almost indefinably — remote, as though he were passing for white; he is, it cannot be too often mentioned, a member (Brian Stableford is another) of a different and exceedingly rare species: an author of Scientific Romances. Hence the long evolutionary perspectives which mark his work, which can be distinguished from US Future Histories by a sense that the March of Progress may well lead us into the cruellest month; and by pithless heroes drenched in twilight; and by the diffusion of affect into a uniformitarian emeritus chill through which genre plots are transformed into models for contemplation. But then, in some recent books — those where much of the actual writing was done by an American collaborator named Gentry Lee — all this seemed to be lost, or abandoned, or never known, the way Disney never knew a duck; and novels signed with Clarke's name, like the spastic *Cradle* (1988), emitted a sad off-the-Interstate air of theme-park dinosaurishness. The first of the Rama sequels, also with Lee, was similarly inauthentic; but *Garden of Rama* (Gollancz) marked a return to the glazed equipoise of Scientific Romance at home with itself. Perhaps the neocytes of UnAmericanism had transfigured the junior partner's episteme, or maybe Clarke himself took a more commanding role in a collaboration which had begun desperately to need a senior voice; whatever happened, a book was given birth to.

For the rest of us — slipstreamers, alpha males, difficult women, neophytes, neighbours, expats — it's down the long chute together, into a heap at the heart of a late year. In *Dracula Unbound* (Grafton), Brian W. Aldiss took time off from the scathing *saeva indignatio* of his latter-day short fiction to diddle a yarn of the old genre, a finger aside his nose, thumb somewhere. Martin Amis gave proper dues, in *Time's Arrow: Or, the Nature of the Offence* (Cape), to the long history of attempts within genre sf, none of them very successful, to write a tale in which time runs backwards, and characters live each moment in reverse from age to infancy. But Amis's protagonist is not Merlin, and the underlying irony of his premise is unmedicable: a man lives backwards into the Second World War, where he had been involved in the Final Solution. Every moment of the book, because it reverses what actually happened this century, therefore marks a redemptive nascence, an epiphanic recovery. Lampshades become violinists, gold fillings are coated in smiles. *The Trinity Paradox* (Bantam), by Kevin Anderson and Doug Beason, is told in a language devoid of much nuance tuning ('Hey, Kev, wasn't it *your* turn to nuance?'), and so nearly fails to awaken the unwary reader to the adult gravity of the story it tells. The premise derives from one of genre sf's favourite gavottes: the time-travel story in which an individual or cadre – as in Poul Anderson's *The Time Patrol* (Tor), which sclerotically repaves old runes in re Wanweird Warriors (Bard Extra) Salvation Corps Inc. – finds it possible to go backwards in time and change (or maintain against change) the course of history. This time it's Los Alamos, 1943, and the consequences of sabotaging the development of the A-bomb, though couched in too much of the blatancy of genre plotting, are threateningly grave. In *A Woman of the Iron People* (Morrow), Eleanor Arnason finally bit into a planetary romance whose scope was great enough to *geographize* her tough but (in the past) self-lacerating edginess. And in *Hunting the Ghost Dancer* (HarperCollins) A. A. Attanasio returned to a Primal Scene of Social Darwinism, the duel between Neanderthal and *Homo sapiens*, but subjected the outcome to doses of ambivalence, densely coloured, without quite showing why he told the tale in the first place.

Just as he did in *Empire of the Sun* (1984), J. G. Ballard gave us, in *The Kindness of Women* (HarperCollins), a confabulated rag-and-bone-shop sight of the artist, this time as a youngish man whose life is a close, but not exact, *doppelgänger* of the author's own. It was not sf. John Barnes's *Orbital Resonance* (Tor) was, on the other hand, nothing but. Written from deep within the shattered house of genre, it could be understood only through race-memories of the Heinlein juvenile leads it paid homage to, but dodged some of the down sides of, in its portrait of an extremely bright girl beset, in an orbital habitat, with rite-of-passage problems, parent problems, future-of-the-human-race problems – all these problems being solved by emissions of chromium savvy from her 'lovable' big mouth; you almost wanted to slap her, but it would break your hand. *The Hereafter Gang* (Ziesing) by Neal Barrett Jr also took the shape of a solution, but of the funnel at the other end, the coriolis dance downwards into the afterlife. Barrett has an ear for the bedlam din of urban Texas, and a story-telling voice which deposes matters of great subtlety with great shouts, and an exuberance which glows in the dark, and he's hilarious. Except in *The Sot-Weed Factor* (1960), the greatest of all twentieth-century picaresques, John Barth expresses his exuberance almost exclusively through the architectonic of conceits, which also glow. *The Last Voyage of Somebody the Sailor* (Little Brown) is like a daylight vision of the Arabian Nightmare (we here christen a newish subgenre, naming it with the title of Robert Irwin's first novel, which exemplifies the mode); a dream (entirely typical of Barth) which has no slumber in it. Stephen Baxter, in *The Raft* (Grafton), wrote an extremely-heavy-gravity-universe novel, but edged sideways from tired expectations through a not-generally-present, not-in-fact-quite-all-there protagonist. But he toted the barge. James P. Blaylock wrote, in *The Paper Grail* (Ace), yet another tale in which a childlike hero with a Wound from a Pacific Rim suburb gets wisdom from a Geezer and a nice sun-chthonic from the New Age, and *still* Stephen Spielberg remains silent. Keith Brooke's *Expatria* (Gollancz) awaited its sequel like a bridegroom whose altar is an *entire planet* (such is sf); John Brunner did another mumpsimus space opera turn in *A Maze of Stars* (Del Rey), earning his crust: it is hard to blame the man; and Lois McMaster Bujold won another of the prizes – what *is* that man's name (Hovis?); or that other one, the prize that's bigger than a star but smaller than a breadbox (Spud-U-Like?) – for *Barrayar* (Baen), a perfectly unobjectionable space opera set in the usual place, without a blemish, or a dare, or a distinguishing mark.

Pat Cadigan's *Synners* (Bantam) was kitchen-sink or Calliope Cyberpunk, cluttered and burly and very smart, and a head-reamer. Orson Scott Card's *Xenocide* (Tor) was – almost unaccountably for a book from Utah's greatest living samurai – smackdab *fuzzy*. The sly sharp steely style of yore had turned into a complacent jog, postprandial and *portly*, and Ender began to bore; the plot was as contrivance-laden as an old tinker; and the ship of story sighed to a cease on its hook (sequel queues are asked to form at the mission gate) like a flounder. *Outside the Dog Museum* (Macdonald) by Jonathan Carroll did not inhabit any sector of the fantastic, but this fourth parable about the costs of answered prayers – costs specifically salient when one thinks about the power of the maker of art to own the made – spoke directly to the inadmissible heart of genre literature: the heart fact that genres are *ownerships* of the tales told. We could go on, and on. But time must have a stop. Jack L. Chalker, George Alec Effinger and Mike Resnick got together and wrote *The Red Tape War* (Tor), a round-robin novel, it bob-bob-bobbed along, then stopped. Those guys! C. J. Cherryh continued, with *Heavy Time* (Warner Books), to write space opera you needed a certificate of fitness to enter: data-dense, swift, allusive, itchy. The tale was set at the beginning of the Union-Alliance Universe, to which almost every sf story she has written now belongs, but *still* seemed *medias res*, almost punch-drunk with stuff to tell. Richard Condon, in *The Final Addiction* (St. Martin's Press), seemed tired of the long chute, motley with the fidgets of age; but still managed to edge his crazed Amerika one step closer to the brink. And Robert Coover's *Pinocchio in Venice* (Simon and Schuster), like Jerome Charyn's earlier *Pinocchio's Nose* (1983), made a fabulistic game out of pining.

Bradley Denton's *Buddy Holly is Alive and Well on Ganymede* (Morrow) was sad and dippy, and might well bring someone (not me) to think hard about the fact that ancient rock and sf are both forms of nostalgia commonly felt by Americans old enough to remember that the Frontier died and everything began to slip downhill to the mall just after the grand opening of the first Interstate, desiccating the arteries of myth: because there's an awful lot of ancient rock sf around, and almost no *roads*. Gordon R. Dickson continued to fail to stop adding great bricks to his **Childe** Shack, though *Young Bleys* (Tor) seemed to be more sand than Dorsai, adding nothing new to earlier volumes, a florilegium of saws. *The M. D.: A Horror Story* (Knopf) by Thomas M. Disch began as a family romance on the curse of suburban Catholicism, moved into a horror fable about sin and answered prayers, ended in an intensely bitter near future, slammed shut. *The Gap into Vision: Forbidden Knowledge* (HarperCollins), which was the second volume of Stephen R. Donaldson's Gap sequence, began to make it possible to conceive that the author might just accomplish something no starship ever will, which is exit from a black hole; because the first volume of this utterly untoward space opera sequence, *The Gap into Conflict: The Real Story* (1990), seemed terminally otiose. Turns out the awfulness was *deliberate*, that it was the nuts and bolts of a space-opera crescendo destined to build over the course of five volumes, a great black-hole-escaping Munch-like bellow of unendurable stress. After the first volume, anything's a relief. George Alec Effinger's *The Exile Kiss* (Doubleday) did not quite sustain the Arabian Nightmare flow of previous titles devoted to its streetwise Muslim anti-hero, but coasted towards something or other; more volumes are needed, to shore this one up. Some penny will have to drop, shaking the world. *Red Orc's Rage* (Tor) by Philip José Farmer was not sf, but could have been written (and read) only by someone deeply immured in the recursive worlds of tiers of genre sf. A troubled lad is introduced by a kindly therapist to Farmer's very own World of Tiers sequence, embraces it in his imagination, and by doing so Orc manages to sort out his problems with the outside world. Sf will make you Virtually Free. And Karen Joy Fowler's *Sarah Canary* (Henry Holt) managed – while at the same time declining any generic gambit whatsoever, allowing no sf premise to shoulder into the knowledge of the text – to give us the impression we were reading a First Contact tale of very great force; it was also a deft needling parable of the male mind-set of Empire.

The Architecture of Desire (Bantam Press) was the sharpest book Mary Gentle has yet written. Set in an alternate-world seventeenth-century England governed by Neoplatonic magic, it finally subjected her over-beloved fantasy heroine, White Crow, to a situation she could not bound out of, like some Temporal-Adventuring cursor in some godawful game. She is a physician; she rapes a woman who has come to her in great distress, and who later commits suicide because of the betrayal and the violation. At the end of the book, however, White Crow is beginning to leap free again: I could have killed her. Alexander Jablokov's first novel, Carve the Sky (Morrow), had a dark compost smell of New England Dying Earth, but was in fact set only a few centuries hence. It depicted a world transformed into an artefact for humans to live like humans in, but also moved outwards, exogamously, from the outgrown gardened planet. In White Queen (Gollancz), Gwyneth Jones finally persuaded herself not to have coughing fits as she chugged over the points of Story, and managed to tell one: aliens arrive on Earth, ask us (maybe) to marry them (or whore). There is a lot of plot, but no full resolution; there will be a sequel. Good. It won a prize. Good. Michael Kandel's Captain Jack Zodiac (Broken Mirrors Press) viewed the aftermath of apocalypse through a congeries of gearloose folk, each of them falling through the blackening day like burning comics. Damon Knight closed off his CV sequence with A Reasonable World (Tor), in which it is seen as possible, though only through the help of the aliens who dominate the three books, for us to inhabit this planet as though we wanted to, as though life on Earth were possible without our constantly trying to chew our legs off to get free. And Nancy Kress continued, in Beggars in Spain (Pulphouse/Axolotl), to build her career into an edifice of chosen stories, each meticulously crafted and spliced, each different from its predecessors. This time she reworked the primal genre sf tale in which the community of super-children (they need no sleep) grows up in secrecy and prepares to rule the world from behind the scenes; but ironies begin to eat at the dream, and the full version of the tale could bite very deep into the inadmissible heart of genre literature (see above) which continues to beat inside the dead meat.

Paul J. McAuley's Eternal Light (Gollancz) – though the disingenuously slapdash style of the thing exposed, once again, the ringer in the fields of corn – soon got down to very serious cosmogonic brass tacks and took its crew up and down and through the timestream, into the wormhole and up the metaphor and down the metamorphosis, and taxied back again; a fine time was had. Tom

Maddox's *Halo* (Tor) gave off a few disillusioned cyberpunk riffs, and slid to a halt as though it had missed the last bus to Mean Street; but it promised a great deal next time. Gustav Meyrink's *Der Engel vom Westlichen Fenster*, which was first published in 1927, was finally translated (very well, by Mike Mitchell) as *The Angel of the West Window* (Dedalus), and proved to have explored the Matter of John Dee long before lots of us were born. Judith Moffett burdened the title of her new fix-up, *The Ragged World: A Novel of the Hefn on Earth* (St. Martin's Press), with an extremely onerous pun designed to offend any reader too polite to notice it until told; but the book itself turned out to be an extremely adult sf embracement of Aids, Hefns, Quakerdom, here on this Earth. There were several 1991 graphic novels, but *Dare* (Xpresso) by Grant Morrison and Rian Hughes, which immured a senescent Dan Dare in the Thatcherite shambles of a UK much like our own dear Now, more plangently mourned the futures of the old sf than any book written or composed during this year in America. And Kim Newman's *Jago* (Simon and Schuster UK) also addressed the Matter of Britain in a horror tale which incorporated almost every trope imaginable: Mummerset gross-outs; Addams Family romances; Christers gone queer; a green man with a sweet tooth; sex and rock'n'roll and politics and Pelion and Ossa – all choreographed to a golgothan, moony nicety.

In *The Cult of Loving Kindness* (Morrow), the final volume of his **Starbridge Chronicles**, Paul Park stewed the Pol Pot of his Long Year, as the great season turned to apogee, a totalitarian fundamentalism blossomed, a new (but very precisely an old) episteme took blood root in dire soil, and a terrible sadness brooded o'er the gulf of time. Marge Piercy paid homage to cyberpunk, in *He, She and It* (Knopf), but couldn't quite disentangle the requirements of her interpolated Golem legend from the legends of our new age, a central one of which is that (unlike the shibboleth-bound Golem of Jewish Prague) AIs Do Good Back-up Disk. The permanent death therefore of the loyal AIs clothed in hunky flesh stuff – but without a download jack to save his soul – did not compute. Charles Platt seemed to try to incorporate in *The Silicon Man* (Bantam) some sense of the sweet flow of intersubjectivity within the veins of a novel that mattered to him, though the storyline – twenty-first-century agent becomes an 'infomorph' or data ganglion in a great computer, and subsequent events lead to a chill metamorphosis of the world – may have lacked Piercy's quasi-humane *je ne sais quoi*: but knew what it was talking about instead. Frank M. Robinson's *The Dark Beyond the Stars* (Tor) had a pocket universe, a generation starship, a lad, a dad, a fight, a god and all the bespoke regalia of Eternal Return opera, including the mind-mirror at the dark End of the tale, out of which pops its very Beginning. And Rudy Rucker, in *The Hollow Earth: The Narrative of Mason Algiers Reynolds of Virginia* (Morrow), wrote the straightest book he has ever published: a recursive tale of the nineteenth-century and Edgar Allan Poe, who journeys to the South Pole, where he and his boon companions enter a Symmesian Hollow Earth, get laid, undergo deep transformation stuff so that more than one of everyone can thicken the plot, and good times are had by alls.

Piero Scanziani's *The White Book* (Eureka) from 1968, now glowingly translated by Linda Lappin, retold the myth of Adam and Eve, again and again and back and forth, until you felt like weeping, out of fellow feeling: Madam, I'm Adam. It all comes to that in the end, *dne eht ni taht ot semoc lla ti*. That's what it all adds up to, in the end, life. Charles Sheffield carried on giganting with a second helping of the **Heritage Universe**: *Divergence* (Del Rey), toying with Uplift (I call it exogamy). Robert Silverberg gazed once again upon the tropes like a headlight hypnotizing a rabbit, assembled in *The Face of the Waters* (Grafton) another immaculate epiphany ferry (burnt-out case sees God after long hegira, sighs, works out visiting hours), overdosed the job with all his air-conditioned skill, asked us to share the tab: so we read it. Iain Sinclair, in *Downriver: (Or, the Vessels of Wrath): A Narrative in Twelve Tales* (Paladin), found runes and labyrinths in the heat-death entrails of a near future East London: Dickens's heir OK. But he still refuses to deign to trifle with the art of telling the tale. In *The Angel of Pain* (Simon and Schuster UK), Brian M. Stableford continued to use the tools of Scientific Romance in an extremely gripping taxidermical evisceration of horror devices (werewolves again this time), a fine mind (Stableford's) gone astray in dreck (you might think). I mean, *werewolves*. I mean, spin-doctoring woof-woofs. And Michael Swanwick published two books of note. *Griffin's Egg* (Legend) neatly expressed a sense that the solar system was part of the continuity (or metastasis) of human life, if no more than an infected sidebar on an inner page; and *Stations of the Tide* (Morrow), which won the Nebula, was a triumph of post-genre sf, though in no particular could it be accused of treason (hence the award). It was set on a Long Year colony planet; it had a cast of the usual suspects; it made intensely imaginative use of the marriage of Virtual Reality and the Theatre of Memory; it quoted (or intrinsicated its substance with) Shakespeare, Budrys, Wolfe, Frances Yates. Like a conjuror's suitcase, it kept on unpacking itself; and stopped far too soon, you felt, though you knew it was done.

As smooth as glass, in which it was possible to discern a variety of Beauties, Sheri S. Tepper's *Beauty* (Doubleday; preferred text

HarperCollins, 1992) conflated fable, fantasy, dream-trek, time-travel sf, and allegory: all without blinking, or drawing breath, or breathing hard. The book comprises the diary of Beauty from Once Upon a Time, who avoids Sleep, who is transported into the horrific near future of all our worst dreams, who escapes into a magical past but who ages rapidly each time she hoicks through time, who travels up a world river, visits her mother in a desolate fading Faerie, who is conversant with a Beast, who becomes a spark in the night we cast. The only problem was the terrifying ease of the thing. I wanted grit, the gasp of a deep pun. It wasn't there: everything else was.

If there were three best novels of the year, this was one, Swanwick's another and Fowler's a third. All three were hatchlings of genre, all three were mutant. They flickered in the mind's eye like outlaws, indecipherable because new. They were dressed in Lincoln green, they stole through the brambles and the scimitars of a new sun. They were the foliage which becomes the map. They spoke to the year.

–It's about time, they said.

The year spoke to all of us.

–O my dearly beloveds, said the Bailiff, who might also be called Time Present. 'Gather round. I have something to show you.'

Afterword

Michael Moorcock

I recently returned from Toronto's thirteenth Harbourfront International Festival of Authors, perhaps the most stimulating and well-run festival of its kind, where I heard wonderful readings from Shulamith Hareven, Clare Boylan, Janette Turner Hospital, Janyce Kulyk Keefer, Diana Souhami and Bill Manhire and to which Toronto resident Michael Ondaatje returned with his Booker at almost the moment the local Blue Jays won Baseball's World Series for the first time in anyone's history.

It was a very good time to be in Toronto, especially since my original reason for going was to attend this year's tribute to a living Canadian author. It was my chance to see a good friend after many years and to say a few of the words which I – and others, such as Kathleen MacLean, Samuel R. Delany, Spider Robinson, Fred Pohl and Elisabeth Vonarburg – felt were long overdue, for Judith Merril was the first important catalyst of what became known as the sf New Wave. Indeed, she virtually created the American sf renaissance of the 1960s and remains, at seventy, as radical in her literary and political tastes as she ever was.

After witnessing at first hand the violent fiasco of the 1968 Democratic Convention in Chicago, she turned her back on the considerable influence and prestige she had discovered as a writer, critic and anthologist and went to help found an experimental college in Toronto, since when her work in sf has largely been advisory and academic. She edited an anthology of Canadian sf, *Tesseracts*, in 1985 and her huge collection of imaginative literature forms the basis of the Merril Collection, one of the largest resources of its kind in the world.

Judy Merril is also writing her memoirs and working on some fiction. A triple bypass seems to have invigorated her. She went down to San Francisco to attend Fritz Leiber's funeral – the *only* one of his contemporary peers to attend. It was an open casket wake and ended with Fritz holding a glass of champagne in one hand, a cigarette in the other – about as good a way to go as any he might have invented. Fritz steered his own sometimes erratic course while producing much of sf's seminal work. His prose was always outstanding and frequently brilliant. With Ray Bradbury and Theodore Sturgeon, he made a huge contribution to sf and, with them, raised the literary aspirations of all its writers.

Judy Merril also demanded our best, in literature as in politics, and continues to do so. She retains her habitual independence, careless of the world's approval or its money, and still takes an enormous pleasure out of life and friendship. She continues to work for women's rights, for the Canadian Writers' Union, and sometimes manages to shift the odds a little further on the side of justice, though she remains as suspicious of praise and apparent altruism as Sam Spade. And like Sam Spade, she still hasn't given up smoking . . .

There were a large number of imaginative writers attending the Harbourfront Festival – William Golding, Douglas Adams, Shulamith Hareven, Robert Drewe, Jim Crace, Edward Al-Kharrat, Margaret Atwood and Neil Bissondath among them – who rather proved the point Merril was making in the 1960s when she claimed that the 'mainstream' of the future was what she was then publishing in her sf anthologies. What was perhaps surprising was how several of those writers recalled *New Worlds* with affection.

Prisoners of Gravity, the Canadian TV show which specializes in popular fiction, took advantage of the presence of so many imaginative writers to do interviews and plan programmes. It seems a great pity to me that British television, with its larger audiences and budgets, can't provide us with a similar show – or at least import the Canadian one. It's a witty and intelligent series which neither patronizes nor diminishes its subject matter. *C'est la vie*, as they say over there.

The Authors

PETER F. HAMILTON is the author of *Mindstar Rising* (1993), which features a psychic private eye in twenty-first century Peterborough. (This is a different twenty-first century Peterborough from the one in 'Spare Capacity'.) His second novel, *A Quantum Murder* (1994), will be followed by a third book in the same series, *The Nano Flower*. His short fiction has appeared in *Fear, Interzone, In Dreams* and various small press magazines; his story 'Candy Buds' was in *New Worlds 2*, and 'Starlight Dreamer' will be in *New Worlds 4*.

GRAHAM JOYCE wrote his first novel, *Dreamside*, during the year he lived on the Greek island of Lesbos. Published in 1991, it was followed in 1992 by his second book, *Dark Sister*, and in 1993 by his third, *House of Lost Dreams*. His short fiction has appeared in *Interzone, Dark Voices, In Dreams, Darklands 2* and *Eurotemps*. He says that, like most authors, he juggles to make a living – but it was a bad line, so maybe he really said 'struggles'.

BRIAN W. ALDISS has had a story in each volume of the new *New Worlds*. 'Friendship Bridge' is part of the Burnell series, the first story of which was 'FOAM' in *New Worlds 1*. Another in the series, 'The Madonna of Futurity', will appear in the Russian magazine *Tomorrow* and the American anthology *Universe*. Revised and rewritten, all of these will become part of his next novel. 'Ratbird', from *NW2*, was reprinted in *The Year's Best Fantasy and Horror*. He is currently trying to persuade the BBC to produce a television version of Philip K. Dick's *Martian Time-Slip*.

GWYNETH JONES made her début in print at the age of nine, with a poem in the *Manchester Evening News*. Her sf novels are *Divine Endurance, Escape Plans, Kairos* and *The White Queen* – which in 1992 became co-winner of the first James Tiptree Jr Memorial Award. She also writes children's books under the name Ann Halam. For some reason, she fails to include 'The Telebugs' on her list of writing credits. He next books will be a *Divine Endurance* spin-off called *Flowerdust* and the sequel to *White Queen* titled *North Wind*. She lives in Brighton with her husband, Peter, a maths lecturer, and son Gabriel, who illustrated her story in this volume.

SIMON INGS is the author of *Hot Head* (1992), and his second novel, *In the City of the Iron Fish*, is awaiting publication. His short fiction has been published in *Interzone, Omni, Other Edens 3* and *Zenith 2*. His story, 'Bruised Time' was in the second volume of the *New Worlds* and was reprinted in *The New Nature of the Catastrophe*, edited by Langdon Jones and Michael Moorcock. His previous collaboration with Charles Stross, 'Something Sweet', appeared in *New Worlds 1*. He has written a short sf film for the British Film Institute, to be shown on Channel 4 in 1994.

CHARLES STROSS, as well as twice collaborating with Simon Ings on stories for *New Worlds*, has had short fiction published in *Interzone, There Won't Be War, The Weerde* and *Villains*. He also writes computer journalism and currently works for a 'Californian lunatic cyberspace multinational'. His ambition is 'to be certified open-system-compliant and run under every operating system', whatever that means.

GRAHAM CHARNOCK had his first story published in the 'New Writers' issue of *New Worlds* in 1968: four issues later he was assistant editor. Other stories have appeared in *Orbit 8* and the first *Other Edens,* but not *The Last Dangerous Visions*. A novel based on his early *NW* stories awaits publication in Germany. He has completed a second novel which he terms a 'Recession Romance' – and wonders why he has failed to find a publisher. As one of the Deep Fix, he wrote and performed with Michael Moorcock on the 1975 album *The New World's Fair*. He and his wife, Pat, live in London with their two sons.

JACK DEIGHTON has a doctorate in chemistry and is a schoolteacher in Fife – but says he is *not* a Fifer. He drags his poor long-suffering wife and weans all over Scotland on Saturday afternoons just so he can watch a duff football team. (His wife is Katrina, and his weans are his two sons.) He is a frustrated song-writer who at last found fulfilment of his *other* secret ambition with the publication of his first story, 'The Face of the Waters' in *New Worlds 2*. 'This is the Road' is his second published story.

PAUL DI FILIPPO is the token non-Brit in this anthology; he has also had stories in both previous volumes of *New Worlds*. His first book will be published in 1994, a collection of three novellas, entitled *Steampunk*. Publication of his novels *Ciphers* and *Joe's Liver* have been long promised – and long awaited. But meanwhile his fiction, reviews and journalism keep appearing in an ever-widening variety of publications. He lives in Providence, Rhode Island, and probably also juggles to make a living. 'Streetlife' is one of his ribofunk stories.

PAUL J. McAULEY is also not a Fifer, although he also teaches there, at St. Andrews University. (His doctorate is in botany.) He was joint winner of the Philip K. Dick Award for his first novel, *Four Hundred Billion Stars* (1988). This was followed by the novels *Secret Harmonies* and *Eternal Light* and the collection *The King of the Hill*. With Kim Newman, he co-edited the anthology *In Dreams,* and his own short stories have appeared in *Amazing, Asimov's, Fantasy and Science Fiction* and *Interzone*. His latest novel is *Red Dust* (1993), and he is now writing an historical novel set in Florence. His ambition is to be a panellist on 'Gardeners' Question Time'.

JOHN CLUTE is the joint editor, with Peter Nicholls, of the totally revised *Encyclopedia of Science Fiction* (1993). Born in Canada, he recently *chose* to become a British citizen. *New Worlds* published his first science fiction story in 1966, and he reviews sf for publications as diverse as the *Washington Post* and *Interzone*. His articles covering the sf novels published from 1987 to 1990 appeared in *The Orbit Science Fiction Yearbook 1–3,* and *New Worlds 1* – and, if he can face it again, he will discuss 1992 in *New Worlds 4.*

MICHAEL MOORCOCK was the second editor of *New Worlds;* he is now the first consultant editor. He has written over eighty books, many of which are currently being reprinted in omnibus editions. His most recent novel is *Jerusalem Commands,* the third in the Pyat series, the final volume of which will be *The Vengeance of Rome.* 1992 also saw publication of Colin Greenland's *Death is no Obstacle*, composed of interviews with Moorcock about his writing and working methods. He played guitar, wrote and sang on Graham Charnock's Deep Fix album. (The Deep Fix were named after a story by James Colvin, uncle of Warwick Colvin Jnr who appeared in *New Worlds 2.)*

DAVID GARNETT edits *New Worlds*. He read a few manuscripts, took half of the photographs, wrote the introduction and the above biographies – and has done enough for this volume.

The Deep Fix: Graham Charnock, Michael Moorcock and Steve Gilmore.

Photograph of Brian W. Aldiss by Leo Birleson.
Photograph of John Clute by Frances Jobling.
Photograph of Jack Deighton by Katrina Skirving.
Photograph of Paul Di Filippo by Deborah Newton.
Photograph of Gwyneth Jones by Trisha Purchas.
Photograph of Michael Moorcock by Linda Steele.
Photograph of *Science Fiction Monthly* by J. Porker.

'Spare Capacity' illustrated by Kate Mason.
'Friendship Bridge', 'Streetlife', and 'Children of the Revolution' illustrated by Neil Evans.
'The Mechanic' illustrated by Gabriel Jones.

Still available . . .
The first two volumes of **NEW WORLDS**

NEW WORLDS 1

VGSF £4.99

NEW WORLDS 2

VGSF £5.99